Prais
JENNY O'CONNELL

PLAN B

"*Plan B*, Jenny O'Connell's first young adult novel, is sure to be a hit. . . . It's full of believable characters, interesting plot twists, and great writing." Rating: 10/10

—Teen Book Review.com

"*Plan B* gets an 'A' for a clever plot. . . . [Vanessa is] a vulnerable and sympathetic character."

—Curled Up Kids.com

THE BOOK OF LUKE

"This fresh, honest novel is full of amazing characters and excellent writing. Jenny O'Connell is a smart, talented author; I'm really looking forward to seeing what she writes next! This is contemporary fiction at its best; readers will not be disappointed." Rating: 5 Stars

—Teens Read Too.com

"[A] fun and charming book that's worth reading."

—Young Adult Books Central.com

"Emily . . . is smart, funny, easy to relate to, and so is her narration."

—The Yayas, Wordpress.com

Rich Boys

An Island Summer Novel

Jenny O'Connell

POCKET BOOKS   MTV Books
New York London Toronto Sydney

Pacific Grove Public Library

Pocket Books
A Division of Simon & Schuster, Inc.
1230 Avenue of the Americas
New York, NY 10020

This book is a work of fiction. Names, characters, places, and incidents either are products of the author's imagination or are used fictitiously. Any resemblance to actual events or locales or persons, living or dead, is entirely coincidental.

Copyright © 2008 by Jennifer O'Connell

MTV Music Television and all related titles, logos, and characters are trademarks of MTV Networks, a division of Viacom International, Inc.

All rights reserved, including the right to reproduce this book or portions thereof in any form whatsoever. For information address Pocket Books Subsidiary Rights Department, 1230 Avenue of the Americas, New York, NY 10020

First MTV Books/Pocket Books trade paperback edition June 2008

POCKET and colophon are registered trademarks of Simon & Schuster, Inc.

For information about special discounts for bulk purchases,
please contact Simon & Schuster Special Sales at 1-800-456-6798
or business@simonandschuster.com

Manufactured in the United States of America

10   9   8   7   6   5   4   3   2   1

Library of Congress Cataloging-in-Publication Data is available.

ISBN-13:   978-1-4165-6336-5
ISBN-10:   1-4165-6336-9

For Tanner, who really did win third place in the South Beach sand castle building contest.

Rich Boys

Chapter 1

DISCARD

I don't play tennis with Jessie anymore. Not since last summer, when she asked me to *just hit it around,* and I naively believed she meant we were simply going to volley the ball back and forth over the net, not that I'd get a forehand to the stomach and end up doubled over gasping to catch my breath. Jessie immediately ran over and apologized profusely (she jumped over the net, which, even though I was nearly suffocating, still impressed me), but that was the end of our match. So now the closest I get to Jessie on the court is the sidelines, not so much because she's so good, which she is, but because she is so much better than me. And as much as I hated getting hit with a ball going sixty miles per hour, I hated losing even more.

"Come on, just one game?" Jessie begged, bouncing the ball against alternating sides of her racquet head. She was between clinics, so we had an hour to kill before her afternoon program. Even after only a week of teaching junior clinics at the Community Center, Jessie was dark, her legs and arms a warm toffee color compared to my mid-June pallor. The thing was, no matter how dark Jessie's skin got, and by the end of the summer she was darker than even the girls who loyally fake-baked at the Sun Tropez, Jessie's hair was always the same color. Almost black. Not a single highlight, no streaks from the sun. Just a solid mass of black curls pulled back into a ponytail, so dark and shiny the color reminded me of licorice jelly beans, which I always thought looked out of place in my pastel-colored Easter basket and always traded with Shelby for the purple, grape-flavored ones. My hair, on the other hand, ended up pale honey blond by the end of the summer, which looked great with a tan. But when my regular old dirty blond started growing in around October and there was no sun and salt air to provide a little assistance from Mother Nature, I had to turn to a bottle to ease the transition to my winter shade of blah.

I shook my head even as Jessie gave me a look that pleaded *pretty please.* "I didn't bring my protective gear."

Jessie rolled her eyes at me. "Well, you'd better remember to bring some tomorrow. You're going to need it."

"I think I can handle a few kids on the beach. Besides, who are you to talk? You just spent three hours teaching a group of ten-year-olds how to rush the net."

"Yeah, but they get out of line, and *whack.*" Jessie let the ball fall to the ground, bounce once, then smacked it away with a killer backhand. Even without her trying, it skimmed over the net and slid down the right side of the court, just inside the tape. She'd made the varsity tennis team our freshman year, all thanks to that backhand.

"If I need your disciplinary skills, I'll be sure to call," I said. Jessie had started teaching junior tennis clinics at the Chilmark Community Center last week, which is why every afternoon I'd come by before her afternoon session to hang out. My complete and total boredom. But today was my last day of unemployment, because tomorrow I started work at the Oceanview Inn, as a camp counselor for the children's program.

"Better you than me," Jessie sighed, looking around for another ball. She taught at the center because it gave her an excuse to hit the court every day, not because she relished explaining the concepts of *love* and *deuce* and *topspin* to a bunch of kids who'd rather be at the beach or at their summer homes playing their Xboxes. "You hear from Shelby?"

"Yeah," I said, then waited while she dug a faded yellow ball out from behind the chain-link fence and resumed bouncing. "She said she doubts there'll be enough time to come home this summer, but she'll try."

Shelby attended the Boston Culinary Institute, turning what had begun as a coping mechanism into an actual vocation. Shelby's obsession with baking had gone into overdrive the summer after her ill-fated and short-lived freshman year at UMass. It was also the summer between my sophomore and junior years of high school, but I was babysitting for the Logans and spent more time at their house than I did my own, so I didn't see Shelby or my parents that much last summer. Which, looking back now, I wasn't sure was a good thing or a mistake. Because maybe if I'd been around more, I could have fixed what was going wrong. If I hadn't been teaching the Logan twins how to craft cardboard sunflowers out of paper-towel tubes and styrofoam plates, maybe I would have noticed how much things were changing.

But I didn't realize what was going on at home until Shelby had gone away to school and it was too late. By that point the silence had become so normal, the hush such a part of my family's daily life, I couldn't remember what it had been like before, and I didn't know how to make everything go back to the way it had been. All I could remember is that it had been different, even if I couldn't put my finger on the exact moment that transformed everything.

There was no grand fight, no battles over the dinner table or dramatic tossing of wedding china, which is why I guess I didn't notice right away. Those were the signs they prepared you for in the movies, the noise of crashing objects, shrill voices, slamming doors. Instead, our house just got quieter as my parents began avoiding eye contact during meals, silently acknowledging requests with a slowly nodding head or a polite smile, passing the salt and pepper without touching fingertips.

And the quieter the house got, the more Shelby baked, as if the sweet smell of blackberry cobbler and banana upside-down cake could fill in the empty space left by my parents' growing silence.

"That's too bad, I miss Shelby's lemon bars. Maybe we could go to Boston and visit her," Jessie suggested. "Like in August, when this place is packed and we can't take it anymore."

I shrugged. "Maybe. I don't know if I'll be able to get time off, but we can try."

"It will have to be after the road race. Nash and I are training together."

Nash. Last year, when Jessie first started helping out at the center, she decided she wanted Nash, a sailing coordinator who was spending the summer on the island before heading off for his freshman year at the University of Vermont. Nash's father was once an economic adviser for the mayor of New

York City, and now he taught at Columbia. It was rare for a summer guy to have a job, but I guess as far as jobs go hanging out on a sailboat all day was about as close as you could get to not working while still collecting a paycheck.

For two months last summer Jessie learned everything there was to know about nautical knots (practiced on her sneaker laces), steering (starboard on your right, port on your left), and rigging (especially the halyard, after she mistakenly wrapped one around her wrist and ended up with a wicked case of rope burn). She played it cool those months, approaching the situation just as she'd approach one of her matches—equal parts strategy, perseverance, and patience. While the rest of the center's staff was fawning over Nash, Jessie hung back, piquing his interest with her disinterest ("They were tossing him lobs," she once told me, "nobody ever wins with a lob."). Finally, with three weeks left to go before he headed off to school, Nash made his move on Jessie. And for the next three weeks they were together, and then he left for college. Now he was back for a second summer and things were on again.

"Want one?" I asked Jessie, holding up the bag of chocolate chip cookies in my hand. Chips Ahoy!—not homemade, which I knew would annoy Shelby to no end. But without my sister around, we had to resort to the baked-goods aisle at Stop & Shop like everyone else.

Jessie reached for the cookie with her right hand while continuing to hold the racquet and bounce the ball with her left. Coordination came so easily for Jessie. She was one of those people who could tap the top of her head with one hand while rubbing circles on her stomach with the other. I knew this because she'd demonstrated the skill to me shortly after we first met. I showed her how I could touch the tip of my tongue to my nose. Somehow I thought that made us even.

I knew Jessie wouldn't be able to eat the cookie while bouncing the ball, though. Jessie eats her food in pieces. It was the first thing I noticed when we met, in the cafeteria, our freshman year. Jessie lives up-island, in Chilmark, which meant that even though we've both lived on the island our entire lives, we didn't actually go to the same school until ninth grade. And on the first day, during lunch period, there she was, tearing off bite-size pieces of her ham-on-wheat sandwich and placing them in her mouth one at a time. I remember thinking how weird that was—why didn't she just bite into the sandwich like a normal person? But then I noticed she did it with everything. An apple couldn't be eaten unless she had a knife to slice it into chunks. Muffins had to be broken apart, each bite-size piece resulting in an equal amount of crumbs that Jessie would press down on with the tip of her finger and lick. I'd even seen her dismantle a slice of pizza, which was messy and not all that appetizing to watch.

So now, to actually eat the cookie she'd taken, Jessie had to lean the racquet against her leg before using one hand to hold the cookie and the other to break off a corner piece.

"What are you going to do with your afternoons?" Jessie asked, her mouth full of cookie.

"I don't know yet. But I can tell you what I won't be doing, and that's sitting around at home."

Jessie knew all about my parents. In the beginning she thought I was nuts. After all, she'd told me, most people complain when their parents fight, not when they *don't* fight. Not that Jess would have any idea what I was talking about. Her parents owned an organic landscaping company and were practically together 24-7 in the summer and even in the winter, when the business closed for the season and the Harrisons plowed through the latest crop of books with titles like *Sow What You Grow* and *Composting: It's Not All Crap*. But then Jess thought I was nuts about a lot of things, my parental situation being just one of many. The others included my summer job corralling kids at the Oceanview, my inability to grasp the significance of wearing a UVM SAILING TEAM T-shirt to bed every night, and my genuine interest in the contrapositive form of proofs—which is why in our geometry class last year Jessie said that, in addition to proving the logical equivalence "P implies Q," I also proved that I needed to get a life.

"What time is it?" she asked now, tossing the last piece of cookie in her mouth. She never wore a watch, which was one of the things about Jessie that drove *me* nuts.

"Almost one o'clock."

"Ugh." She picked up her racquet and laid it over her shoulder. "I'd better go get my students."

I stood up and brushed the loose blades of grass off my legs.

"You know, if you wanted, I could ask Kelsey if they need some extra help at the snack bar in the afternoons," Jessie offered. "It's kind of a cruddy job, but at least you get to snag some free food."

Jessie's sister Kelsey was a year younger than us, but she was already following in Jessie's footsteps as a loyal Community Center staff member. I knew Jess meant well, but she didn't exactly do a terrific job selling me on Kelsey's summer occupation, probably because she didn't know how to sugar-coat anything.

"Thanks, but I think I'll take a pass, even with the free food."

"Okay, well, enjoy your last day of freedom," she said. "And good luck tomorrow."

As if on cue a pack of eight-year-olds burst through the back door of the Community Center, their tennis sneakers kicking up dirt as they ran toward us.

"Looks like you're the one who needs the luck," I told her, wondering how Jessie would survive when up against a pack of eight-year-olds.

"Who needs luck," Jessie replied, showing no fear. "I have a racquet."

Chapter 2

My mom is a first-grade teacher, which is why she's home all summer. My dad is a photographer, which used to mean he was home all summer, too. In fact, summer was his busy time, what with all the tourists looking to have their family portraits taken while their skin was still tawny and little Jack Jr.'s white-blond hair looked perfect against the blue waters of South Beach. But then, a few years ago, while my dad was preparing to take a series of photos of a family from New York, he turned the camera on their golden retriever instead. And the family loved the resulting picture, which had Butch, the retriever, wearing their daughter's pink plastic beach pail on his head, something I have to imagine the very masculine Butch would have objected to had he known that portrait would one day end up displayed in every chain bookstore from Maine to California. But Butch's family loved the picture so much they showed it to their neighbor, who was an editor at a publishing house, and the next thing we knew my dad was shooting a calendar called *The Dog Days of Summer,* for which the lovely Butch was the cover model.

Ever see those photographs of little babies curled up inside blooming flowers or snuggled together like heads of cabbage? Picture that but with dogs, all doing something with a summer theme, like a French bulldog sitting on a lily pad with purple petals curling off his green nylon collar or a beagle seated atop a lifeguard stand, a whistle around his neck and zinc oxide swiped on his nose. That's what my dad does. He takes pictures of people's beloved pets, although he's since branched out from summer to include all four seasons, and from dogs to all four-legged creatures, although dogs remain his specialty.

There's been a new calendar every year since *The Dog Days of Summer,* and my dad's photography studio is pretty much booked every day, which is ironic. I always wondered what his clients would say if they knew we'd never owned a pet because my father is allergic to animals, and it's only thanks to his prescription medication that he doesn't sneeze all over his furry subjects. That's why, even though a few of his clients have called my dad the dog whisperer, Jessie jokingly refers to him as the dog sniffler.

After the first calendar came out, my dad was inundated with requests for pet portraits, but he soon learned that an island only accessible by ferry wasn't the best place for a studio during the off-season. So, for three years now my father has left every Monday morning for Boston, where he spends the week living in his photography studio, sleeping on a fold-out couch set against the back wall and showering in a cramped stand-up stall in the bathroom. I've been to his studio a few times, and I have to say, it seems like a pretty crappy way to spend the majority of your week, staring at the same five hundred square feet of space all day and night. At least during the summer season he comes back to the island on Wednesday nights, instead of Fridays, thanks to the tourists who book him months in advance for a chance to have Zoey the Lhasa apso feel like a supermodel for a few hours.

I didn't notice anything was wrong with my parents until Shelby left for culinary school. At least when she was around, something was always going on: a pan in the oven, a double boiler on the stove, the timer dinging after thirty-five minutes at four hundred degrees. At night we'd sit down to dinner and wonder which of Shelby's latest creations she'd unveil for dessert. It didn't just give Shelby something to do before heading off in January for her first semester of culinary school, it gave us all something to focus on—my sister's burgeoning career as a chef. I mean, who doesn't like to talk about food? Jessie once spent forty-five minutes describing to me a meatball calzone she'd had at Faneuil Hall. I told her she was just probably hungry from following the Freedom Trail around the city all day. She said, no, it was definitely the calzone.

So all through Shelby's fall menu (soup and French casseroles) and into the holidays (Christmas cookies, anyone?), Shelby's food gave us something to talk about. Well, food and Shelby's move to Boston, which we all hoped wouldn't be a repeat of her time at UMass, when she called my mom the first week and told her she'd made a huge mistake and wanted to come home.

The thing about Shelby and me, and maybe why, as far as sisters go, my mother always said she got lucky, is that we never wanted or cared about the same things. When we were younger, I thought I'd die if I didn't get a life-size Barbie head for Christmas one year, the one that lets you comb and style her hair and from that point on never looked as good as when you took it out of the box. Shelby wanted a Snoopy Sno-Kone machine with cherry and very berry flavoring. Maybe that's why I never understood how unhappy she was at UMass, and why I went online and picked the courses I thought Shelby would like, then e-mailed her the list. I needed Shelby to be happy at school the same way I hoped she'd get that Sno-Kone machine under the tree. And just as I'd cross my fingers every time Shelby unwrapped a box covered in red-and-green foil paper, when she called home from school, I'd hold my breath. Because all I could do was picture my sister sitting alone in her dorm room every night or at the back of a lecture hall by herself tuning out the professor as she doodled pictures of cupcakes in a notebook with a ballpoint pen. I didn't just want Shelby to be happy, I needed it, probably in much the same way Shelby needed to bake sunshine muffins and lemon bars.

I never knew if Shelby even looked into the classes I picked, which included Introduction to Sociology and Phonological Theory, and four months later she packed up her dorm room midway through her second semester and came home. She just gave up.

But that's not how Shelby looked at it, even if I did. Then again, Shelby never spent much time lamenting how things should be. She just accepted how they were and figured it out from there.

It wasn't until the drive home from Boston in January, after we'd dropped Shelby off in her new studio apartment on Commonwealth Avenue, that I realized Shelby's cooking had given us more than conversation. It had given us something to focus on, or at least something to take the focus off everything else.

On the ride from the city to Woods Hole my parents continued to talk about Shelby—her apartment's great location, the fabulous kitchen facilities we'd seen on the campus tour, how lucky she was to be studying with Pierre somebody who'd come all the way from Paris to teach a pastry class—until, eventually, without Shelby there to provide new topics of conversation, there was nothing left to say. And by the time we reached the Bourne Bridge the radio had been turned up and we were left listening to the countdown of America's Top 40 instead of listening to the familiar strains of Shelby explaining how premium ingredients are the cornerstone of cooking.

During the week, when my dad was in the city, it was easy to forget how bad it had become. But on the weekends, when he came back to the island, we were all acutely aware of the sudden shift, almost as if the house suddenly shrunk in size like something out of *Alice in Wonderland,* the rooms too small for all of us to sit in, the doorways too narrow to let us pass each other comfortably. It felt as if we were constantly maneuvering around one another, invading each other's personal space. As much as I missed my dad, I had grown so used to being alone in the house with my mother that it had almost become easier when it was just the two of us. We developed our own routines, new habits that accommodated the lives of two people living together rather than three. I was sure my dad felt a vague sense of relief on Sunday nights, an awareness that things would soon return to normal when he was back in his studio the next morning, where he didn't have to ask permission to change the channel on the TV or wait for someone to finish showering before flushing the toilet.

It was Monday, and this morning my dad had left for the city as usual, so I knew that my mom was the only one at home waiting for me. I hit a ton of summer traffic on my way back from visiting Jessie in Chilmark, and it had taken me way longer than I'd expected.

"Hey, sweetie," my mom called out when she heard me come through the front door.

I found her in the dining room tearing sheets of colored tissue paper into half-dollar-size pieces, making sure their edges were as ragged and haphazard as possible. Without nineteen seven-year-olds running around asking her if it was time for recess, my mom had to find other ways to occupy herself. This summer our dining room had been turned into a den of decoupage.

Every summer was like this. Last summer it was stained glass. The summer before that it was wind socks. Before that, soap making, although even I had to admit that my skin had never felt softer than when she made her cocoa-butter massage bar.

"Did you know that in eighteenth-century England decoupage was known as the art of japanning, where they believed it originated?" my mom asked, looking up from a pile of lavender tissues. It was one of the liabilities of being a teacher: she couldn't help but treat every new craft as an opportunity to learn something new and then share what she'd learned. "The traditional technique used thirty to forty layers of varnish, which artisans then sanded to a polished finish." She took a deep breath and let out a sigh, as if just the thought of all that varnish exhausted her.

"Just make sure you put newspaper down on the table this time," I reminded her, remembering the melted-beeswax fiasco. Shelby and I must have spent four hours scraping the kitchen counter with razor blades after the heart-shaped molds had tipped over and spilled molten wax all over our Formica countertops.

"Don't worry," she assured me, and pointed to a stack of yellowed *Vineyard Gazette*s in the corner of the room. "I've been collecting them in the garage all spring, and there's plenty more where those came from. I learned my lesson."

You'd think my dad or I would have noticed a towering stack of newspapers in the garage, but in truth my mom saved all sorts of odd things for her classroom projects. Empty paper-towel rolls. Cardboard egg cartons. The lone sock that lost its mate somewhere between the hamper and the dryer. Newspapers weren't the strangest thing we'd seen her hoard in our garage. That title would go to the collection of old toothbrushes she kept in a shoe box. Apparently toothbrushes, when dipped in paint, made excellent special effects.

People always thought I enjoyed kids because my mom was a teacher, as if in addition to her blond hair, hazel eyes, and size 8 feet I'd also inherited her gene for the art of getting a group of children to sit pretzel-style in a circle. But really it was Shelby who inherited my mother's ability to continually start over, to always be beginning something. I was more like my dad, in that sense. My dad peered through a lens hoping to capture a single moment and save it in time. My mother was happiest when things kept moving.

"All set for tomorrow?" she asked, picking up a lime green sheet and tearing it in half.

"I think so."

"Are your shirts ironed? I saw them on your dresser."

The Oceanview Inn made the camp counselors wear white Polo shirts with the Oceanview logo on the sleeve. White shirts. Children. Paint and glue and fingers covered in rainbow-colored glitter. See where I'm going with this? Normal camps gave counselors cotton T-shirts in blue and green and red to blend in with the assorted stains they'd collect throughout the day. At the Oceanview they dressed us as if we were heading off to Wimbledon.

"I'm going upstairs to iron them now," I told her. "I still can't believe they make us wear white shirts."

"Maybe you could suggest an alternative, or maybe the counselors could wear some sort of smock."

My mom believed a smock was the answer to many of life's potential messes, which is why she was currently wearing a clear plastic one over her yellow top.

"Maybe," I told her, although I had no intention of being the one to suggest the counselors don smocks. I didn't need to be branded a loser on the first day of work.

"Let me know if you want to borrow mine," my mom offered as I turned to head upstairs for the iron.

"Thanks, I'll do that."

Our house isn't very big compared to many of the houses in Edgartown, mostly the summer homes of people who thought the island ceased to exist from October through May. I used to complain that there was never enough room in our house and the walls were way too thin. If someone was taking a shower in the hallway bathroom, you could hear the rush of water in the pipes behind the walls. A running toilet sounded like a series of whitecaps washing away our already dubious floorboards.

When my dad started spending the weekdays at his studio in Boston, the first thing I noticed was the sound of the coffeemaker. Or, more accurately, the absence of it. My mom doesn't drink coffee. My dad can't form a coherent sentence in the morning without it. That first week he was gone, I'd lie in bed waiting for the predictable click of the timer, the sound I'd grown accustomed to hearing every morning, even more reliable than an alarm clock: 7:05, the drip of water, the smell of dark-roasted beans wafting under my bedroom door. When my dad left, the familiar drip ended. The high whir of his electric razor stopped, and the surge of water as he splashed away the last remaining stubble went silent. Oddly, our doorbell also stopped working that week, even though I could never prove the connection, and believe me, I tried.

I learned you can get used to anything and have it begin to feel normal. My father leaving on the nine-o'clock ferry every Monday morning and returning every Friday around dinner? Totally normal. For the past three years it's been the summers that don't seem normal. Having thousands of strangers invade the island you call home is abnormal enough, but we also had to adjust to having my dad around more. June, his first month of summer hours on the island, was always strange. But this year, without Shelby around, it felt even stranger—as if he were a visitor my mom and I needed to accommodate, a guest in his own home while we all got used to living together again as a family. I doubted my father realized he'd one day be asking my mom where she'd moved the butter dish when he'd decided he should get a studio in the city. Or that he'd be apologizing for buying 2 percent milk when we'd switched to skim without telling him.

In the beginning it was an "experiment."

"We're just going to see how it works out," my parents told me and Shelby at a family meeting in the kitchen, during which Shelby and I sat at the table while they stood at the counter, as if standing gave them home-court advantage, the ability to respond to any spontaneous reactions.

They said words like *great opportunity* and *temporary* and *can't pass it up.* I heard words like *leaving every Monday* and *signed a lease.*

Surprisingly, my mother wasn't fazed by the idea of my dad's essentially moving to Boston every week, probably because she didn't envy him the five-hundred-square-foot studio he was renting in Boston's South End, and that was before she even saw the shower stall that required my dad to hold the door shut with one hand while he washed his hair with the other. I hadn't even known my dad had gone to the city looking for a studio, no less that he'd already had new business cards printed up with the studio's address and phone number (he handed one to each of us as physical proof that the place actually existed).

Shelby nodded, said the business cards looked great, and asked what we were having for dinner—she was considering a lemon Bundt cake for dessert and wanted to make sure it would complement our meal.

I sat there with my hands folded on the table and wondered where I'd been when all these plans were being made.

"All this because of a dog calendar?" I blurted out.

"It's not just the calendar," my dad explained, moving over to the dishwasher in a way that made me wonder if they'd choreographed the entire conversation. "It's that with all of the exposure the calendar is getting, we think this is a chance of a lifetime."

I knew that was one of my mom's teacher moves, the "we" thing, like saying "We don't eat glue, do we, Jimmy?" when what she meant was, "Get the glue out of your mouth before it gives you diarrhea."

Was it so wrong that I thought they should at least have talked to us about it before the lease was signed and the business cards printed? Was I the only one who thought the whole thing was a little weird? Maybe it's the analytical side of me, the side that makes Jessie crazy when, instead of enjoying a movie I point out the flaws in the illogical plot, that to get from point A to point Z takes a whole set of steps in the middle, and to go from selling a few calendars to leaving your family alone every week didn't make a lot of sense to me.

"Look, he has a great opportunity," Shelby told me later, practically reciting my mother's words verbatim. "Do you think that when Dad went to art school he aspired to take Christmas portraits for summer families?"

I guess I'd never thought much about what my father aspired to do. He was just a photographer.

"He's taking pictures of *dogs,* Shelby," I pointed out, in case she had him confused with Ansel Adams.

"He's getting his work exposed to hundreds of thousands of people, Winnie. And who knows where this will lead. Maybe one day we'll be seeing Dad's dogs on greeting cards or who knows what. You want him to blow that off so he can spend another year making sure Mrs. Witherspoon from Wellesley looks ten years younger in her family's annual holiday card?"

I got her point.

Everyone made it sound like no big deal, which made me look as if I were either overreacting or being selfish or both.

Maybe that's why the job at the Oceanview appealed to me. Normal, happy families spending a week together doing

normal, happy family things—just sand castles and clam-
bakes and Marco Polo in the pool. There was nothing to try
to understand, no decisions being made behind closed doors,
no one's aspirations clouding the situation.

I finished ironing the last of my four Oceanview Inn–
issued shirts and slipped it onto a hanger, admiring my
handiwork.

Yes, the Oceanview was like real life *lite,* straightforward
and uncomplicated. The most difficult part of my summer
job would be trying to figure out how I'd keep those shirts
clean. Or figuring out how to suggest the counselors wear
smocks without them wanting to impale me with a yellow
plastic beach shovel.

Chapter 3

The Oceanview Inn is the only resort overlooking South Beach. While Edgartown mostly consists of quaint bed-and-breakfasts nestled along the narrow, one-way streets of downtown, the Oceanview stretched across a wide piece of land along Atlantic Drive, just across the street and two hundred yards from the beach. The resort was pushed back behind the cluster of trees lining the road, so you couldn't even really see it until you came to the sprawling grounds that led up to its gray-shingled exterior like a brilliant green welcome mat. Unless you happened to notice the Guests Only sign, in which case you realized that the only people welcome at the Oceanview were those willing to pay for the privilege. But even if you weren't a guest at the resort, you couldn't ignore its presence, how it unexpectedly rose up behind the trees like a mirage, appearing out of nowhere.

Even this morning, as I walked from the bus stop to the resort, I couldn't help but slow down to take in the grounds and the gray-shingled peaks that stretched along the property, each one connected by a brilliant white balcony that looked like something out of a fairy tale—if fairy tales had concierge service and daily yoga classes.

When I interviewed for the summer program, I met with the resort's general manager. He'd asked me why I wanted to work there, and I gave him some line about looking to get solid work experience for my college applications.

"And I love kids," I'd told him. "My mom's a teacher."

The general manager smiled at me as if he'd struck gold. I'd uttered the magic words. "And where are you looking at schools?" he'd asked, already convinced I had the nurturing skills of Mother Goose, which was nothing less than what the children of Oceanview guests deserved. Now he just had to find out if I had a brain in my head.

"I'll probably stay in New England, and I've been looking at schools with strong math programs, Williams, Dartmouth, Bowdoin." I threw Bowdoin in at the last minute, figuring anyone who was willing to spend the winter in Maine wouldn't be the type of person who'd call in sick just because she wanted to catch a good day at the beach. The general manager had to eat that up.

And I wasn't really lying. I had gotten some catalogs from Williams and Dartmouth, although Bowdoin wasn't even on my short list for the aforementioned reason—the Maine winters. And I wasn't making it up when I told him that I was looking forward to spending the summer around the kids at the Oceanview, even if it was just to spend four hours a day with people whose most pressing issue was whether to play croquet or horseshoes, and whose greatest concern would be who'd win the sand-castle-building contest on South Beach.

At that point the general manager had looked down at the application in his hand, reviewing my credentials one last time. "I have to tell you, Winnie, you sound like you'd be perfect for the children's program. There's an orientation training the second week of June."

"That's not a problem," I told him, and I knew the job was mine.

That was over a month ago, and now here I was walking across the impeccably manicured grounds to the door marked Staff Only. The staff break room was off the hallway leading to the front desk, and that's where I found the other counselors, each of us in our white Polo shirts with the Oceanview Inn logo embroidered on our left sleeves. Four round cafeteria tables stood in the center of the room, and each table was surrounded by six aluminum folding chairs that were clearly intended to make breaks as uncomfortable, and therefore short, as humanly possible.

We six counselors, four girls and two guys, had all met for the first time two weeks ago, when we had the day of orientation and training. I knew one of the girls vaguely, a redhead named Rachel who sat in the back of my French class and always had trouble remembering the difference between an *accent aigu* and *accent grave*. I recognized everyone from the training except for a girl standing in front of the vending machine, using her reflection in the red-and-white Coke logo to straighten out her ponytail.

I was the last to arrive, so I slipped into one of the folding chairs and waited to see what happened next.

"Okay, now that everyone's here, I want to say welcome!" The unfamiliar girl spun around to face us, her ponytail whacking against the illuminated Coke machine. "I'm Marla, the Children's Program director, and I could not be any more excited for us to work together."

It takes a certain type of person to be willing to spend her summer catering to every whim and whimsy of pint-size guests, but Marla, it was quickly evident, was born to it. She explained how she'd worked at the Oceanview for four summers before coming back to run the Children's Program, which, from the way she practically genuflected as she spoke the words, had obviously been her life's goal. Marla had just graduated from St. Bonaventure University ("Go, Bonnies!" she hollered, thrusting her fist in the air as if expecting us to do the wave in response), and she was *thrilled* to be back at the Oceanview for another summer.

"We're expecting anywhere from ten to fifteen kids today," Marla told us, straightening the remaining empty chairs around the tables as she made her way around the room. "We're going to begin with a little face-painting and then take the kids to the beach. All of the wagons and sand toys are in the prep area outside. So what do you say? Are we going to have a great day?"

Marla stuck her hand out in front of her, palm down, and waited for us to go over and cover it with our own hands in solidarity.

She wasn't just a cheerleader, she was also the quarterback and coach all rolled into one.

"Are we ready?" she tried again, this time moving over to the door as if getting ready to smack us all on the ass as we walked out to meet the kids.

"Ready," we answered, but from the disappointed expression on Marla's face it was obvious she'd expected a little more enthusiasm.

"Then let's get out there."

And with that, we went to find our campers.

. . .

If I had to describe the Oceanview's decor, I'd call it casual elegance with a nautical twist. *Casual* because the inn wanted guests to feel that they could actually sit on the furniture and feel at home; they were there to vacation, after all. The sofas and overstuffed chairs were upholstered in blues and yellows and pale green plaids that echoed the very colors you'd find if you stood on the resort's patio and looked out over the lawn toward the ocean. *Elegant* because even though the interior was meant to look and feel like a summer cottage, there was no mistaking that every fabric and piece of furniture was handpicked by an interior designer who'd gone to great pains to make sure guests felt that they got what they paid for. And the *nautical twist* because even though the Oceanview didn't go overboard with a nautical theme like most beach resorts, some decorative touches were meant to remind you that the beach was a short walk away—the framed paintings of fishermen hauling in nets bursting with a day's catch, the lobster buoys hanging behind the front desk, even the starfish on the fabric covering the chairs around the fireplace.

Twelve sets of parents were waiting in the lobby to hand off their precious cargo. They were exactly the types of families who booked my dad's services. The kids were impeccably dressed in plaids and stripes and khaki, and the mother of a set of triplets had even gone to the trouble of dressing her boys in matching shorts and LIFE IS GOOD T-shirts. She'd obviously chosen coordination over convenience, and if it hadn't been for the name tags stuck on every camper's chest, I don't think we would have referred to them as anything other than *the triplets* all day.

I looked around at the other counselors, who were flanking Marla on either side and trying to size up the pint-size campers, attempting to figure out which ones would be the problems. Rachel shifted from foot to foot, tugging at her shirt as she stared wide-eyed at the kids.

"Have you ever been around children before?" I asked Rachel, keeping my voice low so Marla wouldn't interrupt her welcome speech to look over at us.

"Does being at the library during story time count?" Rachel looked hopeful.

"Were you actually reading books to the kids?"

"Actually, I was just using the restroom," she admitted.

I paused before answering, "Sure, that counts," even though I think we both knew she was screwed.

With a ratio of 2:1 I was pretty much in the same boat as last summer with the twins. Unlike last summer, when I watched the Logan twins three days a week from June through August, camp at the Oceanview would be a revolving door. Day to day, week to week, we'd see a new set of kids, a new set of picture-perfect parents sending their kids off in our capable care.

Marla introduced us counselors to the parents and kids, and we gave them our best smiles as ambassadors of the Oceanview.

"At the Oceanview Kids Camp every one of us is dedicated to making sure your children are cared for in an environment that is respectful and safe," Marla explained to the parents, laying her right hand across her heart as if pledging allegiance to the small yellow anchors on the blue drapes in the lobby. "And fun," she added as an afterthought. "Respectful, safe, and fun."

As Marla continued to talk about the program, the hours of training we counselors had undergone and the CPR certification we'd all completed, I wondered if she would do this every morning with each new group of parents and kids. Because if that was her plan, she might want to reevaluate her approach. I watched as a few of the parents stopped smiling and looked at each other, wondering if they'd just signed their kids up for the summer-resort equivalent of Bible study. And the kids moved closer to their parents and looked up at them with expressions that clearly cried out, *Help!*

After Marla concluded her obviously well-rehearsed speech, she did everything but fingerprint the parents to ensure that we returned the same number of children to their rightful owners at noon, when the program ended.

"Everyone ready?" Marla called out, and the kids fell into line, ready to march to the activity room to begin face-painting. Parents blew kisses and waved, and we all made our orderly way down the hall.

I knew my way around a face-painting set. It was one of the Logan twins' favorite things to do. We'd usually pick themes—animals, warriors, sports teams (the Red Sox were a big favorite, as were my cat faces). Soon most of the kids realized I was an old pro and formed a line at my table while the rest of the counselors watched, trying to pick up tips for next time.

One by one I selected the right brush for the task—the small, thin brushes for whiskers, the dense, round brushes for covering the kids' cheeks and foreheads in a wash of color. And one by one the kids would hold up the hand mirror Marla had placed on the table. Reactions ranged from "pretty cool" (mostly from the boys, who didn't want to seem too excited in front of everyone else, even though they spent the most time staring at themselves in the mirror) to "Wow, Seymore would freak out" (a little girl who asked me to paint her so she looked just like her tabby cat, named Seymore). And although each of the kids had to eventually put down the mirror and let some other camper have his or her turn, I noticed how they'd stare at their own reflections in the activity room's windows, even though they were supposed to be playing Twister with Marla and the other counselors.

An hour later, all twelve faces were artistically painted and then promptly washed, which didn't make sense to any of us, least of all Rachel, who ended up with the face print of a frog on her shirt when one of the triplets decided that using a paper towel to dry his face was too much trouble. Then we packed up the wagons with beach blankets and umbrellas and bottles of water and headed for the beach.

Each of the counselors staggered along the sandy path away from the property, stopping every ten yards to make sure we hadn't lost anyone along the way. When we reached Atlantic Drive, we reminded the campers to look both ways and made a mass crossing, and even though there wasn't a car in sight, Marla stood in the middle of the road holding up a red STOP sign just in case.

It was almost ten thirty and South Beach wasn't full of tourists yet, just a smattering of families and couples hoping to get a jump start before the rush of people arrived for prime midday sun. As our noisy army marched onto the beach, I noticed the frightened stares of vacationers who saw their visions of a quiet day evaporate into the already humid air.

Marla staked out a spot near the lifeguard stand, and the

counselors carried the sand toys and beach supplies to our designated spot.

For the most part the kids just wanted to get sandy and build stuff. I helped the triplets—Ryan, Randy, and Ross—create a fortress, which they then destroyed with sticks before Marla could remove the weapons from their sweaty, little hands. I saw her shoot me a look as Ryan or Randy or Ross (even with the name tags it was hard to tell them apart) raised a stick over his head and took down an entire turret in one fell swoop, and I had a feeling I'd get the *sticks are not appropriate play items* speech. Probably followed by something about poking their eyes out and the resort's liability insurance.

A few yards away Rachel was at the mercy of two seven-year-old girls who kept begging to bury her in the sand up to her neck. They already had her buried above her ankles.

"I need some help over here," I called over to her, and Rachel gave me a relieved look as the two girls were forced to harass another counselor.

"How are you doing so far?" I asked Rachel as we dug through the bag of toys looking for the blow-up beach balls.

I looked over at her and noticed she'd either contracted a bad case of the chicken pox in the last hour or else was highly prone to freckling in the sun.

"I have sensitive skin," she explained, seeing me examine the connect-the-dots game that had blossomed on her forearm. "I wanted to wear a long-sleeved shirt but they wouldn't let me."

She was already sporting an Oceanview baseball cap (white, of course) and Capri pants, and from the smell of coconut radiating off her skin, she'd obviously lathered herself in sunblock. It had to be almost ninety degrees on the beach, and I figured Rachel, with the hat and pants, was on the verge of heatstroke.

"Why'd you even take this job?" I asked her.

"I know, not the wisest choice, in retrospect. I figured summering families throwing money around, the tips had to be great."

The first thing the general manager had told us during orientation was that counselors were forbidden from accepting tips from guests.

"You could have quit after orientation," I told Rachel, who seemed to be melting into one big freckle right before my eyes.

"It was too late. Where would I have found another job at that point?" Rachel frowned, which only exposed a new cluster of freckles on her forehead.

The girl really needed help.

"Why don't you go hang out under the umbrella with the littler kids and I'll take care of the balls," I offered, and Rachel, and her freckles, seemed thankful.

I sat on the sand and blew up two blue-and-white-striped beach balls and tossed them into the waiting group of anxious campers. Only, watching me spend ten minutes inflating balls had built the anticipation level to a point that the actual balls couldn't live up to, and after two failed rounds of catch, during which the wind blew the balls everywhere but into the hands of the kids trying to grab them, they gave up in favor of Frisbee. And as their ever-loyal counselor and all-around do-everything, I had to chase the balls down to the water's edge when the wind blew them away from base camp and apologize to the woman they hit in the head on the way there.

"Sorry about that," I apologized as I passed the woman on my way to the water. She was alone, watching a little girl play in the waves while trying to keep the sun out of her eyes with a large-brimmed straw hat. Her one-piece bathing suit was navy blue with white polka dots, and it billowed out over her protruding stomach, more like a baby-doll dress than a swimsuit. Only she wasn't being modest. She was being pregnant.

"You've got your hands full." The woman nodded in the direction of the triplets.

"They're not so bad," I told her, wiping the wet ball on my shorts in an attempt to keep my white shirt somewhat white. "Last summer I babysat for a set of twins, and that was harder, they were all about divide and conquer. At least with three they pretty much stick together because one is afraid of being the odd man out."

"I never thought of that before." The woman laughed and then patted her swollen belly. "I can't even imagine one more, no less two."

"When are you due?"

"September. The thirteenth." She must have noticed my expression because she added, "I know, it's a Friday. But what are the chances I'll actually deliver on my due date, right?"

"Right," I agreed, as if my babysitting experience qualified me to comment on gynecological issues as well.

"I'm Anne, Anne Barclay." She pointed to a little girl jumping waves at the edge of the sand. "And that's Cassie. She's six." Anne waved to Cassie, who looked over and smiled at her mom. I smiled, too, mostly because Cassie's purple-and-green-striped bikini top had nothing to keep it in place and she was still unself-conscious enough not to be bothered by it, or the stomach protruding over the ruffled skirt of her purple-and-green-striped bottoms.

I looked from Cassie back to Anne, noticing the resemblance between them, their round faces and shiny brown hair, although Cassie's was up in pigtails.

"Nice to meet you, Anne. I'm Winnie." Over by our blankets the other camp counselors were beginning to gather the toys and pack up water bottles. "I better go, the natives are getting restless."

"Well, it was nice meeting you, Winnie." Anne smiled at me and I smiled back.

"You, too, Anne."

I made my way up to the campers, who had stolen Rachel's baseball cap and were tossing it back and forth, making her monkey in the middle.

I had a feeling Rachel's days as an Oceanview camp counselor were numbered.

Chapter 4

"**I**s this what you're going to do every day? Come here and loiter while I attempt to explain the finer art of the ground stroke to a bunch of ankle biters?"

Jessie and I were sitting under a tree by the tennis courts eating our lunches.

"No," I answered, even though I hadn't come up with any better options yet, which is why as soon as camp ended at noon I took the bus from the Oceanview to Chilmark.

"Not that I mind, it's nice to talk to someone who doesn't know every word to the *SpongeBob* theme song, but there's got to be something else you can do."

Actually, I did know every word to the *SpongeBob* theme song. *SpongeBob* was one of the twins' favorite shows last summer, and every afternoon at two o'clock you could find the three of us hunkered down in front of the TV with a bowl of popcorn and the twins' *SpongeBob* pillows. I didn't say that to Jessie, though, and instead just thanked her for the compliment and spared her my knowledge of a guy who lived in a pineapple under the sea.

"I promise I won't be bothering you and Nash every day. Maybe just every *other* day."

Jessie tore off a piece of her turkey sandwich and stuffed it in her mouth. "He'll actually be here in a couple of minutes. You can say hi."

"Great." I smiled and tried to look as if I meant it.

It wasn't that I didn't like Nash. I didn't *not* like him, I just hadn't bought into the idea that he was as flawless as his skin made him out to be (I didn't trust a guy who never, not even on weekends, said *screw it* to his razor and went with a little stubble). Nash is charming, able to carry on a conversation with anyone and comfortable around everyone, a skill he undoubtedly picked up from being around politicians most of his life. And in a way that's what he reminded me of, a politician, someone who knew the right things to say to the right people. I wanted to believe that he really liked Jessie, but a part of me wondered if half the reason he went after Jess was that he wanted to prove he could get her, the only girl at the Community Center who didn't fall over herself trying to get his attention. I think that's what appealed to Jessie at first. The conquest. Proving to herself that she could get Nash even though everyone else was trying so hard and getting nowhere.

Jessie didn't take crap from anyone. It was one of the things that made her so great on the court and why the tennis coach loved her. The harder her opponents hit the ball at her, the harder she returned it. I think that was one of the reasons why Jessie never had a boyfriend until Nash came along. He was the first guy she didn't scare the hell out of, the first one who seemed up for the challenge.

Nash was always pleasant enough to me, acting as if he

didn't mind having me around and seeming at least mildly interested in what I had to say. Maybe a part of me just needed to get used to the idea of Jessie's having a boyfriend, someone who needed some of the space that I usually occupied. Last year they were only together three weeks, but they were the last three weeks of the summer, our last free days before school started. But instead of going to the beach with Jessie I ended up either going straight home after babysitting the Logans or sitting in the backseat of Nash's Saab, learning forward over the center console, trying to include myself in their conversation.

It wasn't that I felt as if Nash had swept in and brushed me aside, but more like I'd been moved a little to the left and back some. Shelby would probably say I was jealous or envious of Nash, but that would be Shelby, who wasn't used to looking at things in shades of gray.

Last summer I kept my ambivalence to myself, if only because I knew Nash was taking off for Vermont in less than a month and Jessie was enjoying her victory way more than I had anticipated. It was unnerving in a way. By the end of the three weeks Jessie was different, as if Nash had worn away her edges, somehow softened the calluses she'd gone to so much effort to build up. I don't think anyone but me noticed because it wasn't as if she became one of those girls who agreed with everything her boyfriend said or asked his permission to go out with her friends instead of him. It was more the little things, how she'd reach for his hand, holding her outstretched fingers toward him until they touched, and how the expression on her face relaxed, her shoulders settled down, as if something inside her had been calmed. In those three weeks Jessie laughed a little easier and walked a little slower.

When he left for school, Nash never promised to e-mail Jess or offered to have her up to visit him in Burlington once he got settled into his dorm. And he didn't suggest they not see anyone else while he was at school. Not even after Jessie slept with him the night before he left.

As soon as Nash was gone, Jess wasted no time going on the UVM website to buy herself a Vermont sailing-team T-shirt. She wore that T-shirt to just about every tennis team practice and any other time she could get away with it (her mother swore she'd use the shirt as a garden rag if she saw Jessie wear it one more time). At first I thought maybe Jessie just wanted a souvenir, like the huge stuffed dogs you win at the carnival as proof of your ability to knock down a milk bottle with a small rubber ball. But whenever anyone asked why Jessie was wearing a Vermont sailing shirt, she'd cast her eyes down at the block letters on her chest and smile to herself before telling them about Nash. And that's when I noticed a crack in her veneer, just from listening to her voice and how it softened. Jess never came out and said it, but usually people walked away from her thinking the obvious—that Nash had given her the shirt before he went back to school. I was the only one who knew she'd ordered it off the Internet using her mother's credit card, but I never clarified the point. Instead I let people believe what I knew Jessie wanted to believe herself. That Nash wanted her to wear that shirt, even if it hadn't cost him $19.99 plus $3.50 in shipping and handling.

"Did you ask if he was with anybody else this year?" I asked Jessie.

Jessie shook her head, no.

"Aren't you curious?"

She shrugged. "He's here now, right?"

I watched for a sign that she was fooling herself, but Jessie just chewed her turkey sandwich as if she actually believed that what Nash had done at school this past year didn't matter. I didn't get it. I'd want to know whom Nash was with—her name, how tall she was, what she was majoring in, how she kissed, if he liked her more than me.

"There he is." Jessie waved to Nash, who was making his way across the grass in our direction.

Nash was like the straight white-blond hair that fell across his eyes and the tanned arms his white T-shirt exposed—in a word: smooth. And he swaggered. I swear. There was no other way to describe the low-slung way he moved his body, as if exaggerating every stride. He actually reminded me of someone out of an old western movie. All that was missing were the spurs on the back of his shoes and a bandana around his neck.

Jess thought Nash was gorgeous. That's all I heard from her last summer, how gorgeous this sailing instructor was. And there's no denying Nash is cute. He just wasn't my type. Nash was so good-looking he was almost pretty, is the only way I can explain it. His features seemed finely drawn, painstakingly perfect, from the straight nose that had never seen a stray elbow in a basketball game to the cheekbones that sat high and sloped down at an angle that would require two black diamonds on Mount Snow. He was the kind of guy who could make a girl feel ugly. At least, any girl but Jessie. Leave it to Jessie to pick the best-looking person in the room and not feel the least bit intimidated.

Jessie was pretty but in a different way, the kind of pretty that snuck up on you, such as when she walked off the tennis court, her hair matted back from constantly pushing it out of her eyes, her cheeks flushed.

"What's up?" Nash greeted us, taking a seat on the ground next to Jess. "Hey, Winnie."

Nash reached over and lifted a potato chip out of the bag on Jessie's lap. Jessie never liked to share food, which was maybe one of the reasons she sliced and diced her food until nobody would actually want her to share. But when Nash pulled a chip out of her bag, Jessie didn't even react.

"We were just talking about Winnie's lack of afternoon activities," she said.

"Aren't you working?" he asked me, reaching for another chip.

"Yeah, but the camp gets out at noon." Even if Jessie didn't want to know, even if she acted as if what happened at UVM stayed at UVM, I knew better. And that's why I watched Nash and tried to detect a movement or inflection in his voice that would provide a clue as to what he did during his year in Burlington, signs that Jessie needed protecting. But Nash didn't give me any.

"Sounds like the perfect job to me," he said.

"Believe me, after spending all morning watching those rug rats at the Oceanview, she needs time to recuperate." Jessie took the last chip out of Nash's hand and popped it into her mouth.

I had to smile because Nash actually looked surprised. But instead of complaining, he leaned over and kissed her, pretending that he was trying to get the chip back.

"I better go," I told them, balling up my sandwich bag

and reaching for the crumpled-up napkin Jessie had set on the ground.

Jessie turned her attention back to me. "Hey, Nash is helping out with the Menemsha Pond Races this summer," she announced as if Nash would be curing cancer while he was here. "I can't go, I have travel team, but you could go watch."

"Maybe," I told them, wondering if that was what my summer would be, afternoons spent watching Jessie's boyfriend at the pond races when I wasn't watching Jessie play tennis. "I'll have to see what happens."

Jessie nudged Nash.

"You should come," Nash told me, taking Jessie's not so subtle hint. "Really."

I smiled as if I'd consider Nash's offer, but I had no intention of spending my Wednesday afternoons at Menemsha Pond. And I definitely couldn't spend every day watching Nash and Jessie use snack food as foreplay. I had to find something to do after camp every day, because compared to watching Jessie and Nash, even Kelsey's snack-bar job was starting to look pretty good.

Chapter 5

The second day of camp the schedule was much like the first day's, although face-painting was replaced with kite-building. There were only ten kids, and even though we knew most of them from the first day, a few were new. It's always amazed me how quickly alliances are formed between kids, and even though they'd spent a mere four hours together the day before, the campers from yesterday acted as if they'd been best friends since birth, as if building a sand castle together was a lifelong bonding experience.

The kids fell into two groups, the ones who wanted nothing to do with the counselors and the ones who clung to us like magnets, climbing up our backs every chance they got in hopes we'd give in and carry them around on our shoulders. While most of us managed to redirect the kids toward the craft table to begin their kites, the neediest kids found Rachel, almost as if they could sense she was the weak link. And Rachel gave in, mostly because the kids kept tugging on her sunburned arms and she decided a piggyback was probably the less painful option.

Luckily once Marla heard four kids chanting Rachel's

name at the top of their lungs, she stepped in and prohibited piggybacks as a form of camper transportation, then reminded everyone to use his or her indoor voice.

My mom had never actually attempted kite-making, at least not yet, but I figured wind socks were a close relative on the craft family tree. And once again, when the campers realized I could cut and staple and glue a kite in half the time the other counselors took, I was inundated with requests for help.

"You're making the rest of us look bad," Rachel commented, running a stream of glue along a Popsicle stick and getting glue on just about each of her fingers.

"I've had some practice," I explained, handing a completed kite over to a little girl who'd requested one in the shape of a ladybug.

The little girl, Grace, took the kite and grinned at her ladybug before standing on her tiptoes and cupping a hand against my ear. "You're my favorite," she whispered so quietly even I could hardly hear her voice.

I should probably have told her that she shouldn't have favorites, that all of the counselors were nice and helpful, and she should like everyone equally.

Instead I pushed the blond hair away from Grace's little ear, leaned down, and whispered, "Thank you."

"Is there anything you can't help with?" Rachel asked, her fingers now sticking to everything she touched, including the tail she'd just attempted to attach to the kite. When she tried to separate herself from the yellow construction paper, it tore in half, and five-year-old Elizabeth looked as if she was trying to decide whether to cry or dig her fingers into Rachel's red arm.

I winked at Elizabeth, squeezed a dollop of glue onto the end of a new tail, and handed it to Rachel. "The summer is still young, I'm sure there will be something."

When all of the kites were completed, and their streamer tails stapled in place, we piled them into the wagons and headed to the beach to see how aerodynamic a few pieces of construction paper held together by Popsicle sticks could be.

We staked out our spot next to the lifeguard stand, and each of the kids took his or her kite out of the wagons. But if yesterday the wind was too strong to play catch with the beach balls, today the wind had decided to die down completely. With the wind's lack of cooperation the campers quickly lost interest in the kites and went for the shovels and pails.

Without the breeze the beach was stifling, and even stacking the abandoned kites up in the wagons produced beads of sweat that trickled down my face. And if I was overheating, I figured Rachel had to be about ready to melt into a puddle right there on the sand.

"You've got to be kidding me," I told Rachel, who had resorted to a white stripe of zinc oxide on her nose and a long-sleeved jacket to keep the sun off her arms. "Aren't you dying in that?"

"It's the official windbreaker of the Oceanview Inn," Rachel explained, pointing to the logo plastered across her back. "I found it in a box in Marla's office. She told me I could wear it."

"How come I didn't get one?"

"They didn't actually give them out to anyone. Who'd need a windbreaker when it's eighty-five degrees with fifty percent humidity?"

"Are you seriously going to wear that the entire time?"

"What choice do I have?"

"Find another job!"

"I told you, I can't." Rachel glanced across the sand at Marla, who was helping the kids dig a moat around their sand castle. "At least the jacket's white, right?"

"Sure, Rachel." I laughed. "At least it's white."

I noticed Anne sitting in a beach chair beside a *Dora the Explorer* beach towel, the wide-rimmed straw hat tilted down over her eyes, shading her from the sun as she watched Cassie digging for shells down by the water. Anne squeezed a dollop of suntan lotion into her hand and began rubbing the cream along her leg. She caught me looking at her and waved.

I left Rachel to sweat alone and went over to her.

"Hi, Winnie," Anne greeted me, rubbing the last of the lotion into her arms in circular motions. "Boy, it's a hot one today. I don't know how much longer I'm going to be able to do this."

A drop of sweat slid down her chest and disappeared inside her bathing-suit top.

"Cassie seems to be enjoying herself." I pointed to the edge of the water, where Cassie had made friends with another little boy, who'd decided to share his Nerf football for a game of catch.

"I know, I feel horrible about this. A summer on the Vineyard and all I seem to do is sleep. And sweat," Anne added, wiping her chest with her hand. Her hair was held in two braided ponytails, which made her look younger than she probably was. Although she was carrying around an extra thirty-five pounds and her ankles were swollen to the size of mandarin oranges, I could tell she was pretty, even if she was also sweaty and puffy and obviously miserable.

"Oh, shoot." Anne let out an exaggerated sigh and gripped the arms of her beach chair as she attempted to stand up. "Coming!" she yelled to the kids.

I looked toward the water and noticed Cassie and her friend wading into the water as they attempted to keep the football from floating away.

"Stay here, I've got it," I offered, and jogged down to the water's edge, where I retrieved the ball before Cassie and her friend got out too far.

"Here you go." I handed the ball to the little boy and then turned to Cassie. "Hi, I'm Winnie."

"Thanks for getting our ball." Cassie wore matching braids in her hair and an orange one-piece, which struck me as being much better for football than her purple-and-green bikini. "Do you want to play?"

"I can't, but thanks." The boy was looking anxious to get started again, so I left them alone and went back to Anne. "They're all set."

"Thanks. You know, Winnie, I hope you don't think this is strange, but would you be interested in some babysitting? I know you probably get your fill of chaos with the camp, but I was thinking how nice it would be for Cassie to have someone to do things with. As you can tell, I'm not exactly the best company these days. I think she's bored with me already."

"What did you have in mind?" I asked, thinking that Anne was on the verge of giving me an option that wouldn't just get me out of watching Nash sail Menemsha Pond every Wednesday, but would also pay well. "Camp goes until noon every day."

"The afternoons would work for us. That's when I really start to fade, and, of course, Cassie starts to get going again after lunch." Anne took the bottle of suntan lotion and slipped it into the canvas beach bag beside her foot. "What's your schedule look like?"

"I could come over today after camp," I told her, and she laughed.

"I wasn't thinking of something so soon, but I'm game if you are."

Cassie yelled to her mother, and when I looked over, she held up a shell the size of her hand. Anne signaled her approval with a thumbs-up.

"Our house is in town, on South Water Street," Anne said, then told me the address.

I could immediately picture the house, one of the massive summer homes set beside Edgartown harbor, their backyards offering a view of the water and the boats docked at the yacht club.

"I can take the bus and probably be there by one."

"Perfect."

I turned to leave but stopped. "Hey, Anne, there's one more thing. Can I ask where you got your hat? I have a friend who doesn't do so well in the sun."

Anne raised her hand and slid a finger along the smooth rim. "This hat is the best, and believe it or not, I got a bunch of them in town last year on sale, so I doubt they even sell them anymore."

"Oh, okay." It looked as if Rachel was going to have to stick to the baseball hat and windbreaker. I just hoped she didn't turn up in sweatpants tomorrow, although at the rate she was going, I wouldn't be surprised. "I'll see you at one o'clock."

Anne took a deep breath and laid her hands on her bulging stomach. "See you then, Winnie."

•   •   •

Everything is brighter in the summer, as if the island were a professionally lit stage designed to exaggerate every color, every shadow that changes throughout the day as the sun makes its way west. Off-season the summer sun is replaced with a fluorescent bulb, the imperfections are more noticeable, the reality of island life is exposed.

All of the homes in downtown Edgartown are old, and the preservation society makes sure they stay that way. They're also white, at least most of them, which makes them perfectly matched to the white picket fences lining the sidewalks all around downtown. It's like something out of history class, the houses with their small wooden plaques noting BUILT IN 1765 and THE CAPTAIN ABRAHAM OSBORNE HOUSE CIRCA 1840, and even though every summer tourists drive up and down the narrow, one-way streets jockeying for spaces to parallel-park their luxury SUVs, you can just imagine that hundreds of years ago there was more than enough room for horses and buggies.

The homes downtown were of the type your parents walked by and muttered aloud, "Wow, it must cost a fortune to heat that place." The truth was, it did, but it also didn't matter. The summer people who owned those homes either closed the houses off-season, or, if they actually ventured back for the holidays, it wasn't money they were worried about, but how to fit all of their presents into the car for the ferry ride over. But more often than not they spent the holidays at their ski houses, trading waterside for slopeside in the off-season.

The interiors of those houses always intrigued me, how

they were close enough to the sidewalks to let passersby see inside the impeccably decorated rooms, to identify shadows of people walking past the windows at night, martini glasses in hand, and yet, set behind those white picket fences, they were politely removed from us—look but don't touch.

But even if on the outside the homes looked as if they'd been there forever, on the inside the rooms were *Architectural Digest* perfect, their overstuffed couches and armchairs tastefully upholstered in current designer fabrics.

I was sure the Barclays' house would be like that, lining the water side of South Water Street, perched above Edgartown Harbor, set back just far enough to keep the envious passersby from getting too close, their voices whispering, "Who can afford to live in a house like that?"

The Barclays' house wasn't white. It was the other option, natural wood shingles stained a yellowy brown, like maple syrup. The dark green shutters added to the au naturel look, but anyone who lived on the island knew that every year those shingles were stained, the shutters painted, in an effort to combat the sun and wind and salt water that faded the facade and wreaked havoc on the tourists' version of what a Vineyard house should look like. Luckily the summer families who owned these homes could afford the annual painting and staining, the weekly landscaping to keep the purple and blue hydrangea looking as if they'd just nestled below the windows in haphazard perfection. The house next to the Barclays' was like that. Only we all knew that if you pushed aside the hydrangea and rhododendron bushes beside the garage, you'd discover three gravestones the owners had moved when they decided to turn the garage into guest quarters and learned their summer house had also been the burial site of some of the Vineyard's first founders. Needless to say, moving gravestones was not a smart thing to do. Which is why admirers didn't just stop to gawk at the gorgeous house, but the Edgartown ghost tour also made a stop there every Tuesday night.

I turned left and made my way up the stone walk toward the front door. Because the Barclays' house was on the harbor side, they had more land than the others downtown, which meant they had a front yard. It also meant the backyard faced Edgartown Harbor, a view tourists coveted but only a few could afford. Obviously the Barclays could.

As I stepped on each stone of the front walk I mentally checked off the list.

Manicured bushes, check. Mercedes SUV in the driveway, check. Potted flowers decorating the front steps, check.

I rang the doorbell and waited for a housekeeper or some other help to answer so I could check one more item off my list. Instead, Anne appeared, her hair pulled back into a ponytail, which only made her head seem smaller and her stomach even bigger. If not pregnant, Anne would be tiny, probably just a few inches over five feet, which meant she was at least five inches shorter than me.

"Winnie!" she exhaled, as if grateful to see me standing on her doorstep. "Come in. I told Cassie you were coming and she's been dying for you to get here."

Anne stepped aside, inviting me into the foyer, a large circular area dotted in the middle by a round table that was empty except for the vase of giant yellow sunflowers in the center. Over against the far wall, where a curving set of stairs swept up to a second-floor landing, a side table held framed photographs of the Barclays.

Anne must have noticed me staring at the photos because she walked over to the table and pointed to each frame, one by one. "That was Cassie when she was just six months old. And that's our nephew, they were born a few weeks apart. Cassie adores him."

"I'm sure she'll love having a little brother or sister, too," I told Anne.

"Six years apart isn't ideal, I realize that, but hopefully Cassie won't feel too displaced. She's always been the baby."

"My sister is three years older than me. My mom always said it was a little like having two families. Just when I was old enough to start enjoying what my sister enjoyed, Shelby would move on to something else."

Anne nodded. "That's sort of what I've been preparing myself for, as much as I have this vision of the two of them playing together peacefully."

"Do you know what you're having?"

"I wanted to, but Jim, my husband, wants to be surprised."

I looked more closely at the picture of Anne, Cassie, and a man I assumed was Jim. They were sitting together on the sand, dune grass springing up around them, their matching white shirts contrasted against the stalks of green and the cornflower blue sky.

"That was last year. We used that picture for our Christmas card." Anne pointed to Cassie, tapping the glass with the tip of her finger. "Looks lovely, right? It was six thirty in the morning, barely sixty degrees, so we were all freezing, and Cassie hated the photographer because she wouldn't let Cassie say cheese."

I laughed. "You'd never know it, you all look great."

"Anything can look great for the time it takes to snap the shutter closed. Between shots we were miserable."

"Is Mr. Barclay here this summer, too?"

"He'll be coming to the island every Friday to spend the weekends, but other than that he'll be home in Connecticut, so it's just us girls most of the time." Anne turned away from the table and led me down a hallway toward the back of the house.

As we wove our way through the labyrinth of rooms, I wondered what it was like to wake up every morning in a house that most people could only imagine, from the flawlessly polished hardwood floors to the immaculate color-coordinated rooms, the expansive windows offering views in every direction, to the framed pictures displaying what could only be described as the perfect family.

When we finally reached the back of the house, we found Cassie sitting at the kitchen table licking jelly off her fingers. "Cassie's been waiting impatiently for you to get here."

"Winnie!" she cried when she noticed me, as if we'd met a million times before. "What are we going to do today?"

"I'm not much fun these days." Anne looked down at her stomach. "Cassie keeps complaining she's bored and we've only been here for two weeks."

"Well, what would you like to do?" I asked Cassie.

Cassie looked to Anne, who had pulled out a chair and sat down, wedging herself up against the kitchen table. "Can we go to the candy store?"

"Is she allowed to have candy?" I asked Anne, knowing how some mothers thought sugar was the childhood equivalent of crystal meth.

"Sure," Anne told me, and she must have seen my surprise

because she added, "I know, I'm probably ruining her, bad mother, all that. But you know what? I had Froot Loops and chocolate milk for breakfast every day until I was twelve and I turned out okay, even though I'm probably lucky I still have all my teeth."

"What'd you switch to when you turned twelve?" I asked, curious.

Anne smiled sheepishly. "Pop-Tarts. The brown-sugar-and-cinnamon kind. I still love them."

We both laughed and Cassie joined us, even though I was sure she didn't really understand what we were talking about.

"So what do you say, Winnie? Are you up for a walk into town and taking Cassie to the candy store?" Anne sighed, as if she wasn't up for much of anything. "I was hoping to do a little grocery shopping while you two have fun."

"That works," I told her.

Anne gave me a ten-dollar bill and I handed it to Cassie, who slipped it into her pink-flowered purse for safekeeping.

It only took us a few minutes to walk to Main Street, but once we got there, our pace slowed. As the day wore on, downtown became busier and the sidewalks more crowded.

"So your dad is in Connecticut all week?" I asked Cassie as we walked behind a family who stopped about every ten feet to ooh and aah over another display of madras shorts and matching thirty-dollar flip-flops.

"And New York. That's where he works. He's a lawer."

I knew she meant *lawyer*, but I didn't correct her.

"My dad works in Boston. He's gone all week, too, so I don't get to see him except on weekends."

"I like weekends," Cassie told me, and I agreed.

As we made our way up Main Street, I watched Cassie take in all the activity, the bikes passing by, the tourists with their brightly colored shopping bags slapping together, the storefront windows displaying colorful T-shirts emblazoned with MARTHA'S VINEYARD across the front. I tried to see the town through her eyes, how it existed solely for her enjoyment, a place that transformed during her presence.

To Cassie it was all temporary, the summer house, the island, the father who flew in for a few days and then left again. I wondered if I could ever be like her, able to enjoy what was fleeting.

Anne came home a few minutes after Cassie and I returned from town.

"You were such a huge help today, thanks." Anne smiled at me as she placed the grocery bags on the kitchen counter. "So, what do you think? Interested in making this a permanent thing? I could use you during the week, if you're willing."

Cassie slapped her hands together in prayer and jumped up and down on her tiptoes. "Oh, please, Winnie? Please? We'll have so much fun."

"That would be great," I agreed. "I could be here by one, if that works for you."

"That's perfect. Can you start tomorrow?" Anne asked, then laughed. "Not that I'm desperate or anything."

"That's fine." I turned to Cassie, who already had a box of Fudgsicles in her hand and was trying to tear open the cardboard flap. "Anything special you'd like to do tomorrow afternoon?"

Cassie looked up from the box. "Go get some ice cream?"

"Would that be okay?" I asked Anne.

"Terrific. You're a lifesaver, Winnie. Thanks."

"No problem."

"Hey, before you leave, I have something for you." Anne disappeared down the hallway and returned a few minutes later. "Here."

She handed me a wide-brimmed straw hat, identical to the one she'd had on at the beach. "I found the extras upstairs in my closet, and I don't think I'll be needing all of them this summer."

"Thanks, Anne, that's nice of you." I took the hat, surprised at how light it was.

"No problem. I hope your friend likes it."

I grabbed my backpack and turned toward the hallway.

"There's a key under the front mat, just let yourself in tomorrow," Anne called after me. "I'll get a key made for you at the hardware store."

Anne had offered to walk me to the door, but I told her I could let myself out. I figured the less walking she did, the better. As I closed the front door behind me, I noticed someone coming up the front walk, a duffel bag slung over his shoulder. I didn't recognize him from any of the pictures in the foyer, but he seemed to know exactly where he was going, as if he lived here. But since he looked to be barely older than me, was wearing brown cargo shorts and a T-shirt, and obviously hadn't shaved in several days, I assumed he had to be helping out around the yard or something. Someone had to trim all those bushes, right?

He continued up the walkway, coming toward me without even offering any sort of acknowledgment we were about to pass each other—not a smile or a wave or a nod in my direction. Instead he avoided my eyes and looked the rest of me up and down before passing by me and heading into the house without even knocking. And that's when I realized, unless he had a pair of hedge clippers and a bottle of Miracle-Gro in that duffel bag, that guy wasn't doing any landscaping.

Chapter 6

"Hey, where were you today?" Jessie asked when she called me after dinner. "I've gotten used to having you around."

"I got an afternoon job." I could hear my mom downstairs in the dining room tearing sheets of tissue paper.

"Does this mean I'll be eating lunch alone from now on?"

"It means I'm making thirteen dollars an hour to hang out and eat ice cream," I told her. "I'm babysitting a little girl for a summer family in town."

"Okay, when you said the thirteen bucks an hour thing I was jealous, but the word *babysitting* got me over it really quickly."

I laughed. "I figured it would."

I told Jessie about Anne and Cassie and the Barclays' house, but I knew no matter how great I made it sound she wouldn't envy me in the slightest.

"Nash and I are going out tonight, want to come with us?" Jessie offered when I finished telling her about my new job.

As much as I appreciated the offer and knew Jess was trying to include me so I didn't feel left out, I actually had plans. "Thanks, but I have to do something for work."

"They give you homework at camp?"

"Not homework," I hedged. "Just a little project."

As soon as Anne gave me the sun hat, I knew what I had to do. I couldn't let Rachel melt before my eyes every day, and if she wasn't willing to find another job, there was only one thing left for me to do: give the girl a decent hat.

I found my mom in the dining room brushing the first layer of glue onto a glass lamp base she was converting from plain white to multicolored. "Hey, Mom, where's your glue gun?"

"The hall closet, why?"

I held out my hands. Anne's hat dangled from one, and the white sleeve I'd cut off one of my standard-issue Oceanview Inn polo shirts hung from the other. "I have a little project for us."

I knew my mom was torn between admonishing me for cutting up my shirt and getting me the glue gun herself. The woman can't resist an opportunity to wield the supreme power of hot glue. In the end she just stood up, left the room, and returned carrying the glue gun.

"Shelby called today," she said, also handing me a pair of shearing scissors so the edges of the fabric wouldn't fray.

"How's her job going?"

"Good, she's been working both lunch and dinner shifts so most days she's exhausted." My mom reached over the table and held the fabric down flat as I cut across the edge in as straight a line as I could. "But she says she's learning a lot."

"Do you think she'll come home next summer and get a job on the island?" I asked, remembering how Shelby hadn't even wanted to leave the island in the first place. She'd been totally content with her job cooking at the Willow Inn, although I think part of it had to do with Wendy, the owner. Wendy loved Shelby almost as much as the Willow's guests loved Shelby's breakfasts.

"I don't know," my mom answered, reaching for the sun hat and placing two paper towels inside the rim so they'd soak up any glue that seeped through the woven straw. "I guess we'll just have to wait and see."

When Shelby brought home the brochure for the Boston Culinary Institute, she didn't show it to any of us, which is why when I found the pamphlet, I wasn't sure what to do. I figured if Shelby was really interested in going to cooking school, she would have told us. But I'd discovered the brochure stuffed inside the pocket of her sweatshirt, so how excited could she have been?

"What do I need to go to Boston for?" she'd replied when I asked her about the brochure. "I'm doing fine at the Willow, everyone loves my cooking."

It was true, Shelby had turned breakfast into something of a fine art at the Willow Inn, and she'd pretty much run the kitchen. But I didn't think Shelby's dismissal of the Culinary Institute had as much to do with her knowing her way around a western omelet as it did her experience at UMass. I knew that if she stayed on the island, she'd still be a great breakfast chef, and if she continued to consume the *Gourmet* and *Bon Appétit* magazines in her room, she'd probably get even better. Still, she'd never be as good as she could be, and that's why

I called the school and had them send an application to Shelby, and then I made sure she filled it out.

"What do you think?" I asked my mom when we'd finished the cutting and gluing and the band was securely fastened around the base of the sun hat. I knew she was probably concocting all sorts of plans in her head, maybe even debating whether she should get out her BeDazzler and spiff up the straw rim a little.

But instead of suggesting we add a ribbon on the back or a Velcro chin strap, my mom appraised my work and nodded her approval. "I think you'd be great at decoupage."

I found Rachel in the break room, where we all met each morning before going out to greet the guests and their kids.

"Here." I held out the hat. "Maybe this will help."

"Thanks, Winnie, I appreciate the thought," she told me, but didn't move to take it. "The thing is, it's not *official*. Marla will never let me wear it."

I turned the hat around so Rachel could see the front. "What's that say?" I pointed to the white band of fabric around the base of the hat, and that's when she noticed the blue Oceanview Inn logo embroidered in the center.

"How'd you do that?" she said.

"When your mom's a teacher, you learn how to use a glue gun at a very young age."

"But where'd you get the logo?" she wanted to know, this time taking the hat from me.

"You're better off not asking. Just tell Marla you found the hat at the front desk or something."

"It's great." Rachel put the hat on her head, pushing her

bangs under the brim to keep them out of her eyes. "I bet the brim is wide enough to even cover my shoulders."

"That's the idea. Now you don't have to wear the zinc oxide on your nose."

Rachel looked over her shoulder, checking to see if we were alone. "Can I tell you something?" she asked, once she determined it was just the two of us. "That wasn't zinc oxide. I found some Desitin in the kids' playroom and I was so desperate I figured it was better than nothing."

"Diaper rash, sunburn, they're sort of the same thing, right?" I asked, hoping to give Rachel some consolation at a time she obviously needed it.

Rachel stooped down, trying to catch her reflection in the glass on the break-room door. "Regardless, I'll take the hat."

That afternoon I took the bus downtown and walked to the Barclays'. I'd brought an extra shirt in my backpack and changed before I left the Oceanview. I may have been forced to wear that shirt from eight to twelve, but as soon as camp was over, my obligation ended.

When I got to the door, I bent down and lifted up the mat, which was tan with a rough texture and a solid black *B* in the center. A single silver key was lying there, just as Anne had promised.

I took the key, but before slipping it into the lock, I turned around to see if anyone was watching me, ready to dial 911 and report a girl breaking into the Barclay house on South Water Street. But it was just me and the azalea bushes. I slipped the key in and pushed the door open.

"Hello?" I called out, making my way toward the kitchen, where I figured Anne and Cassie might be finishing up lunch. Only when I walked into the room, I found someone else at the table, and this time he didn't ignore me.

"So who are you?" he asked, his eyes sweeping across me as if taking inventory.

"Winnie. Who are you?"

This made him laugh, but it didn't make him answer my question. I didn't have enough time to get a good look at him yesterday, but now I couldn't help but notice that he was cute, even if he still hadn't shaved. His hair was lighter than the stubble on his face, which was a dark brown compared to the disheveled mass of long, pale brown waves on his head, which were just past the point of needing a haircut. The wispy ends bent enough that I could see the beginning of a real curl. He must just have woken up because he still had that rumpled look that only came from being pressed against a pillow. And then there were his eyelashes. His brown eyes were flecked with a yellowy gold and framed by the most amazing lashes, the kind you drew on smiley faces in elementary school, thick and dark and long, curling up at the very edges. They were exactly the kind of lashes on guys that made girls think life wasn't fair.

"Does Anne know you're here?" I glanced through the arched doorway toward the family room, hoping to find Anne or Cassie on the couch or playing a game on the floor, but the room was empty.

"Does she know I'm here?" he repeated, laughing and shaking his head as if he found me vaguely amusing and yet annoying at the same time. "Um, yeah, she knows I'm here."

I waited for further explanation, but he didn't offer any, instead enjoying my obvious discomfort as I stood there trying to determine what I should do next. "Is she around? Anne? Or Cassie?"

He jerked a thumb over his shoulder toward the French doors behind him, stood up, and left me standing there alone, his cereal bowl still half full of milk on the table.

Through the French doors to the backyard I could see Anne kneeling beside one of the gardens, her bulging stomach resting on her thighs as she bent over, plucking weeds from the soil and tossing them into a bucket.

For a second I considered taking the cereal bowl to the sink, but then thought, *Screw it*. I was the babysitter, not the maid. And I was here for Cassie, not some strange guy who couldn't get out of bed before noon.

I opened the French doors and went outside.

The Barclays' backyard sloped down to the harbor, a seamless carpet of green interrupted only by a path of scattered stones leading to the water's edge, a stone birdbath, and flowerbeds, the largest of which was off to the left, where Anne and Cassie, each on her own padded rubber mat, knelt with shovels in hand.

"Do you know there's a guy in your kitchen eating cereal?" I asked.

Anne looked up at me and wiped her gloved hand across her forehead, leaving a streak of dirt. "I see you met Jay."

"Actually, I didn't. He didn't bother introducing himself. Who is he?"

"My brother," Cassie chirped, as if she actually took pride in her relation to the guy. "He's nineteen."

I did some quick math. If Anne was in her mid to late

thirties, which is what I suspected, then there was no way that guy was her son.

"He surprised us yesterday." Anne's voice wasn't nearly as enthusiastic as Cassie's. "Jay told us he had plans to spend the summer in Colorado with some friends mountain biking or something, but I guess his plans fell through."

"So he's here for the summer?" I asked, realizing that after just one day I might be out of a job, and also realizing how much I'd been looking forward to spending my afternoons at the Barclays'.

"Yep. The whole summer." Anne made it sound like a very long time.

"Will you still need me to watch Cassie, or will Jay be helping you out in the afternoons?"

Anne's lips parted, as if she was about to laugh, but then she glanced over at Cassie and stopped herself. "Yes, we'll still be needing you, Winnie."

"Good," I found myself saying. "So what do you say, Cassie, ready for that ice cream? I'm starving."

Cassie tugged on Anne's arm, leaving a set of muddy fingerprints on her mother's bare shoulder. "Can we go, Mommy? Please?"

"Go, have fun. I think I'm going to lie down for a while." Anne attempted to stand up and I held out my hand to help her. "Cassie, why don't you run inside and wash your hands."

Cassie did as she was told, and Anne and I walked, or in Anne's case waddled, toward the house.

"I guess I should explain about Jay," Anne began once the back door closed behind Cassie and she was out of earshot. "Jay is my husband's son from his first marriage, my stepson. I don't really know how to say this without feeding into every stereotype about stepmothers, but Jay can be difficult. Since his mom died last year, it's gotten worse, and it wasn't like he was especially easy to get along with before. So I don't know what to expect this summer, but if he gives you any trouble, make sure you tell me. Sound good?"

I wasn't sure that sounded *good*, exactly, but I nodded anyway. "Okay."

The back door swung open and Cassie stood there, her clean hands planted on her slim little hips. "Come on, Winnie!"

"We'll be back before three," I told Anne, who stopped beside the patio table and rested her weight against it.

"There's money on the desk in the kitchen. Take your time and have fun."

"I have a big sister," I told Cassie on our walk into town. "It must be neat to have a big brother."

Jay was the same age as Nash, and I found myself comparing the two of them—Nash's polish to Jay's raw edges, Nash's clean-cut exterior to Jay's scratchy surface. While it was easy for anyone to see why Jess was attracted to Nash, I couldn't help but think that something about Jay made him more interesting. With Nash you got exactly what you saw. With Jay, I had a feeling what you saw was just the beginning.

"Jay goes to college, so we don't get to play much. He thinks I'm boring."

"Oh, I very seriously doubt that. I don't think you're boring."

Cassie smiled. "Me neither."

I was still trying to figure out what Anne meant by her comment to tell her if Jay gave me any trouble. What kind of trouble was she talking about? I considered asking Cassie about Jay, but it didn't seem fair pumping a little girl for information. Besides, I wasn't sure I'd get a true read on Jay from Cassie. She actually appeared to like her brother, which I guess was natural, considering she didn't spend much time with him. I was sure that spending more time with Jay would cure her of any good feelings she had.

When we got to the corner of Water and Main streets, we came face-to-face with the vacationing crowds as they vied for position on the sidewalk. Mothers clutched the hands of their little kids, holding them back as they attempted to break away and run down the sidewalk toward the harbor or some other distraction that caught their eye.

"So which way?" I stopped, letting Cassie choose where she wanted to go for ice cream.

"Scoops." She pointed to her left, and we crossed the street.

After we got our ice-cream cones, Cassie and I wandered around town, eventually heading over to the observation deck at Memorial Wharf, where we watched the Chappaquiddick ferry go back and forth six times before calling it an afternoon and heading home.

I had to admit, although I was curious about Cassie's brother, I wasn't exactly looking forward to running into him again so soon. A part of me thought Anne might say something to Jay about being civil, if nothing else, but I wasn't all that hopeful. From the way Anne talked about him, it didn't sound as if she and Jay were on the best of terms, and if he was there all summer, she probably had more to worry about than how Jay treated the babysitter.

When Cassie and I arrived back at the Barclays', she went into the kitchen to get a drink and I went to find Anne to tell her we were home. But when I walked into the family room, I found Jay reading *Sports Illustrated* on the couch.

"Is Anne around?" I asked.

Jay barely looked up to acknowledge me. "She's upstairs sleeping."

"What happened?" Cassie stomped into the room holding a miniature glass teapot in her hand. She held up both hands, each grasping fractured pieces of porcelain. "It's broken."

"You left it on the hallway floor and I didn't see it. You shouldn't leave your toys lying around," Jay answered, not even a hint of remorse in his tone.

Cassie handed me the teapot, which was smashed into three pieces. "Look."

It was broken, all right. The spout had snapped off, and the handle, which was decorated with small, pink, hand-painted rosebuds, was no longer attached to the pot.

"Just throw it out," Jay told her. "I'm sure your mom will buy you a new one."

Cassie reached out and took the pieces from my hand. "Where's Mom?" Cassie asked me, not her brother.

I knelt down on the floor so that Cassie and I were on eye level. "Why don't you tiptoe upstairs and knock lightly on her bedroom door. That way if she's asleep, you don't wake her up. Okay?"

Cassie nodded and disappeared silently down the hallway.

"The least you could have done is apologize," I told Jay once I was sure Cassie had gone out of earshot.

"She left it right in the middle of the floor. And if you're actually worried that Cassie won't have any toys for teatime, I'm sure there are plenty more where that came from."

"That's hardly the point." I stood there waiting for him to say he was wrong, but he didn't.

"So what's *Winnie* short for?" Jay asked, still not looking up from the magazine. I was surprised that someone so totally self-absorbed had actually remembered my name.

"Winifred," I answered, my tone clipped. He wasn't going to make me forget about the teapot that easily. "I was named after my grandmother."

Jay nodded, laid the magazine facedown across his lap, and looked up at me. "I see."

I assumed Jay put down the magazine in an attempt to engage me in conversation. "You're here for the summer?"

"Is that what Anne told you?" he asked, as if he knew there would be more to the story.

"That's all," I lied, figuring my allegiance to Anne was more important than attempting to make friends with her stepson. "Why, is there something else I should know?"

Jay didn't answer. Instead he watched me intently, his head cocked to the left as if he was assessing whether he should tell me something.

"Nah." He shook his head and went back to reading, officially ending our first conversation.

Chapter 7

"**C**assie has a brother," I told Jessie. Nash had some sort of sailing-instructor meeting so Jess had offered to meet me at my house after work. We were in my room, where I was ironing my Oceanview shirt. Maybe cutting the sleeve off one of my shirts wasn't such a brilliant idea after all. Now I only had three left, which meant making sure I didn't forget to do a wash almost every other day.

"He's old enough to be potty-trained, I hope." Jessie was lying on my bed picking at a callus on the palm of her left hand. Even after only two weeks of tennis lessons she had plenty to choose from.

I set the iron down on the ironing board and went to retrieve the garbage can beside my desk.

"He's nineteen," I said, placing the can next to the bed just in time to catch the flap of skin she'd flicked toward the carpet.

"Oh, that makes it a little more interesting." Jessie turned over onto her side to face me. "How come you didn't know about him before?"

"He was supposed to be away for the summer but he showed up here instead."

"And?" Jess asked, knowing there had to be more to the story.

"And I don't know. Anne mentioned something about having a bad first year at college, but she didn't share any of the specifics."

Jessie had obviously wanted more information than I could provide, because as soon as she learned I wasn't going to get into the sordid details, she went to work on her right hand. "Maybe there are no specifics. Maybe he just had a bad year at school. It happens, you know. Not all of us are academically inclined."

Jessie hated to ask for help, but when it came to school, she knew it was either let me explain the difference between inverse trig derivatives and arctrig functions or sit out a season of tennis. She couldn't afford to do that if she was going to get a scholarship to UNC, which she was counting on, even though I hadn't seen her wear the UNC Tar Heels T-shirt she got for her birthday sophomore year ever since she'd traded in Tar Heel blue for UVM green. It was a good thing Jessie had tennis because she definitely wasn't getting into UNC for her grades.

"I got the feeling it had to do with more than just academics."

"I sure hope so, it would make him more interesting at least."

"The way Anne talks about him, there's definitely more to the story. And he's not the nicest person in the world." I told Jess about the teapot and the cereal bowl.

"Okay, I might give you the teapot thing, even though the

kid shouldn't be leaving her stuff in the middle of the hallway. But a cereal bowl on the table? You're going to condemn the guy because he didn't feel like washing his breakfast dishes?"

When she put it like that, I saw her point. Maybe it wasn't so much *what* Jay did as *how* he did it. Even though he kept himself scarce, Jay's presence hung over every room. "I don't think he likes Anne."

"You've known the woman for three days," she reminded me. "Maybe he knows her better than you do."

Jessie wasn't getting it. I debated whether to tell her about a conversation I'd overheard that day between Anne and Jay, an exchange that left me feeling that I'd glimpsed a part of the Barclays I shouldn't have and almost wished I hadn't. The whole thing had left me with a weird feeling, as if I knew more about them than I was supposed to.

After my brief conversation with Jay, I'd left the family room and gone upstairs to find Cassie. We were in her room playing with her stuffed animals, pretending to have a birthday party for a stuffed, white bear named, aptly, Bear. But when we went to hang the SURPRISE sign up across the closet door (Bear wasn't supposed to know what we were planning), I realized we'd forgotten the tape downstairs. I left Cassie in charge of the seating arrangements and started down the hall toward the stairway. As I neared the landing, I recognized Anne's voice coming from Jay's room, which I thought was strange because as far as I could tell, Jay avoided Anne as much as possible. Still, I heard the strained tone of her voice coming from the doorway to Jay's room, and even though I knew I should have kept walking down the steps, I stopped and listened. I was unable to make out most of Anne's words, but I heard her say something about "this weekend" and "your father." But when Jay spoke, there was no mistaking his words.

"Do you think I care what he thinks?" Jay's voice was terse, its volume rising as he spoke. "I don't even know why you care, Anne." He spat out her name as if he found it distasteful, and I could almost imagine him staring her down in the same way he'd looked at me that day on the front walk, a look that dismissed her as irrelevant. "You're not my mother, so stop trying to act like it."

Jay's words stung, and I held my breath, waiting for Anne's response. But there was none, and Anne walked out of Jay's room a moment later, going straight to her bedroom without even looking back to see me standing on the first step watching her, wanting to go after her to see if she was all right.

Only I didn't move. I stayed there on the step listening for Anne until I felt someone's eyes on me, waiting for me to turn and notice. And that's when I looked over toward Jay's room and spotted him standing in the doorway, his gaze fixed on me, his mouth a flat line. He had to know I'd heard their conversation, and so I opened my mouth to apologize, but he stepped back into his room and closed the door behind him.

Even now, in my room with Jessie, just thinking about their exchange made me uncomfortable. Maybe that's why I decided not to tell Jessie the whole story. Or maybe it was the look on Jay's face as he watched me, the gravity in his eyes, the way he made sure I knew he'd seen me, almost as if saying, "There, now you know."

"I overheard him saying some pretty mean stuff to Anne the other day," I told Jessie instead, and she swung her legs off the bed and sat there waiting for me to finish ironing.

"Well, if he's that much of a jerk, it doesn't matter what his deal is, right? Just steer clear." Jessie looked up at the clock on my dresser. "I better go. I told Nash I'd meet him at his house at six."

I unplugged the iron and took a cushioned hanger from my closet (four summers ago my mother's projects included replacing every wire hanger in our house with handmade cushioned ones). "How are things going with you guys?"

Jessie smiled. "Things are really good," she told me, her answer shorter and more ambiguous than what I was used to. *Really good* might not seem that vague for most people, but Jessie wasn't someone to use words that could be left up to interpretation, which is why if you asked her how her match went, she was more likely to say "I kicked her ass" than "good." And then she'd likely spend the next five minutes giving you the details of the match to demonstrate the extent of the ass-kicking.

But Jessie didn't offer any additional information about Nash, and that made me think she wanted to keep the details to herself, as if sharing them with anyone else would somehow diminish their importance. Only I wasn't just anyone, I was her best friend. And her not wanting to share them with me made me wonder what else she was keeping from me now that she had Nash.

"So, I'll call you later?" Jessie stood up and reached for her sneakers, slipping them on as I pushed down the lever on the underside of the ironing board and let it fold down flat.

I wanted Jessie to stay, not to talk about anything in particular, just to talk. But I didn't ask her not to go and she didn't offer.

"Sure," I agreed, and she smiled at me before leaving my room.

"I'll talk to you later," I said, but she was already on her way downstairs and I don't think she heard me.

"Is Jessie gone?" my mom asked when I went into the dining room to see her.

"Yeah, she had to go meet Nash."

"Why don't you come join me then?" My mom picked up a dry brush and held it out to me. "Choose something and try a little decoupage."

I didn't take the brush. "That's okay."

"Come on, it's fun. Pick something." She nodded toward the corner of the room, where she'd stacked her latest findings. Every week my mom attended no less than four garage sales in search of someone's unneeded, unwanted trash, or, as she called them, *discards*. I guess she couldn't justify buying new lamps and vases and assorted wooden boxes to decoupage when all she was going to do was varnish the outsides until all the hideous pink roses, black polka dots, and rotting wood were completely covered.

"Do you suggest anything in particular?" I asked, taking inventory of other people's junk.

"Why don't you start with something simple, like that jewelry box over there."

I walked over to the corner and bent down looking for something, anything, that even remotely resembled a jewelry box. I found what looked like a round hatbox, a serving tray, and even a set of nesting boxes, the kind where you open one box only to discover another smaller one inside, and then still another. "Where?"

"Right there, by your foot."

"This?" I held up an orange rectangular box with blue stars carved into its lid. It wasn't more than six inches long and the top wasn't even hinged. The jewelry boxes I was used to either had dancing ballerinas in the lids or at least faux leather. This looked more like a wooden box for children's shoes.

"That's it," she confirmed. "Bring it over here."

"This is the ugliest jewelry box I've ever seen," I told her as she rubbed the orange wood with a soft cloth, removing a layer of dust before lifting the top off and cleaning out the spiderwebs.

"It might be the ugliest jewelry box now, but wait until you're done with it. It will be gorgeous."

I had to take her word for it. "So where do I begin?" I asked, pulling out a chair and sitting next to her.

One by one, my mom explained the simple materials, including a bottle of Elmer's glue, a pastry roller that I recognized as Shelby's (I couldn't imagine she'd be too thrilled to know our mom was using her pastry roller to smooth out her Elmer's glue), and sponges.

"But first you have to sand the outside, to make sure you have a clean surface." She handed me a sheet of sandpaper.

"Like this?" I asked, rubbing the sandpaper in circular motions and watching as the fine shavings fell onto the table.

"Exactly."

An hour later I had sanded all of the paint off the box and created a smooth surface to begin gluing on the torn pieces of paper.

"I think I'm going to call it quits," I told my mom.

"But you're just about to start the fun part," she protested, already gluing the third layer of tissue on her lamp base.

I didn't have the heart to tell her I wasn't exactly a fan of the torn-tissue look and its kaleidoscope of mismatched colors.

"Next time," I said, and she didn't try to get me to stay. I think she was just glad I said there'd be a next time.

I didn't need to look under the doormat anymore. I just let myself in with the key Anne had made for me at the hardware store.

I heard a noise in the kitchen, the sound of silverware and plates clanking together. My first thought was that it had to be Cassie trying to make herself lunch.

But when I got there, I saw it was Jay, standing at the kitchen counter in nothing but blue-and-white-striped boxers and a faded gray Wesleyan University T-shirt.

"They're upstairs," he informed me, reaching for two bagel halves that had just popped up to the ding of the toaster.

After just two days around Jay it was obvious he wasn't a morning person.

"Careful," I warned, but either he didn't want to listen to me or he didn't hear me, because as soon as he gripped the edges of the bagels he dropped them onto the counter, swearing under his breath.

"They're going to be hot," I explained, thinking it was pretty obvious from the orange coils still glowing inside the toaster.

Jay blew on his fingertips twice and tried again, this time placing the bagel on a plate with no problem.

"So you go to Wesleyan?" I asked, making every effort to keep my eyes focused above his waist. It didn't take much imagination to figure out that Jay, even covered by the wrinkled T-shirt and the baggy boxers, had a great body. I could usually tell from a guy's calves, and judging from Jay's, which were perfectly toned and just muscular enough to make me think he had to be some sort of athlete, but not so big that I thought he was one of the guys who spent hours in the gym kissing his biceps, I had to say I was right.

He walked over to the refrigerator and removed a container of cream cheese. "Yes, I do."

For some reason Jay didn't seem the least bit fazed to be walking around in front of me in his underwear. Just a thin piece of striped cotton between me and him.

"Do you like it?" I asked, moving my eyes up to the faded red letters stamped across his chest.

"It's not Harvard," he answered, as if I was supposed to know how that actually answered my question.

"No, I guess it's not."

"And if it's not Harvard, it doesn't matter, or at least that's what my dad thinks."

I wasn't sure how, or even if, I was supposed to react to that. So I just watched Jay spread a dollop of cream cheese on both bagel halves.

"Is that where he went?"

"Undergrad and law school." Jay raised the bagel to his mouth, took a bite, and walked out the back door to the patio, leaving me standing there staring at the open tub of cream cheese, a cream-cheese-crusted knife, and a balled-up paper towel. Not to mention brown, crunchy crumbs creating a trail from the toaster to the edge of the counter. It didn't make any sense to me that someone could have everything and act as if he cared about absolutely nothing.

Through the French doors I could see him standing at the edge of the patio, his bare feet just grazing the grass where it met the squares of flagstone. His back was to me so I couldn't see what he was looking at, but it was something out in the harbor, maybe a seagull or a duck skimming the surface of the water. He kept still, not even moving his arm, which stayed by his side, the bagel still in his hand, and for some reason I wondered what he was thinking, why he was standing outside in his boxers with a half-eaten bagel he eventually tossed over toward the birdbath, providing breakfast for the sparrows who flocked to it, pecking the sesame seeds off the crust.

I knew I didn't have to do it, but I went over to the counter, placed the lid on the cream cheese, and returned it to the refrigerator. Then I took the paper towel and tossed it into the garbage, where I found the shattered teapot, exactly where Jay had told Cassie to put it. I reached in and removed the pieces, laying them out on the granite countertop. The tube of Krazy Glue was in my backpack, and I reached for it, carefully aligning the porcelain pieces and running the glue along the cracks, careful not to squeeze too much and make a mess, but just enough so that if you didn't look too closely you'd never know the teapot had ever been broken. In just a few minutes I had it back together, minus a few small chips of porcelain that had probably fallen to the bottom of the garbage can or were still in the hallway, kicked to the crevice where the molding met the hardwood floor.

Jay was still outside on the patio and I counted six birds clustered around the bagel he'd tossed to the ground.

I wiped away any excess glue and left the teapot on the kitchen table to dry. Then I went to find Cassie.

When I got to the foyer, instead of climbing the stairs I stood there, halfway between Jay outside on the patio and Cassie upstairs in her bedroom. Two people who lived in the same house, shared the same family, and yet you would have thought Jay was a total stranger, expect that he always seemed to be eating the Barclays' food.

Even the family photos on the side table in the entry didn't provide any clues. I went over and picked up the picture of the Barclays, the one of them on the beach that they'd sent as last year's Christmas card. Where was Jay last summer when that picture was taken? Or even the picture of the Barclays skiing, maybe in Vail or Aspen or wherever it was that people like the Barclays went in search of perfect powder. But Jay wasn't in any of them, not in the picture of Cassie and her cousins or in the photo of everyone in front of a Christmas tree, wrapping paper strewn around them in haphazard crumpled-up balls.

"That was a crazy morning," Anne said, coming down the stairs. She held on to the banister for balance. "We had my brother and his kids visiting from Chicago, and they got up at some ungodly hour. I think Jim had just finished putting together Cassie's dollhouse and barely got to bed before the kids were yelling and screaming that Santa had arrived."

I placed the frame back on the table and waited for Anne to reach the bottom step. "Can I ask you a question?"

"Sure." Anne let out a breath as if the long trek down had worn her out.

"Why isn't Jay in any of the pictures?"

Anne bit her lip, then lowered her weight onto the bottom step, sitting down as if preparing for a long explanation. "There are a few reasons, actually. I guess mainly because he never spent much time at the house with us."

"Not even the holidays?"

She shook her head. "His mom got sick the year Jim and I were married, and I think Jay felt like he'd be deserting his mother or she'd think he was choosing us over her. I don't know. As you can tell, Jay doesn't exactly have a lot to say to me." Anne's words were matter-of-fact, as if it was a situation she didn't think she could do much about. But I remembered that scene upstairs in Jay's room, how she'd been in there trying to talk to him about something that obviously mattered to her and he had completely shut her out. Anne was still trying, even if Jay responded with hurtful words. And they were definitely hurtful words, there was no denying that. But as much as I wanted to side with Anne, to see Jay as the bad guy, I also remembered the look on Jay's face when he locked eyes with me from his bedroom doorway, how he held my gaze as if trying to explain himself to me. And for some reason that made me believe there was more to Jay than Anne's explanation would have me believe. I just had no idea what it was.

"Well, I better go upstairs and find Cassie," I told Anne, excusing myself from our conversation.

Anne scooted to the side of the step and let me pass.

I found Cassie coloring at the miniature table and chair set in the corner of her bedroom. The room was exactly what you'd picture for a little girl who spent her summers on the Vineyard and the rest of the year in Greenwich, Connecticut. Shades of pinks and greens colored the walls, the bedspread, the curtains, and the overstuffed rocking chair beside the window seat. Even the table Cassie sat at was white with pink-and-green stripes.

"What are you doing?" I asked, pulling out the other undersize chair and fitting myself on the seat. My knees came up past the tabletop, but I leaned over and admired Cassie's artwork.

"It's for you. Here." Cassie handed me the piece of paper. "I hope you like flowers."

In the middle of the page Cassie had drawn a small pink flower in crayon, its petals big and round and surrounding a yellow smiley face at its center. "I love flowers, especially ones that look so happy."

"I knew you would. Jay said you wouldn't, but I didn't care."

"Well, Jay was wrong. This is going straight into my back-pack, and I'm saving it forever." I took my flower drawing and stood up. "I was thinking we could go for a walk in town and then maybe go to the playground. How's that sound?"

Cassie agreed that it was a great idea, and she got up from the table and led me down the hall toward the stairs. But when we got to the steps, I didn't stop. Instead I kept going until I came to Jay's room on the right. I paused and leaned through the doorway, just far enough to see the blue plaid comforter on the queen-size bed against the wall and Jay's duffel bag on the floor, his clothes still folded neatly inside. I hadn't expected that; I guess given the cereal bowl and the tub of cream cheese, I thought Jay would carelessly toss his clothes around the room, letting them stay where they landed. In-stead, his shirts and shorts lay in an orderly pile inside the duffel bag, his socks folded into tidy balls.

If it weren't for the duffel bag, I wouldn't have known anyone was even staying in the room. The dresser top was empty except for a lamp, and the sole item on the night table was an alarm clock, its green numbers displaying the time for an empty, immaculate room. If he couldn't even be bothered to unpack, I figured Jay wasn't planning to stay long.

"Ready?" Cassie asked, waiting for me on the top step.

"Coming," I told her, turning my back on Jay's room and following Cassie down the stairs.

On our way back from the playground Cassie and I passed the fudge shop on North Water Street, and even before we got there we could both smell the rich fudge, almost as if they intentionally let the scent seep out onto the sidewalk knowing it would make us stop in our tracks.

In the front window of the fudge shop an almost life-size puppet dressed in a chef's outfit stirred a pot of fake fudge and winked at us every ten seconds like clockwork.

"Do you think we could taste every flavor?" Cassie asked, her nose pressed up to the glass as she winked back at the puppet.

"Well, we have until the end of the summer, we could sure give it a shot."

As we stood there, a group of tourists came out of the store. Cassie and I stepped aside, and the smell of chocolate and nuts and marshmallows swept over us. Before the door could close, I reached out and grabbed hold of it.

"Let's start now," I suggested, and Cassie ran under my outstretched arms and straight up to the counter.

We decided our first time we should start out simple with

plain chocolate fudge. I ordered enough for each of us and a little extra to bring home to Anne. And Jay, too, if he wanted some. It was just past four o'clock, and in Jay's world that probably meant it was lunchtime.

When I got home from the Barclays', my dad was in the backyard with a client and her black Lab, who was reclining on a home plate while wearing a Red Sox hat on his head (they'd cut holes in the hat for his ears) and a catcher's mitt on his left paw. I dropped my backpack on the kitchen table and went outside to see.

"Who's this?" I asked, bending down to pet the dog. As soon as he'd seen me coming out the back door, the Lab had ditched his home-plate pose to greet me.

"That's Marley," my dad told me, coming over to give me a hug. "And this is Mrs. Conrad."

The woman, a tall blonde in her late fifties who was holding a baseball bat under her arm, held out her hand and I shook it.

"So Marley's a baseball fan?" I stood up and Marley ran in circles around me.

"Mr. Conrad is the baseball fan," Marley's owner explained. "The portrait is Marley's present to his dad."

To anyone not accustomed to talking about dogs as children who give their father a portrait for his birthday, our conversation would seem bizarre. But I was used to having dogs in our backyard dressed up in any outfit imaginable. An actress had even hired my father to take pictures of her pug dressed like Tinker Bell, a role the actress had once played on

Broadway. So a black Lab in Red Sox gear? That was down-right tame by comparison.

"Want to hang around and watch?" my dad asked, leading Marley back to his spot on home plate, where he gave the dog a snack to keep him still.

"Sure," I agreed. "What can I do to help?"

My dad started giving me directions, guiding me as I moved the lighting and he snapped some test shots.

"Wouldn't this have been easier in a studio?" I asked my dad.

"Probably, but Fenway still has real grass, and Mrs. Conrad wanted the shoot to be as authentic as possible."

Mrs. Conrad sat down on the green plastic lawn chair my dad had set up for her in the shade. "Mr. Conrad would recognize artificial turf in a heartbeat."

For the next two hours my dad and I posed Marley in every conceivable baseball-themed situation possible, even managing to get Marley to hold up a foam finger as we all chanted, "We're number one," although the dog did balk at wearing the catcher's mask, and I couldn't blame him. My dad and I didn't talk about anything but Marley and the lighting and whether the shadows helped the shot or hurt it, but it was the most fun I'd had with my dad in ages. The afternoon reminded me a lot of when I was younger and he used to let me tag along on his shoots.

I didn't actually help out then, and I was probably more of a pain than anything else because all I wanted to do was play with all of his equipment, but he never told me no unless I wanted one of his lenses, which were super expensive. Back then, before he went digital, my dad would develop the film in the darkroom he'd built in our basement. I'd stand next to him, our skin tinged pink in the red glow of the safelight, and wait for the picture to develop as my dad swirled the rubber-tipped tongs in the solution, distributing the chemicals evenly over the soggy paper. As the timer ticked off the minutes, my dad and I waited for the subjects of his most recent shoot to appear, the dot of an eye, the swirl of waves in the background, the wide, white smiles, until eventually the whole picture was clear, a perfect family seemingly appearing out of nowhere. Now, in the end there was always a perfect glossy portrait of a dog posed in an implausible situation, and I knew that his photographs would soon end up on someone's mantel or a coffee table or even hung on a wall. I also knew the owners would have guests come over and they'd marvel at the photo, amazed at how a dog could be made to look exactly like Tinker Bell, gossamer wings and all. The guests would have no idea it had taken hours to get the wings affixed to the dog's back, or how the first magic wand broke in half when the dog decided to use it for a chew toy, or that it had taken a combination of wires and pulleys to loft the dog in the air so it could look appropriately fairylike. The guests would suspend reality because that's what they wanted to see—a pug in a green tulle fairy skirt floating in the air, her magic wand just grazing the fairy wings on her back as she cast a spell.

Chapter 8

When I got to the Barclays' after camp the next day, the house was empty.

"Hello?" I called out, but instead of an answer all I heard was my voice echoing up to the foyer ceiling where the chandelier hung high above my head.

I didn't remember Anne telling me she wouldn't need me or that they had other plans, so I went back to the kitchen, thinking maybe she was out in the garden with Cassie. But when I peered out through the kitchen windows, I didn't see anyone in the garden, and when I opened the door and stepped outside, I couldn't hear Cassie's or Anne's voice anywhere in the yard. All I heard was the sound of birds jumping from branch to branch and the water shifting in the harbor.

It was an amazing view, looking out over Edgartown Harbor with the sun's reflection skimming the surface of the water, creating flashes of light where the current ebbed and flowed out toward the cut at Norton Point.

And that's when I spotted him, sitting in one of the white Adirondack chairs where the back lawn met the harbor wall. I could only see the back of his head, and I noticed for the first time how his hair curled up where it met the collar of his shirt, almost echoing the curl of his lashes.

From behind he didn't look to be doing anything but staring out at the sailboats bobbing in the wake of a massive yacht that had just pulled into the harbor. I couldn't tell exactly what he was looking at, but his head never moved, and I almost thought he might be asleep.

I noticed the chair next to him was empty, the way Jay usually preferred it.

In the days since Jay had arrived, he was always alone. I hadn't even seen him talking on the phone to anyone, no less with a friend or spending time with Cassie and Anne. He was always by himself, and if someone joined him as he sat at the kitchen table or on the family-room sofa, in minutes Jay stood up and exited.

I found something about Jay both perplexing and intriguing. I couldn't figure him out. If he wanted to be alone, why'd he come to spend the summer on the island? And if he really disliked Anne so much, which was pretty obvious, why'd he come to live in a house where she was the only person around all week, other than Cassie?

I hadn't decided if I should feel sorry for Jay or disregard him altogether; tell him he was a jerk or ask what bothered him so much.

I went back inside the kitchen to see if Anne had left me a note or something and found a piece of paper hanging on the refrigerator door, held there by a magnet in the shape of a dragonfly. A dragonfly in the bottom corner of the paper matched the magnet.

Ran over to Vineyard Haven, the note read in Anne's tight script. *Be back by 1:30.*

I removed the magnet and took the note down, slipping it into the front pocket of my backpack before walking back over to the French doors and considering my options. I had a half hour to kill, which wasn't really enough time to do anything but walk into town for a few minutes before I'd have to come back. Or I could hang out in the kitchen by myself or even go into the family room and watch TV. And then there was the other option: I could go talk to Jay.

I glanced at my watch: only twenty-five minutes before Anne and Cassie were expected home. How bad could he be?

I opened the door and started down the rock path toward Jay.

"Hi," I said, startling him, which I have to admit I kind of liked. It was the first time I saw Jay's eyes widen, his guard down.

"Hey."

"Anne and Cassie went to Vineyard Haven?" I asked, even though I already knew the answer.

"Yep." He turned his eyes back to the boats and I had two choices. I could either continue to hover over him, or I could sit in the chair next to him.

"Mind if I take a seat?" I asked, letting Jay decide if I stayed. I figured he wouldn't remain for long regardless.

He shrugged. "Go ahead."

I took this as an invitation and sat down. This time Jay was wearing more than boxers, and he'd shaved for once. In a pair of jeans and a dark green polo shirt he actually looked as if he'd been up more than a few minutes.

I followed his gaze until I found the boat he had been watching, a wooden day sailer with a navy blue hull. Its cream-colored canvas sails were rolled up and tied in place, and although it was pretty, with its polished mahogany transom and seats, it wasn't the most impressive boat in the harbor by any means. In fact, it couldn't have been more than fifteen feet long.

"Do you sail?" I asked.

"I used to, on Nantucket."

It figured. Most people would give anything for one summer house, and Jay had two. "You had a house on Nantucket, too?"

"My mom's house. When they got divorced, my mom got Nantucket, my dad got the Vineyard."

"We don't even have an island in our kitchen for my parents to fight over, no less an actual mass of land." I thought I saw Jay smile, but because he wouldn't look over at me I couldn't really tell.

"You're better off, fewer lawyers to get involved."

As Jay continued looking out over the water, I observed his profile, the fringe of his lashes, how they swept up and down as he blinked, appearing almost capable of creating a breeze that would fill the sails in the harbor. "I thought your dad was a lawyer."

"A mergers-and-acquisitions attorney, whole different breed. He deals with companies, not people."

"My dad deals with animals. Now they're really a whole different breed."

This time when he smiled, Jay looked over at me. "What is he, a vet?"

"A photographer. He photographs people and their pets."

"Are there really that many people who want their picture taken with their pets?"

"Are you kidding me? People think it's the greatest thing

ever." I angled my body toward Jay, pulling my knees up to my chin and wrapping my arms around them. "He works in Boston during the week, that's where his main studio is. He has one on the island, too, but mostly he sees clients in the city."

"Mine, too," he said, then clarified, "I mean, he sees his clients in the city, too, only New York, not Boston."

"At least his clients don't crap on his office carpet."

Jay laughed. "You never know. They can be a tough crowd."

We were both quiet then, the only sound coming from the water pushing up against the harbor wall and then subsiding again. "So why'd you stop sailing?" I asked, breaking our silence.

Instead of answering, Jay shrugged.

"My friend's boyfriend teaches sailing on the island. She teaches junior tennis clinics over at the Chilmark Community Center."

"Do you play tennis?" Jay asked.

"I can. I have. I don't play much anymore."

"You gave it up?"

I shook my head. "I don't give up."

"Really?" Jay laughed. "If you asked my dad, he'd tell you that's all I do."

"What I meant was, tennis just wasn't that important to me. Besides, my best friend's really good."

"So what you're really saying is that you don't like to lose."

"Winnie?" a voice called from the house, and Jay and I turned to find Anne standing in the doorway, the screen door resting against her stomach. "We're back."

"I should go inside," I told Jay, and stood up.

He shifted in the chair, almost as if he'd decided to join

me, but then he leaned his head back, resting it against the hard white slats. "See you around."

"Daddy's coming today," Cassie told me.

"Is he?" I asked Anne, who nodded.

"Every Friday. He usually leaves the city early and gets here around two."

"Is he driving?" I asked Anne, but before she could answer, Jay, who had come in the back door, answered for her:

"He takes the plane out of Westchester."

"The plane?"

Anne shook her head at Jay, embarrassed.

"My dad keeps his plane at Westchester Airport," Jay continued. "Always ready to take off at a moment's notice."

"Anyway, if you could have Cassie back by four at the latest that would be great. Jim will be here by then and I know he can't wait to see her." Anne stopped and looked over at Jay. "He's looking forward to having everyone together for the weekend."

Jay didn't react, just opened the refrigerator door and stared inside as if it were only a matter of time until what he wanted appeared out of nowhere, right next to the low-fat yogurt.

Anne ran a brush through Cassie's hair and wrapped an elastic around her ponytail, then she left us in the kitchen, where Jay was still inspecting the contents of the refrigerator.

"Do you want to come with us?" I offered, expecting him to say no. "We were going to get some ice cream."

Jay turned around to look at us, his arm still holding the

door open, letting the cold air seep out into the warm kitchen, the frigid air dissipating before it could even reach us. I swear I could see the condensation forming on the milk cartons as Cassie and I stood there waiting for him to make up his mind, and just when I was about to suggest he close the door, Jay spoke.

"Where are you going?"

"It depends. We kind of like to mix it up, makes it a little interesting."

He hesitated, taking one more look at the shelf on the side of the refrigerator door as if weighing his options. "Okay, I'll go."

Cassie decided that we'd go to Mad Martha's, which meant waiting in line behind tourist families before finally making it to the counter, where I ordered Cassie a cookies-and-cream cone and a chocolate cone with rainbow sprinkles for myself.

"Have you decided what you want?" I asked Jay, who was still peering into the refrigerated case reading the labels on the tubs of ice cream.

"I'll have the same as you," he answered. "A chocolate cone. But make it a large."

When we left Mad Martha's, we followed Cassie down to the harbor and then walked over toward Memorial Wharf, where we sat beside the huge whale-tail sculpture submerged in the grass. Jay didn't talk a lot, but rather than feeling uncomfortable from the lack of conversation, I felt as if we'd come to a mutual agreement, if not exactly a comfort level with one another, then at least an understanding. Mostly

Cassie did the talking, acting as a conduit between Jay and me.

Cassie didn't seem to notice one way or another. She was just excited to have me and her big brother all to herself, not to mention the extra scoop of ice cream Jay had suggested she add to her cone.

"Hey, thanks for fixing the teapot," Jay said as we watched Cassie reach over the fence as she attempted to touch the tail.

I hadn't expected Jay to acknowledge the teapot, much less thank me for gluing it back together.

"How'd you know it was me?" I peeled away the blue-and-white-striped paper cone wrapper and folded it up before stuffing it into my pocket and taking a bite of my cone.

Jay shrugged. "You seem like the kind of person who doesn't like broken teapots."

I was going to say "You're welcome," but instead I found myself saying, "Anne told me about your mom. I'm sorry."

"Thanks," Jay said, for the second time in less than a minute. I hadn't been sure of how he'd react. I figured he'd tell me it was none of my business, but just as with the teapot, Jay had surprised me.

Jay sucked the last of the chocolate ice cream from the bottom of his cone, then checked his watch. "It's almost four o'clock. We should probably get back to the house."

I noticed he didn't call it home.

When we reached the Barclays' house, I could hear laughing as soon as we walked through the front door, a deep, genuine chuckle that was joined by Anne's familiar voice. The living-room windows were open, and as the door opened, a breeze swept into the foyer, picking up speed as it met the air from the living room. The sunflowers in the centerpiece shivered in the wind.

"He's here." Jay's voice was flat.

Cassie let go of my hand and ran down the hall toward the back of the house.

Jay stopped next to the foyer table and focused on a sunflower that was turned toward him as if waiting to hear what he had to say.

Then he headed toward the stairs and started climbing.

"Aren't you going to go say hello?" I asked.

Jay laid his hand on the banister and stopped halfway up, his right foot poised on the step above him. He glanced up at the landing before turning to look at me. "I wasn't planning to."

"But you haven't seen him for a week," I reminded Jay.

"Actually, I haven't seen him since school ended three weeks ago." Then Jay turned around and ascended the stairway without looking back.

A part of me wanted to go after Jay, to stop him and take him downstairs with me, bring him out to the patio where his father was probably sitting, Cassie perched on his knee asking him to bounce her as if on a horse. Only I wasn't sure Jay wouldn't shake my hand loose, free himself from me the way he'd seemingly freed himself from everyone else in his life, and tell me to butt out.

I didn't know if I was afraid he'd say no, or even more afraid he'd take my hand and pull me along with him, but it didn't matter. Jay was already gone, and so I went to the back of the house to meet his father.

"You must be Winnie." Mr. Barclay stood up and came over to shake my hand. His khaki pants were creased around his thighs from sitting on the plane, but his blue golf shirt with the small polo player looked crisp, and I decided he must have changed when he got to the island. "Cassie's told me all about you. And Anne thinks you're a lifesaver."

From what Jay had said, I'd almost expected Jay's father to be wearing a crimson shirt with a big H on his chest. But he just looked like a normal dad—if normal dads traveled on private planes. Mr. Barclay reminded me of an older Jay with thinning hair, the slight curl long gone, the wave only visible around his ears where the longest hair was combed back.

When he stood up, I realized how tall he was, a good three inches taller than Jay, who had to be six feet himself. I wondered if Jay's mom had been six inches shorter and Jay ended up equidistant between the two.

"It's nice to meet you, Mr. Barclay," I replied, wondering if Anne saw the resemblance between her husband and her stepson, and if, through her eyes, Mr. Barclay was still as good-looking as Jay.

"It's Jim," he told me, and sat back down, pulling Cassie onto his lap.

"Would you like some?" Anne pointed to the pitcher of lemonade on the patio table.

It was family time, and no matter how welcome Anne and Mr. Barclay tried to make me feel, I knew I should leave them alone even if I wished I could take a seat at the table with them and stay. It was a Friday, so my dad would be home, but like every other weekend so far this summer, he'd be in his office catching up on client billing or outside in the yard trying to make up for the neglect it suffered during the week. My mom might be in the dining room with her latest discard or visiting a friend, but wherever she was, it wouldn't be with my father. And tonight when we sat down for dinner, they'd exchange information—not talk, not have a conversation, but merely provide each other with a variety of facts and maybe a few observations. The kitchen faucet was leaking. The studio's landlord had talked about raising the rent when the lease came up for renewal. Did you see that the ferry was already booked solid for the July Fourth weekend? Whatever it was, the topic would be innocuous, something we could all chime in on, provide an opinion, then continue on to another subject of equal safety. And at the end of our meal we'd all get up to clear the dishes, piling our forks and knives on our plates in one hand while balancing a saltshaker or a bowl half full of carrots in the other, and if you didn't know what it used to be like, you'd think it was an average dinner for the Dennis family. What you wouldn't know was that my mother didn't affectionately rib my dad for putting barbecue sauce on his chicken potpie or that when my father told us a joke he heard from one of his clients, my mother politely smiled but failed to laugh, and even though I pointed out that barbecue sauce on chicken potpie was gross, and even if I laughed loud enough for both of us, it was just my attempt to take up the slack.

Mr. Barclay reached for the pitcher of lemonade and started to pour me a glass until I shook my head no. "Thanks, but I better be going. See you on Monday?"

Anne smiled. "Have a good weekend, Winnie."

On my way through the foyer I glanced up at the second-floor landing, a part of me hoping to see Jay standing there, looking for me, knowing that I'd be looking for him. But the landing was empty, and Jay was nowhere in sight.

Chapter 9

"So which ice cream spot will it be today?" Jay asked me on Monday when I stepped outside onto the patio, where he was lounging with his feet up on the table. Cassie was on the back lawn playing croquet by herself while Jay turned his face to the sun.

"I hadn't thought about it yet," I answered, even though I had. I liked ice cream as much as the next person, but if I kept this up, by the end of the summer I'd have more to show for my days at the Barclays' than a nice bank account balance. Every single day Cassie wanted to go for ice cream or candy or fudge. And I took her because that was my job, and, well, it was nice to wander around town for a while.

Cassie came over to me, swinging her mallet like a baton. "Are you in the mood for ice cream today?" I asked, and of course she nodded.

"Actually, I had an idea," Jay announced, swinging his feet off the table. "What about Dairy Queen?"

Cassie dropped the mallet and clapped her hands together, applauding the idea. "I'm having a cookie-dough Blizzard."

"I take the VTA here from work," I told Jay, thinking he

must have noticed the empty spot in the driveway where my car would be.

He shrugged. "I can drive."

Now Cassie was practically cheering. "Come on, Winnie, Jay will drive."

Anne had never mentioned anything about not taking Cassie out in Jay's car, although I'm pretty sure she never expected that Jay would actually offer to take either of us anywhere. But at least Dairy Queen was a change of scenery, even if it was just a few miles down the road.

"Okay," I told Jay, and Cassie did a cartwheel, which I took to be her seal of approval.

Jay's black Jeep was parked in the gravel driveway, its canvas top down. It was a beautiful day, all blue sky and not a cloud in sight, and even though I would have loved to drive around with the top down, I wasn't convinced Anne would approve.

"Can we put the top up?" I asked him. "I don't know that Anne would want Cassie in the backseat with the top down."

"I'm not going to kill us," Jay said, as if he knew that was my concern, his reckless driving. That it was his first thought should probably have worried me. "Besides, it's barely a mile away."

Before I could stop her, Cassie placed her foot up onto the back tire, swung her other leg over the side of the Jeep, and climbed into the backseat.

I considered asking Cassie to wear her bike helmet but decided against it. What was the point of riding in a convertible if you couldn't even feel the wind whipping through your hair?

I opened the passenger door and stepped into the front

seat. "Buckle your seat belt," I told Cassie, then twisted around to make sure the nylon strap was pulled tight across her lap.

With the top down and the radio on, I didn't have to worry about making conversation with Jay. I just enjoyed the feel of the wind blowing and the sun beaming down on us. As we drove toward Dairy Queen, I looked back over my shoulder at Cassie, who held her arms up in the air, waving her hands over her head as if we were on a roller-coaster ride.

The thing about Dairy Queen is that it doesn't exactly provide the scenery of one of the shops downtown. Instead of slowly working our way along Main Street as we tried to keep our cones from melting down our wrists or sitting on a wooden bench beside the harbor, we sat at a picnic table with a view of Stop & Shop across the street.

"Good?" Jay asked me, watching as I licked the last of the rainbow sprinkles off my chocolate cone.

"It's a nice change, thanks."

"Didn't you get the same thing the other day at Mad Martha's?"

"Same thing," I told him. "A chocolate ice-cream cone with rainbow sprinkles."

"So how exactly is this a nice change?"

"Soft ice cream."

"I see." Jay started to smile. "You don't like Bizzards?"

"I've never had one."

Jay was about to spoon a glob of his Oreo Blizzard into his mouth but stopped. "You've never had a Blizzard?"

I shook my head.

"Are you an ice cream purist or something?"

"I guess I just really like chocolate ice-cream cones."

I thought he was about to offer me a taste of his Blizzard,

but instead he said, "Well, you've got to respect someone who knows what she likes."

Cassie was quiet as she concentrated on her cookie-dough Blizzard.

"Hey, look." Jay pointed to a black Lab coming toward us from the parking lot, its owner tugging back on the retractable leash in an effort to keep the dog from charging straight toward us. "A subject for your dad."

The black Lab finally reached us, pushing its nose against my outstretched hand as I stroked its head. "Hello, Marley," I cooed, and the dog fell onto its side and stretched out, exposing his belly to me.

"Hi, Winnie," Mrs. Conrad said when she reached us, and Jay looked shocked to hear her say my name. "Would you mind watching Marley while I go inside and order?"

I took the leash from Mrs. Conrad and she left him there with us by the picnic tables.

"Marley had his picture taken last week," I explained to Jay, as Cassie came over and knelt beside Marley, rubbing his stomach.

"I was just kidding about the subject thing," Jay confessed. "Your dad really took Marley's picture?"

"In our backyard. It was a sports theme, Marley with a baseball, Marley wearing black paint under his eyes, a Red Sox hat on his head and a mitt on his left paw. They dressed me up as the home-plate umpire."

Jay had been about to take another spoonful of Blizzard, but he stopped, his hand poised in midair. "You've got to be kidding me."

"Only about the umpire thing," I said, smiling at the look on Jay's face. "The rest, all true." I crossed my heart earnestly.

"Does your dad come back to the island every weekend?" Jay asked, continuing to eat his Blizzard.

"During the summer he comes home on Wednesday nights and leaves Monday mornings." I explained the logistics to Jay, the studio in the city, how my father had two sets of everything rather than lug supplies from one place to the other, from toothbrushes to slippers.

"So when's he going to stop?" Jay asked. I looked over at him as he waited for my answer. Only I didn't have one, because, honestly, I'd never thought to ask that question before. I just assumed at some point it would end and he'd come home for good, and everything would go back to the way it was before *The Dog Days of Summer*.

"I don't know," I admitted.

"So your parents are just going to live apart for the rest of their lives?" Jay scooped the last remaining ice cream from the bottom of his Blizzard cup. *The rest of their lives*. The way Jay said it the whole thing sounded so bleak. "Why even bother being married?"

His last question stabbed at me, although I knew it was a rhetorical question and Jay wasn't really asking me to respond. But I wanted to. I wished I had the answer. Because the truth was, knowing what it was like between my parents when my dad was around, knowing that they'd seemingly run out of things to talk about, how their lives had begun running in parallel lines that never touched no matter how close they got, I couldn't think of one single reason.

"Thanks a bunch, Winnie." Mrs. Conrad had appeared beside me, vanilla cone in one hand, the other reaching for Marley's leash. I handed it over and Cassie waved good-bye to the dog.

"Ready to go home?" I asked Cassie, who frowned and shook her head.

"Do we have to?" It was the closest I'd seen to a whine in the whole time I'd been babysitting for the Barclays.

"We don't *have to*, but we probably should." I got up from the picnic table, tossed my napkin in the trash barrel, and started walking to the car.

Cassie and Jay reluctantly followed.

"Actually, we don't have to go straight home, do we?" Jay asked when we reached the Jeep. Then he turned to Cassie. "Where else would you like to go?"

Cassie looked as if she were going to combust with the variety of options running through her head. "Can we go to the beach?" she finally suggested.

"What do you say?" Jay opened the car door, but stood there staring at me, his hands gripping the foam-covered roll bar overhead. "Do you want to take her to the beach?"

Anne wouldn't be home for at least another hour, and I had to admit it was actually pleasant having Jay hang out with us. "Sure," I answered. "Let's go to the beach."

We decided on South Beach, primarily because it was closest and we figured we'd hit the least amount of traffic considering it was getting late in the afternoon and most people were leaving Katama and heading toward town. Jay, Cassie, and I removed our flip-flops and carried them as we walked from the parking lot and then past the Porta Potties and up the sandy path to the beach. The beach was different now than when we took the Oceanview kids there, not just emptier but calmer, as if the anticipation of the day had subsided and with it the pressure for the perfect wave, the cloudless sky, the ideal spot in the sand.

Cassie ran ahead of us, joining the last remaining group of kids as they chased greedy seagulls away from the remains of lunch left behind by this afternoon's beachgoers.

"This is my first time at the beach since I got here," Jay told me, kicking the sand ahead of him as we walked.

"I come practically every day. See that lifeguard stand over there?" I pointed up toward the white structure in the distance. "I can tell you how many feet exactly it is from the water's edge to where the lifeguard's float is stuck in the sand right there."

"So how many feet is it?" Jay asked, testing me.

"Fifty-four."

"Exactly?"

"And a half."

Jay grinned.

We found a good spot on the sand and watched Cassie run around after the seagulls, laughing when she'd eventually get herself so dizzy she'd fall down.

Our conversation from Dairy Queen still echoed in my head. Over an Oreo-cookie Blizzard he'd found out more about me, from doggy dress-up to my greatest fear, than I'd learned about him the entire time I'd babysat for his sister. Whether it was real or just wishful thinking, I felt as if Jay and I had gone from two people who spent the afternoons together by chance to something verging on friendship.

"How did your mom die?" I asked him, my eyes still on Cassie.

"Breast cancer," he told me, his voice flat but soft and lacking the edge I'd become accustomed to before the past couple of days. "Last October."

Now that I'd asked, I wasn't quite sure how I was supposed to continue the conversation, what I was supposed to do with the information.

"I wasn't there, at home, when it happened," Jay added, almost as if he knew I was stuck.

"She was home?"

"At that point she was receiving hospice care. We knew it was getting close to the end. And she hated the hospital."

"Were you at school?"

He nodded. "I know," he told me before I could even figure out what I wanted to say next.

"You know what?"

"I'm a horrible son, I should have been there."

"I didn't say that." However, my thinking might have been heading in that direction, just a little.

"I wanted to go home to be with her, but I'd barely been at school five weeks at that point." Jay almost seemed to be trying to convince himself as much as he was trying to explain the circumstances to me. He reached for a stick and dragged it through the sand as if writing something I couldn't quite make out.

"Well, that makes sense," I agreed, although I wasn't sure I did.

"It's Herbert," he said, continuing to write.

"What is?"

"My name."

"Your name is Herbert?" Just saying the name out loud sounded funny to me.

"Not just Herbert. Herbert James Barclay the third."

I laughed. "Were your parents trying to punish you?"

"It's a family name."

"Well, Herb, I guess I know why you went with Jay."

"Actually, it was always Jay. The Herbert thing is just tradition."

"Keeps you in the will, right?"

This time Jay laughed and turned to me. "Is that what Winifred does?"

"Oh, yeah. I'm banking on that inheritance to keep me in dog portraits for the rest of my life."

Jay stopped writing with the stick and tossed it away from us toward the water.

"Herbert," I repeated, trying to reconcile the old man's name with the guy sitting beside me. "I like it. From now on you're Herb."

"Fine with me, Fred, if that's how you want to play it." Jay smiled at me and I smiled back, and if it weren't for Cassie calling our names to go for a walk down the beach, I think we would have stayed that way for a while.

Chapter 10

I finally decided enough with the ice cream. Twice a week, fine. Even three times a week, but every day had to stop. Working for the Barclays was supposed to earn me extra money, not twenty extra pounds, and at the rate we were going, that was exactly what was going to happen. Granted, I could always take Cassie and not get anything for myself, but as much as I'd like to think I could actually resist ordering something, I knew once I got a whiff of a waffle cone, I'd be a goner. So I had an inspired thought that would kill two birds with one stone, so to speak.

"My friend Jessie teaches over at the Chilmark Community Center, and I was thinking it might be fun if Cassie took a couple of tennis lessons," I told Anne when I got to the Barclays' the next day. I'd had the idea the night before and thought it was brilliant, a way to do something other than going for ice cream, and I'd get to see Jessie, too. "I thought Cassie might think it was fun. We could meet Jessie over at the public courts or something."

"That sounds like a great idea," Anne agreed. "Talk to your friend and let me know."

And that's how I ended up on the phone trying to convince Jessie to spend one afternoon a week with me and Cassie.

"Want to make some extra money?" I asked Jessie when I called her on my way home from the Barclays'. She'd just finished her lessons and I could still hear the kids in the background.

"Is this a trick question?"

The bus was crawling along in afternoon traffic, and as we stopped in front of Stop & Shop, I looked to my left, thinking about yesterday afternoon at Dairy Queen with Jay. "Anne wanted to know if you could give Cassie private tennis lessons." So what if it was an exaggeration of the truth. "I thought you could use the public courts in Edgartown after work."

"So it is a trick question. You know I don't do the whole one-on-one kid thing. They're too needy. Besides, I have travel team Wednesday afternoons."

"So do it some other day. Just give it a chance, she's a cute kid. I promise. Not needy at all."

Jessie hesitated, and I could almost hear her calculating the dollars in her head, mostly because she tended to multiply out loud. "Fine, but I'm charging twenty bucks an hour."

"I'm sure Anne won't have a problem with your fee."

"What about thirty an hour, then?" Jessie asked, testing me.

"I think twenty is fine."

"Fine," she agreed, then changed the subject. "So what's up with the crazy brother?"

"His name's Jay. And he's not crazy."

"Then what's his deal?"

"I don't know, I can't figure him out." *I can't figure Herb out,* I said to myself, and couldn't help smiling.

"Uh-oh." Jessie stretched the words out for effect, indicating a serious problem.

"What's wrong?" The bus stopped and I held on to the seatback in front of me to keep from smacking my head on the window.

"It's the rat all over again."

"The rat?" I repeated, thinking if a rat were in the vicinity of Jessie's feet she'd be saying more than *Uh-oh*.

"Last summer, that rat in the woodpile? The brother is this summer's rat."

It wasn't a rat, actually, it was a mouse, but even last summer Jessie had failed to see the distinction. My dad had been outside one Saturday restacking the woodpile to make room for more logs when he came across a baby mouse, just a tiny gray thing no bigger than a strawberry. The poor thing was all by itself, so I'd decided to rescue the mouse and take care of it until the baby was big enough to be released back out into the woods.

"I just said I couldn't figure him out," I explained. "That's it. Nothing more." I told Jessie about Dairy Queen and our talk on the beach. But I left out the part about his real name being Herb. I knew she'd enjoy it way more than she should.

"We'll see. In any case, how about I meet you over at the courts on Thursday for the first lesson? Nash is picking me up in a few minutes so I should go wash up." Jessie stopped talking and took two deep sniffs. "I think I stink."

"Okay," I said reluctantly, "I guess I'll see you on Thursday."

"Hey, we're going to the movies tomorrow night, do you want to come?" she asked, probably sensing I wasn't ready to hang up yet. "We'll meet you in Edgartown."

The bus started moving, and as the Dairy Queen sign disappeared into the distance, I wondered what Jay was doing as I sat on the bus talking to Jessie.

My first inclination was to say no, but I thought about how much I'd learned about Jay in just two days and I realized how little I knew about Nash. Last summer Jessie and Nash had all of three weeks together, so it wasn't as if I'd had a ton of time to get to know the guy who had Jessie practically yelling "Ahoy, mate" as she tried to learn everything there was to know about sailing. Maybe I needed to give him the benefit of the doubt. If Jessie saw something in him, there had to be something worth getting to know. "Sure. Where and when should I meet you?"

We made plans to meet in front of the theater, and for the first time all summer I didn't mind the idea of sharing Jessie with Nash for the night, even though I couldn't exactly figure out why.

"Big plans tonight?" Jay asked me as I collected my backpack and got ready to leave for the day.

"I'm going to the movies with my friend Jessie and her boyfriend."

"And who are you bringing?"

"Nobody. Just me." I started to walk toward the hall and Jay followed me. He wasn't walking me out exactly, more like he just happened to be heading in the same direction.

"What are you going to see?"

"I don't know. I assumed they'd decide."

"I haven't been to the movies in ages."

Jay and I stopped at the front door, my hand on the

brushed-nickel handle, feeling its smooth surface, while Jay stood waiting as if for an invitation.

I kept my hand on the doorknob but I didn't turn it. "Are you saying you want to come to the movies with us?"

"Well, I'd help you even the ratio, wouldn't I?" Jay pointed out. "What time are you meeting them?"

I assumed that meant he was going to join us.

"We're meeting in front of the theater at seven forty-five."

"So I'll pick you up around seven o'clock?"

I must have seemed surprised because Jay laughed at me. "Well, if I'm taking you to the movies, I think I should at least pick you up."

Jay could walk to the theater on Main Street in less than five minutes. It didn't make any sense for him to pick me up at my house and then go back into town, where he'd park his car in his driveway and we'd walk to the theater anyway.

"That's okay, it's probably easier if I just meet you there. I can take the VTA."

"If that's what you want. At least I offered."

"You're such the gentleman, Herb," I joked.

"Nothing but the best for you, Fred," he replied.

Jay was in front of the theater when I arrived. I saw him standing there as I turned the corner onto Main Street.

"I already got us tickets," he told me when I reached him.

"How'd you know which movie we're seeing?" I asked, completely confused.

"I didn't." Jay fanned out four tickets, two for each show. "So I got us two tickets to each. Whichever ones we don't use we can give away, right?"

As we stood there, a Saab slowly followed the line of traffic down Main Street and then stopped beside us.

I recognized Nash in the driver's seat. "Forget the movie, we're heading over to Fuller Street beach," Nash called to me through the open window, his elbow resting on the ledge of the door, his hand tapping the roof as he spoke.

I walked over to the car, bent down, and looked across the front seat to Jessie. "It's too nice to sit in a movie theater," she explained, then nodded toward Jay and mouthed, *Who's that?*

The cars in front of Nash were beginning to move, and I knew we had to make a decision before the car behind his started getting antsy.

"Jay was going to come with us," I told her, already feeling bad that Jay had purchased tickets for not one show, but two.

"It's fine, we'll meet you there," Jay told them, appearing beside me. "We can walk."

Nash waved at us and pulled away, leaving Jay and me standing by the curb, close enough to hear the driver in the car behind the Saab mutter, "'Bout time."

"So that's the boyfriend?" Jay asked.

"His name is Nash. She met him last summer when he taught the Community Center's sailing program." I noticed Jay still had the movie tickets in his hand. "Hey, I'm sorry about the tickets. I can pay you back if you'd like."

Jay shook his head. "Don't worry about it. I'm sure we can unload these with no problem."

He was half right. In less than five minutes we'd found a taker for two of the tickets, but rather than waste any more time Jay decided he'd take a loss on the other two. He looked around for a garbage can.

"Here, I'll take them," I offered, and Jay handed the tickets over. I took the two yellow stubs and placed them in my front pocket.

"If you don't feel like walking, we could always go back to my house and get the Jeep," Jay offered. "It doesn't matter to me."

"No, we can walk. Jessie was right, it's too nice out to be inside."

Jay and I had walked through town together before with Cassie, but this wasn't the same. This was just the two of us, and even though the absence of a six-year-old shouldn't have made that much of a difference, it did. When our shoulders bumped, it wasn't because the sidewalk was too crowded, but because we walked close together, our hands brushing together as we headed away from town toward the beach.

Fuller Street dead-ends at the beach. It's not a beach most of the tourists visit, probably because it's shorter and narrower than their other choices, and it faces Vineyard Sound so the waves are pretty much nonexistent. As Jay and I got nearer the end of the road, we passed Nash's Saab parked off on the side, half on the pavement, half on the grass. The sun was setting but I could still make out Jessie and Nash on the sand, their silhouettes close together and what looked like Jessie's head resting on Nash's shoulder.

The full moon hung low in the sky casting white highlights on the ripples of water lazily lapping the shore. When we reached them, Nash held out a six-pack of Corona and a bottle opener in the shape of a lobster.

"Thanks." Jay took two bottles and popped off the caps before handing one to me.

Jessie gave me an impressed nod, as if Jay had scored some points by demonstrating that chivalry wasn't dead. At least when it came to opening a beer.

I sat down on the sand and introduced Jay to Jessie and Nash. Jay took the spot next to me, his legs stretched out in front of him, his hand in the sand beside mine. We formed a sort of half-circle facing the water, Jay and me on one side, Jessie and Nash on the other.

It was irrational, I knew it, but I felt as if the scales had been leveled, that I wasn't outnumbered by Jessie and Nash for once. That I had Jay on my side.

Nash asked Jay where he was from, where he went to school, the vital stats everyone asked while searching for common ground.

"Jess and I are running the Chilmark Road Race in August," Nash told Jay, then paused and sipped his beer. "Do you run?"

"I used to," Jay answered. "But not anymore."

"Well, Jess and I have been training." Nash then reviewed their routine, how they met up every day after work or, when they couldn't, got together before work for a run.

"What time?" Jay asked.

"We'll meet around six thirty and do four miles," Nash said, and I could imagine Jay thinking they were crazy getting up that early to do anything, no less run.

In the red glow of the setting sun I could make out Jessie's face, and I wondered if she could see mine, if she was looking at Jay and me the way I'd first looked at her and Nash, with a mix of curiosity and skepticism. I wondered if Jessie was comparing the two boys as they talked, not so much listening to their conversation as watching the way they interacted, the differences between two people who seemingly had so much in common, summer guys, rich boys who would only be around as long as the warm weather and the sunshine lasted.

But even in the dim light of the beach Jay and Nash stood in stark contrast to one another. It wasn't simply the conversation, how Nash could seamlessly weave the conversation from one topic to another, while Jay lingered on a subject, taking his time. It was more that Nash seemed to use all the space around him, punctuating every sentence with sweeping arm movements that left little room for anyone else. Jay's gestures were more subtle, a slight tilt of his head, a slow nod, a faint shifting of his shoulders, and because of that I felt that I had to watch him more closely, pay careful attention in case I missed a movement that spoke louder than any of the words coming out of Nash's mouth.

Jessie and I didn't say much, instead sitting back and observing, as if we could learn about each other by watching Jay and Nash. In the past two weeks I'd spent more time with Jay than with Jessie, and in an odd way he knew more about what happened to me every day than she did. For Jessie, it was the same way with Nash, who, on the days they trained in the morning, had spent almost two hours with my best friend before I was even awake.

With Jay there I was able to see Nash and Jessie differently, maybe because instead of focusing on my conspicuous role as third wheel, I could step back and truly see them as a couple, not a guy I had to yield my best friend to for a night. And for the first time I could see why Jessie enjoyed being with Nash, who brought a kind of energy to everything he did, from handing Jay a second beer to describing how one of his students tipped over a Sunfish in class. In a way Nash's energy seemed to give Jessie permission to sit back for once, to be the one who rides shotgun. And even though I wouldn't have thought she was cut out for that role, Jessie almost appeared to savor the part.

"Hey, Winnie, come see the water with me," Jessie suggested, standing up and waiting for me to follow. I did.

We walked next to each other on our way down to the water, but neither of us said anything, and I wondered if, like me, Jessie was still trying to listen to the conversation between Jay and Nash. Jessie waited until we were far enough from the guys so that they couldn't hear us before she started talking. "So what's up with that? I thought you said he was a jerk."

Actually, it was Jessie who'd called Jay a jerk. I just didn't disagree at the time. "He offered to come to the movies."

"And you accepted the offer," Jessie finished for me. "Is something going on with you two?"

"No," I answered, even though I wasn't sure that was the whole truth. Even if nothing was going on between Jay and me, it felt as if something was happening. "What about you and Nash, how are things with you guys?" I asked, turning the tables on her.

"Things are fine." The word was so ambiguous I was surprised she could even get it out while keeping a straight face. "We've been spending a lot of time together training. You're going to come watch us race, right?"

"Sure. If you can run a 5K, I can be there at the finish line to cheer you on."

Jessie and I watched the guys sitting on the sand, the empty six-pack case marking the halfway point between them. I could make out the Corona bottle in Jay's hand, the glass glistening in the moonlight as he raised it to his mouth.

"I'm really glad things are working out with you and Nash," I told Jess, and I meant it.

"Thanks, Winnie." Even in the dark I could see her smile. "That means a lot."

I knew she meant it, too.

Jess and I started walking back toward the guys.

We spent the next half hour hanging out, until we finished the last of the beers and Nash mentioned that he and Jessie had to get up early to run.

"We're going to take off," Jessie announced, dusting the sand off her butt as she stood up. "Do you guys want a ride home?"

"That's okay," I answered, not so much because I didn't want to be in the backseat of Nash's Saab but because I knew Jessie probably wanted some time alone with her boyfriend. "I can walk to the bus."

"I'll take her to the bus stop," Jay offered. "Don't worry, she's in safe hands."

Jessie didn't argue with him.

"Don't do anything I wouldn't do," Jessie whispered dramatically in my ear as she hugged me good-bye.

"Don't worry, I won't," I whispered back.

Nash collected the empty bottles and slipped them back into the cardboard six-pack before taking Jessie's hand and leading her back to the car.

Jay and I continued to sit on the beach even after we heard Nash's car drive away.

"How'd they get together?" Jay asked me, even before I had a chance to ask him what he thought of Nash.

"She stalked him." Then I laughed at the look on Jay's face. "No, really, she met him last summer, and then she went about things the way she always does."

"Do you like him?"

"I don't mind him." I sifted sand through my fingers and found a bottle cap Nash had left behind. I ran the tip of my finger along the rough, creased edge, then pushed it down into my pocket next to the movie tickets. "I guess I just miss hanging out with her as much as I used to."

"They seem pretty close." He got to his feet and brushed the sand off his shorts. "Especially for having been together such a short time."

Jay held out his hand for me and helped me up.

"The bus stop is this way," I said, walking toward Fuller Street, but he reached out and placed his hand on my elbow, stopping me.

"Come on, I'll take you home."

Jay must have known I was about to protest, just as I had when he'd offered to pick me up, because he put his finger to my mouth, touching it lightly against my lips in the universal sign of *stop talking*. "I know I don't have to, I want to. Okay? Besides, you can't tell me you'd rather take the bus."

Well, I could, but I'd be lying. "Are you sure?"

"As you know, my social calendar is pretty full, but I think I can spare fifteen minutes to make sure you get home okay."

"Okay," I agreed. "Lead the way."

He started walking up the beach in the direction of the Edgartown Lighthouse and the outlet onto North Water Street.

The short, white, squat lighthouse stood there like an upside-down styrofoam cup. My mother's first-grade class made a replica of the lighthouse every year using exactly that

and a black-painted Dixie cup for the top. Pipe-cleaner railing optional. Farther out the Cape Poge Lighthouse looked
lonely on the northeast tip of Chappaquiddick, where the flat,
windswept land made the beach surrounding the Edgartown
Lighthouse look downright cushy by comparison.

"My mom liked lighthouses," Jay told me as we neared
where North Water Street met up with the beach, which would
give us a straight shot to the Barclays' house. "She used to collect photographs of lighthouses from all over the world. Our
house on Nantucket had this one room we called the lighthouse room because she'd covered the walls with the photos."

"What happened to them?"

"Well, the house on Nantucket was sold and everything
was put into storage back in Connecticut. I guess the pictures
are there, along with the little lighthouse statues and orna-
ments she used to line up on the windowsills of the room.
She'd buy one every summer and write the year on the bottom of the statue in black Magic Marker so she wouldn't forget when she got it."

"And you have no idea where all her lighthouses are? Except maybe in some storage locker in Connecticut?"

He shook his head and I found it hard to believe that he'd
remember a detail such as the handwritten dates and yet not
even know what had happened to his mom's collection.

"So if your mom got Nantucket and your dad got the
Vineyard, how'd they work Connecticut?"

"It's much harder to divide a state than it is two islands. So
my dad got Greenwich and my mom got New Canaan. I guess
you could say they used I-95 as the border, minus the guard
shacks and the lookout towers."

"Yeah, but I hear the barbed wire is a bitch."

Jay laughed and bumped my shoulder.

"Why'd they get divorced?" I asked.

Jay fell quiet. "Good question. They were young and stupid, my mom used to say. She joked about it, but I think when they finally decided to split, she realized it was really over."

"So that was it? There was no big event? No huge surprise? No pointed fingers?" I thought about my parents as I waited for Jay's answer.

"Nope."

"Oh." I thought about this. For some reason I'd gotten the impression there was more, that somehow Anne was the cause. It was the only reason I could think of for Jay's overt animosity toward her. "I thought there might have been something else."

"Like an affair or something? As far as I know, it was nothing like that."

"Then why do you have such a problem with Anne?"

At this point we were crossing Main onto South Water Street, and Jay's house was just twenty yards away. He stopped walking and turned to face me. "Don't you spend enough time with my family all day? Do we really need to talk about them at night, too?"

He was right, and I let it drop.

The Jeep's top was down, and as Jay drove, I tipped my head back and looked up at the stars, trying to make out the Big Dipper. But I was never good at telling the difference between one cluster of stars and another, so instead I found the brightest one in the sky and focused on that.

"Take the next right," I told Jay, pointing up ahead.

He slowed down and pulled into my driveway, cutting the headlights so they wouldn't shine into the house.

Jay put the Jeep into park and turned to me, resting his arm on the back of my seat. "I had fun, thanks."

"No problem, I had a good time, too."

He hesitated a moment, then removed his arm from my seat and slid the car into drive. "Good night, Fred."

I sat there for another minute, waiting for his hand to leave the gearshift again and move in my direction, but it stayed there.

"Good night, Herb," I said, hoping he didn't recognize the disappointment in my voice. "I'll see you tomorrow."

Chapter 11

"**S**o did Jay make a move on you?" Jessie asked when I got to the tennis courts with Cassie. She'd immediately sent Cassie out to the baseline to practice bouncing the ball with her racquet.

"Nope."

"Come on, tell me. Something happened, right?"

I shook my head. "Nothing. He took me home, said he had a good time, and drove away. Officially, nothing happened."

"As long as we're being official," Jessie joked, rolling her eyes at me. "I guess it's for the best, right? Because wouldn't making out with your charge's big brother be a blatant violation of the babysitting code of ethics?"

"I'm not doing anything wrong."

"If you say so, but what do you think Cassie would say if she knew you were getting friendly with her big brother in the front seat of his car? Talk about years of therapy."

"Well, Cassie is not going to need therapy because nothing happened."

"At least he offered to drive you home, which is better than taking the bus, so he can't be all bad."

That was exactly what I'd been thinking last night as I watched the taillights of the Jeep fade into the distance until they disappeared altogether. He *wasn't* all bad, and that's why I had a hard time reconciling the Jay I was with last night with the Jay that Anne had warned me about, the guy who could be so cruel to her one day and yet so kind to me the next.

Jessie left me and went over to Cassie, who looked to be getting bored just bouncing balls. I wondered if that was part of Jessie's grand plan to tire her out so she could call it quits early.

For the next fifteen minutes I watched as Jessie taught Cassie how to hold the racquet and make a ground stroke. Despite what she said, Jessie was actually quite patient with Cassie, even when she missed the ball five times in a row. As I watched Jessie clasp her hands around Cassie's, spacing her fingers just right along the leather-wrapped grip and explaining the importance of rolling her wrists, it occurred to me that last summer I could never have imagined Jessie agreeing to do this. Teaching a class of six kids at the Community Center was one thing; they were happy just smacking a ball against the chain-link fence while Jess practiced her serve for fifteen minutes. But Cassie required her undivided attention and a level of tolerance I hadn't seen Jess demonstrate with anyone else but Nash. It made me think that even if I had to share Jessie with Nash all summer, maybe it wasn't all bad. Just like Jay.

"Think she'll make it to the U.S. Open?" a voice behind me asked, and I turned around to find Jay coming toward me. He was wearing the same faded orange T-shirt and brown cargo shorts he'd had on the first time we almost met, when he passed me on the front walk of the Barclays' house. Only this time he'd shaved, and he seemed to have gotten his hair trimmed, if not exactly cut. The ends still curled up around his neck, and the front was almost long enough to cover his eyes, but he'd pushed his bangs back, and this time instead of noticing how scruffy he looked I realized how really good-looking Jay was. It made me almost glad I didn't get the full effect that afternoon on the front walk, as if every day I discovered something new about Jay, much like those nesting boxes my mom had in the corner of the dining room.

"Cassie or Jessie?" I asked Jay.

"Either one."

"With Jessie as her coach, I'd say Cassie had a chance."

Jay stood next to me and watched as Jessie held her hand on Cassie's shoulder and drew her arm back, demonstrating the proper form for a forehand. "I came by to give you this." Jay handed me a twenty-dollar bill. "Anne forgot to give you money for the lesson."

Jay didn't have to bring the money for Jessie. Anne could have brought it herself or even just given it to me when I got back. I seriously doubted she'd asked Jay to walk all the way to the courts when she could barely ask him to clean up his cereal bowls without getting a dirty look. The only reason I could think of for Jay's visit to the courts was that he wanted to see us. And that also probably meant he wanted to stay.

I took the money and waited for Jay to tell me he had to go. But he didn't.

"Take a seat." I patted the ground next to me, and Jay sat down.

We watched as Jessie left Cassie on one side of the court and walked around to the other. Jess lobbed the ball across the net to Cassie, who awkwardly pulled her racquet back before swinging it forward and connecting with the ball.

I knew Jessie would call it a pop fly, but from the way Cassie reacted you would have thought she'd won the match.

Jay clapped and Cassie beamed at him, noticing her brother for the first time. "Nice shot," he called out, and she set herself up for the next ball.

Jay's encouragement buoyed Cassie's confidence, and she managed to return about every other ball Jessie hit toward her. I thought about Anne's explanation for Jay's absence from their family pictures, and it made me think, even though Cassie no doubt had ballet recitals and gymnastics performances and ice-skating shows, that this was probably the first time Jay had ever sat down and cheered for his sister.

Every time Cassie took her racquet back, Jay's eyes were on her as if he really cared whether she connected with the ball, the look on his face a mix of anticipation and hope as he waited for her to swing. And when the racquet head did connect with the ball, Cassie would turn toward her brother and yell, "Did you see that, Jay?"

"That was the best yet," he'd yell back, almost every single time.

"She likes you," I told Jay, just in case he didn't know.

"You say that as if you're surprised." Jay was looking at me, waiting for an answer, and even though the sun was shining down on us and we were at the public tennis courts, it felt so much like last night in my driveway, in the darkness, when it was just he and I.

I shook my head. "Actually, Herb, I'm not."

I placed my backpack on the dining-room table and unzipped the front pocket, reaching my hand all the way down to the bottom of the pouch, feeling around until I found what I was looking for. One by one I pulled out the items. The white-and-blue-stripped wrapper I'd removed from my Mad Martha's ice-cream cone. The sheet of paper with the pink flower Cassie had drawn for me my second day with her. The sticker from our package of fudge and the dragonfly notepaper Anne had put on the refrigerator the day she'd gone to Vineyard Haven. The two yellow movie-theater tickets Jay had wanted to throw out. Even the Corona bottle cap Nash had left on the beach. I laid each piece of my summer out on the dining-room table, and with the soft, flat pad of my pinkie I smoothed them out until the creases had faded but not disappeared completely. I set the bottle cap aside, not quite sure what I'd do with it.

The jewelry box was on the table, its sanded exterior still rough to the touch. I reached for it, placing the box on a sheet of newspaper to protect the flawless mahogany surface from the glue, much the same way my mom used to lay down a tablecloth before Thanksgiving dinner, shielding the wood from spilled gravy and creamed spinach and cranberry sauce.

I dipped the brush in the glue and ran the bristles over the outside of the box, creating a clear, shiny coating that would hold the torn pieces of paper. The idea had come to me last night, as I took my Oceanview shirt out of the backpack. All the little pieces I'd unwittingly collected over the past two weeks were still in the front pocket waiting to be either thrown away or put to good use. I chose the latter. Each item represented a first, a beginning of something, either my job at the Barclays' or Cassie's and my quest to sample every flavor of fudge. Even the cone wrapper from Mad Martha's reminded me of a first: the first time Jay decided that being with me and Cassie was better than being alone.

"Hey, what are you doing in here?" My dad stood in the doorway to the kitchen watching me. "I never knew my daughter was so crafty. Is your mother finally rubbing off on you?"

"Not exactly."

He came over to me and ran his hand over the top of my head, pulling the hair off my face before giving me a kiss on my forehead.

"How was your photo shoot?"

"Chihuahua," he answered, and I immediately understood. My dad pretty much liked every dog, even if his allergies didn't. But Chihuahuas always tested his talent, or at least his patience. Not only were they spindly little things that required a seamstress as much as a professional photographer to make their costumes fit right and stay that way for an entire shoot; they were also unable to sit still and take orders.

I made one final gluey stroke with the brush before setting it down on the newspaper. "What is that?" my dad asked, pointing to the wet glue and the small torn pieces of paper beneath it.

"Just some stuff I've been collecting this summer."

"Not exactly the hodgepodge of colors your mom prefers, but I like it. There's a sort of subtlety to the design." He walked around to my left, inspecting my handiwork from the other side. "Looks like you need to do a little more collecting, though."

He was right. The glue had soaked through the torn papers, making them almost transparent and exposing the bare wood where the edges didn't meet.

"The summer's barely halfway over. I still have time."

My dad nodded. "So, I have some exciting news," he announced, a huge grin on his face.

"You're giving up the studio in the city?" I guessed, and he shook his head, the grin dissipating. "I've been asked to show my work at a gallery in town. They're going to have a whole opening-night event and everything."

"That's a big deal, Dad," I said, trying to make up for my initial guess. "I can't wait to go."

"It's not until the end of the summer, but it should be good. Maybe Shelby will even come back for it."

"Does Mom know?"

"Not yet," he told me, not even seeming bothered by the fact. "I need to start thinking about which pieces I'll include in the show. Have any favorites?"

I tried to think back to all of the portraits my dad had taken over the past three years, but the only one that stuck out vividly in my mind was Butch. Because without him in the pink plastic beach pail, my dad would still be photographing weddings and anniversary parties and families on the beach for Christmas cards.

"I'm sure whatever you choose will be great," I ended up saying, and he seemed pleased, as if he almost believed it, too.

Chapter 12

The week leading up to the Fourth of July always feels a little different from the rest of the summer. Energy is in the air, an anticipation that people carry around with them as if the entire island is gearing up for something big. Everyone is making plans and buying red-white-and-blue-striped paper plates, filling up shopping carts with hamburger patties and hot dogs and every condiment under the sun. The stores downtown are decorated in Stars and Stripes, and signs announcing the fireworks over Edgartown Harbor are taped up around town just in case someone forgot about the festivities. And even though fireworks are illegal in Massachusetts, you get the feeling everyone has a stash of Roman candles and bottle rockets and sparklers in a brown paper bag at the back of a drawer, just waiting for the sun to disappear and the sky to grow dark to be broken out.

The Fourth was on a Saturday this year, and Mr. Barclay had decided to make a long weekend of it, which is why when he walked into the kitchen Friday afternoon I wasn't surprised. It was nice having another person around, even if, in a way, Mr. Barclay's presence canceled out Jay's. With his dad in the house, Jay spent most of the day in his bedroom by himself, venturing out only when he knew he wouldn't run into his father. If Cassie and I were playing in her room, Jay would wander in to see what we were up to, but other than that he kept himself scarce.

"Ready for the big weekend, Winnie?" Mr. Barclay asked me, pulling out a stool and sitting down at the kitchen island next to Cassie. "You know we get a great view of the fireworks from the backyard. You're more than welcome to come over and watch with us tomorrow."

In the past the Fourth of July usually meant a traditional barbecue at our house. My parents invited their friends over, and my dad would spend most of the day standing beside the grill stoking the coals and flipping burgers while Shelby baked corn muffins and shortbread for dessert. We hadn't talked about plans for this year, though. Shelby obviously wasn't coming home, and my mom hadn't mentioned inviting anyone to the house.

"Thanks for the offer, but I'll have to see what my parents have planned."

Mr. Barclay tilted his head to the side as if he'd just realized the two-liter Coke bottle on the island wasn't filled with soda and we'd peeled the label off the side. Cassie and I had decided the granite island was a better work surface for our experiment, in case it went awry. We didn't want to ruin the wood on the kitchen table. "What are you two doing?"

"We're building a rocket," Cassie told him, leaning her elbows onto the counter as she watched me attempt to force a cork into the mouth of the bottle. "It's an experiment."

Mr. Barclay gave her a dubious look.

"It's something my mom does with her students," I explained, figuring he was envisioning a stealth bombing on the neighbor's house. "It's actually easy."

"Can I join you in this little experiment, then?" he asked. "I have to admit I'm curious. Almost as curious as what you did with all of the soda in that bottle."

Ten minutes later we had the bottle filled halfway with water, a cork stopper in its mouth, and a bicycle pump connected to the valve I'd stuck in the stopper. The three of us went outside to the backyard to the center of the lawn, hoping we'd given ourselves enough margin for error if the bottle decided to explode out rather than up.

"If this hits any of the neighbors' houses, I'm denying I had anything to do with this." Mr. Barclay winked to let me know he was kidding. "We'll just tell them it was all Cassie's idea. Who could be angry with that face?"

Cassie stuck her bottom lip out and gave us a big, sad-eyed look to demonstrate her best get-out-of-jail-free face.

Mr. Barclay and I laughed, and I tried to fathom why Jay had such an attitude toward his father. As far as I could tell, Mr. Barclay was a decent guy. Sure, he wasn't around most of the week, but when he was on the island, he seemed to really want to spend time with Cassie. But maybe that was the problem, although it seemed sort of ridiculous for Jay to hold a grudge against his father for having another child with Anne. Even if Jay had acted as if Cassie were more of an annoyance than anything else when I'd first started babysitting, if yesterday's display at the tennis courts was any indication, he obviously didn't think that so much anymore. From what I'd seen, it was Jay who wanted nothing to do with his dad, not the other way around.

"Are you ready?" I asked Cassie as I screwed the bicycle pump connector to the valve stem and silently prayed the rocket would work the way it was supposed to. Cassie's pouty face was cute, but I didn't really think it would have much effect if the rocket smashed through the window of the house next door and exploded water all over their living-room rug.

"Ready," Cassie announced, beginning her countdown from five.

I started pumping as hard and fast as I could, and about a second after Cassie yelled, "Blastoff," the pressure in the Coke bottle reached breaking point and our makeshift rocket shot into the sky.

Cassie gasped as the bottle flew straight up overhead, and I thought I heard Mr. Barclay mutter, "Holy shit," as he stepped even farther away from the house and shielded his eyes from the sun to get a better look.

I shielded my eyes from the sun, too, attempting to follow the rocket as it grew smaller and smaller against the backdrop of the blue sky. But as I stepped back from the house and turned my back to the harbor, I noticed someone standing in a second-floor window. Jay was watching us from his bedroom, a hand holding the curtain back to give him a better view.

Mr. Barclay must have noticed Jay at that moment as well, because he waved for Jay to join us. "Come on!" Mr. Barclay implored, loud enough for Jay to hear through the screen that separated him from us.

Cassie was still squealing and running around on the lawn trying to guess where the rocket would land when it finally ran out of water, completely unaware of her father's exchange with Jay.

I almost wished Cassie had noticed Jay first and screamed for him to come down and watch the experiment with us. I wondered if she would have made a difference, because Jay didn't even acknowledge his father's invitation. He just observed us for another minute before walking away from the window and letting the curtain drop, shielding him from our view.

"Over here, Dad!" Cassie yelled, running down toward the harbor wall. "It's going to land by the chairs!"

Mr. Barclay hesitated briefly, still looking up at the window, then turned away from the house and followed Cassie's voice.

Cassie and Mr. Barclay decided to walk into town to see if they could find a little Fourth of July present for Anne. "Something with stars on it," Cassie told me, and I was sure she'd have more than enough gifts to choose from.

"You can go, Winnie, there's no reason for you to stick around." Mr. Barclay offered to walk with me to the bus stop, but I told him I should probably straighten up Cassie's room first, so they left without me.

The room wasn't that much of a mess, but we'd played dress-up earlier in the day, and I knew that at least three princess dresses, six pairs of sequined shoes, and one sparkly crown were strewn around, and I figured the least I could do was hang the dresses up so they didn't get wrinkled. Or more wrinkled, considering Cassie tended to stuff clothes into the corner of her closet rather than attempt to fold them and put them away where they belonged.

"That doesn't look like it's your size," Jay said from the

doorway, pointing to the pale blue Cinderella dress I was slipping onto a hanger.

I held the lace sleeves in place while I zipped up the back. "It's not, but I can't fit into the matching glass slippers either, so it really doesn't matter."

Jay came into the room and bent down to pick up the satin, pink Sleeping Beauty dress Cassie had left on the floor under her green-and-pink table. He walked over to the closet and removed a hanger.

"You don't have to help," I told him, but he set the hanger down on the table and started smoothing out the creases in the pink skirt.

"I saw you today, watching us." I didn't look at him as I spoke, instead concentrating on the zipper, which had gotten stuck halfway up and wouldn't budge.

"Nice job on the rocket." He sat down on the corner of the table, beside the teapot and cups Cassie and I had set up for our princess party.

Jay hadn't even acknowledged the watching part, focusing on the water-filled Coke bottle instead of the implication that he could have been on the lawn with us instead of observing from his window. "Why didn't you come down?" I asked.

Jay stopped working at the wrinkles, letting his hand rest against the smooth fabric stretched across his lap. "Look, Winnie, it's no secret that my dad and I don't get along."

"He doesn't seem to feel that way." I remembered how Mr. Barclay had looked at the vacant window, how he'd continued staring at the window even after the curtain had fallen closed and shut Jay off from him. "He told you to come down."

"Yeah, well, I've learned that it's best not to listen to everything he says." Jay reached for the hanger and held it in his hand, tapping the wire frame against the surface of the table as he spoke. "It's just the way it is, Winnie."

I didn't believe him. I didn't know Mr. Barclay well, but if what I'd seen this afternoon was any indication, he wanted to have a relationship with Jay. And no matter how Jay acted, the guy who'd cheered Cassie on yesterday at the tennis courts could not just disregard that. Nothing was irreparable, not if you really wanted to fix what was wrong. "I don't think that's true."

"You don't know what happened, so it's not like you even have a clue what I'm talking about." Jay was tapping the hanger harder now, its wire frame leaving small gray marks on the pink-and-green-striped paint. "Just drop it."

"No, I won't." I went over to him. "Your dad obviously isn't as angry with you as you are with him, so why don't you just talk to him. He seems like a totally reasonable guy."

"God, can't you just leave it alone!" Jay leaped up and threw the hanger down onto the tea set, where it skidded across the table with such force it sent the cups and pot flying off the side, smashing them against the hardwood floor.

I backed away, leaving space between Jay and myself, a buffer to absorb the shock waves.

"I told you to just drop it!" Jay yelled again, pushing past me on his way out of the room.

The tea set lay cracked and broken on the floor a few feet from where the Sleeping Beauty dress sat in a crumpled heap. A door down the hall slammed, and I knew Jay was hiding in his room again, shutting himself off from me just as he did everyone else.

I went over to the tea set and knelt on the floor, picking up the pieces of the pot and holding them in my palm to see if Jay had broken the porcelain in the same places as last time. My hand was still shaking as I thought about how angry Jay was, how he'd pushed past me as if I were just something in his way instead of someone who mattered. The Krazy Glue had held together in some spots, but new fractures had appeared, smaller ones that would be more difficult to align and possibly even too fragile to hold.

As I collected the shards of white and pink porcelain and walked them over to the garbage can, I started to think that maybe I was totally wrong about Jay. Maybe the person who'd just destroyed the tea set and stormed out of the room was the real Jay, not the guy who'd driven me home the other night. The idea that I'd let him lure me into believing he was different made me feel foolish and furious and completely confused, but most of all it made me sad. Because while I hated the Jay who'd just broken Cassie's tea set, I liked the guy who'd walked with me on the beach. The one who'd driven me home and sat with me in the Jeep that night, the one who'd made me think he'd slide his arm down from the seatback and let it fall over my shoulders, just as I'd wanted.

But I'd been wrong, and instead of moving closer, Jay had backed away from me and said good night. So maybe I didn't really know him at all, even if I wanted so badly to believe I did.

"So what are we doing today?" I asked my mom the next morning. She was at the kitchen counter waiting for two slices of whole-wheat toast to pop up. It wasn't as festive as last year's Fourth of July breakfast, when Shelby made pancakes with blueberries and strawberry syrup, her culinary version of red, white, and blue.

"Are you girls making plans?" My dad came over to the table and kissed me on the head before moving over to the counter and standing beside my mother.

I waited for my dad to lay a hand on her waist, pulling her closer to him, but instead he reached for the butter dish and passed it to my mom.

"Would you like some toast?" she offered, removing the lid from the butter dish just as the toaster dinged.

My dad nodded and my mother took two more slices of bread from the open bag to her right.

It was just two people making breakfast on a Saturday morning, a couple sharing a kitchen. I can't say that my mom and dad used to blow each other kisses while making scrambled eggs or whisper intimate nicknames to one another while frying up French toast, yet their interactions now were so controlled, as if they shared the same room but not the same space. I'd almost hoped that today would be different, the way it used to be, with my mom boiling a huge pot of macaroni for her pasta salad and my father trying to figure out how many bags of hot dog buns he needed to match the number of hot dogs in the Ball Park franks package.

But no pot of macaroni was bubbling was on the stove and my dad hadn't asked me to calculate today's hot-dogs-to-buns ratio.

"Who's coming over this afternoon?" I asked them, finishing my glass of orange juice.

My parents looked to one another, then over to me.

"You know, we didn't invite anyone," my mother explained.

"I guess because it was a Saturday the whole day just felt like any other weekend."

Sure, just like any other weekend when Edgartown Harbor is lit up by ten thousand pounds of explosives.

"So we're going to hang around here all day?" I asked.

My dad went to the refrigerator to get a jar of jelly. "I guess we could ask some people over, but I'm sure everyone has plans. Why don't you call Jessie and see what she's up to?" he suggested.

"Jessie is sailing all day with Nash," I told him. "So what are we going to do?"

The toast popped up and my mom waited a minute for the bread to cool before taking it between her fingers and setting it down on my dad's plate. "I don't know. Do you have any ideas?"

"We could go out for lunch, at least," I suggested, having an inspired idea. "Let's go to the Pot Belly Deli. Maybe they have some of Shelby's lemon bars out for the holiday."

My mom turned to my dad. "What do you think?"

"I think that's a great idea." He bit into his jellied toast and made a less than satisfied face. "And if this is my breakfast, you can be sure I'll be hungry for lunch."

That's how, at noon, my mom and dad and I ended up waiting in line at the Pot Belly. I knew it would be packed, with everyone picking up sandwich orders for the beach, and my parents knew, too. But I think they realized that going to the Pot Belly would give us all something to do, and even if it didn't make up for our traditional family barbecue, at least it was something.

Last summer Shelby worked at the Willow Inn with Kendra Bryant, who was working behind the counter today when we finally made it to the front of the line. Kendra's family owned the Pot Belly, and one day Kendra had brought Shelby's lemon bars to the deli to share with her parents and sister. Somehow they ended up next to the cash register, and even though they weren't intended to be sold, all of the bars were gone in minutes. They still carried the lemon bars whenever Shelby could send a batch over.

"Do you have any lemon bars?" I asked Kendra.

She shook her head. "We wish. Shelby sent us a couple dozen last week, but they didn't even last a day." Kendra leaned her elbows up on the counter. "Not that I didn't save a few for myself. Do you know what you'd like?"

My parents were still staring at the blackboard up against the wall behind the counter.

"I guess I'll go first," I said. "How about a Santa Fe Gobbler."

"And I'll have a Kendra with a Pickle on Top," my mom chimed in.

My dad nodded. "Make that two."

When we sat down at an empty table, I had a good feeling. They'd picked the same sandwich, which I thought was positive. They talked about a cute little girl in line, complimenting the girl on her Stars and Stripes sundress, even striking up a conversation with the toddler's parents and laughing together as the mother explained how difficult it was to get little Darcy up the flagpole. Maybe my parents just needed to be forced to spend time together to remember what it used to be like when they spent every day together, when they shared seemingly mundane tasks that, when accumulated over time, actually made up the fabric of our family life.

My plan had been to get us all together in a place we used to visit as a family, and when a few minutes later Kendra came over and set a plate down on our table, I actually thought my plan might work after all.

"Here," she said. "I was saving the last lemon bar for myself, but you can have it."

"Are you sure?" my mom asked, even though her finger was already making its way to the excess powdered sugar covering the rim of the plate.

"Sure." Kendra nodded. "I'm sure there will be more where that came from."

But if I thought my sister's lemon bar and a couple of roast-beef sandwiches would make all the difference in the world, I was wrong. We ate and talked, telling stories about past July Fourths, remembering the summers before my dad had the studio in the city, but I soon realized that everything we remembered, every story we told, was from a long time ago, as if we had nothing worth remembering from the past few years. And eventually, without any new memories to recall, our conversation went back to innocuous topics and pleasant observations. It was just like at home, only we had bigger sandwiches and a better dessert.

I almost wished I could say they acted like strangers, but even that wouldn't be true. Strangers weren't expected to have anything in common, to know what to say and share. It was more as if my parents had become old friends who hadn't seen each other in a long while, able to touch on the few subjects they had in common, respecting certain boundaries that had been agreed upon but never venturing outside the lines.

"All set?" my dad asked, wiping his hands on the paper

napkin he'd removed from his lap. He'd finished the entire roast beef sandwich, leaving just a few stray crumbs behind on the plate.

My mom nodded and started stacking our empty plates on top of one another. "I think so. Winnie, this was super. Thanks for suggesting it."

"How about I go get the car and pick you girls up?" my dad offered, pushing his chair back from the table. "That way we all don't have to wait in traffic."

My mom thought that was a great idea, and before I could tell him we should all walk together, my father was gone, lost in the crowd waiting to place their lunch orders.

Together my mom and I cleared our table and made our way toward the door, just the two of us. You'd think by now I'd be used to it.

"Winnie?"

Looking up, I found Jay standing alone in line.

"What are you doing here?" I asked before I remembered I shouldn't even be talking to him after what he did yesterday in Cassie's room.

"I'm getting some lunch." Then, because he probably realized my mother was staring at him, he said, "I'm Jay."

"This is Cassie's brother," I explained, looking away from Jay and toward the line snaking through the front door and down the street.

"Do you recommend anything special?" Jay asked me, moving to his left so I couldn't ignore him. He kept ducking down, trying to force me to look him in the eye, but I managed to slip between the line of people.

"Whatever you pick will be fine," I mumbled, then turned

to look over my shoulder at my mom. "Come on, Dad is probably waiting for us."

I reached for my mom's hand and pulled her behind me as we made our way through the line and out the front door.

I didn't look at Jay again until I was outside and a plate-glass window separated us, but for a split second I caught him watching me before he looked away.

Chapter 13

"Where's Cassie?" I asked Jay on Monday afternoon. It was the first time we'd seen each other since the scene on Friday aside from our encounter at the Pot Belly. I'd spent at least fifteen minutes cleaning up the remains of his outburst, but he'd never come back into the room to apologize and never offered to help me clean up the broken tea set.

"Didn't you get Anne's message?" he asked, acting as if nothing had even happened, choosing to ignore the whole ordeal. "Cassie's got a fever. She took her to the doctor and they think she has an ear infection."

I took my phone out of my backpack and set it on the kitchen island. Sure enough there was one voice mail.

"Is she upstairs?"

"No, they're not back yet, but I guess you have the afternoon off."

He looked at me as if I was supposed to act as if I wanted to stay, but I didn't. "Okay, well, I guess I'll go then."

Jay got up from the kitchen table and came over to me, standing on the other side of the island as if he knew I needed some distance between us. "Cassie wanted you to go to her room before you left. She had something to show you."

"I can wait until she's here." I swung the backpack over my shoulder, prepared to leave.

"She made me promise you'd go upstairs," Jay said. "Don't make me look like a liar."

He didn't want to look like a liar, but he had no problem looking like a jerk.

"Fine," I agreed, turning my back and leaving him standing alone by the kitchen island.

I didn't notice anything different in Cassie's room at first. Except that it looked really, really clean. Not a princess dress or Magic Marker anywhere in sight, or at least not on the floor. And then I noticed the table and knew it wasn't Cassie who had wanted me to come upstairs. It was Jay.

The small table was set with four pale yellow teacups set atop coordinating yellow-and-white-polka-dotted saucers. In the center of the table a matching teapot and sugar bowl sat beside a small oval platter where four pink-frosted sugar cookies waited to be eaten. He'd even placed one of Cassie's four favorite stuffed animals in each of the chairs, and they looked as if they were enjoying themselves if only because Jay had appeared behind me and asked, "They look as if they're enjoying themselves, don't you think?"

I turned around to face him, but before I could say anything he started talking.

"Look, I'm sorry, I lost it and I was totally wrong. I know the new tea set doesn't make up for my reaction, but if it's any consolation, Cassie said she liked it even better than the old one." Jay waited for me to respond, and when I didn't, he went over to the table and picked up the yellow-and-white-polka-dotted platter. "Aren't cookies the universal food of forgiveness?"

I tried not to smile, but he looked so ridiculous next to Cassie's animal tea party I couldn't help it.

Jay smiled back. "I really am sorry, Winnie."

"Okay. I heard you." I believed he really meant it.

Jay invited me to stay until Cassie and Anne got home, but I still thought I should leave.

"I can walk into town with you, if you'd like," Jay offered as he followed me down the stairs toward the front door.

I considered declining his offer, if just to prove I wasn't going to forget that quickly what he'd done, but he seemed so repentant I decided he deserved a second chance. "Just don't tell me you want ice cream, because honestly, I've had enough ice cream this summer to last me a lifetime."

Jay held up two fingers as if he were making a solemn oath. "I promise, Fred. No ice cream."

"Am I supposed to believe you were a Boy Scout?" I asked, smacking his fingers down.

"Only if you don't ask me to start a fire with two sticks and a piece of flint."

"I wouldn't even know where to find a piece of flint."

"Then it's safe to assume you weren't a Girl Scout?" he asked, holding the door open for me.

"No, I was," I told him. "Just not a very good one."

As we walked toward Main Street, I almost asked Jay why he was by himself at the Pot Belly. It was Fourth of July, after all. I knew Anne and Mr. Barclay were having people over for a cookout and to watch the fireworks over the harbor. They probably had enough food to feed half the people crowded down by the harbor that day, so Jay didn't need to get a sandwich from a deli. But that's exactly what he'd done. It made me realize that even if Jay was sorry he'd lashed out at me in Cassie's room, he still wasn't ready to let go of whatever made him so angry with his father. And even though I wanted to ask if he watched the fireworks from the backyard with his family, I had an idea what the answer would be. And I didn't feel like getting into it with him because at that moment, walking along the sidewalk together, things almost felt normal again.

"Do you feel like going for a bike ride?" Jay asked as we passed Island Wheels.

With an empty afternoon stretching out before me, I wasn't looking forward to going home. "Where to?"

"I don't care, we can just go wherever we want. Doesn't matter to me."

"Okay. Do you want to go back to the house and get one of the bikes out of the garage?" I'd seen the bikes in the Barclays' garage, shiny European models with heavily padded seats and what looked like thirty gears.

"No, I can just rent one with you."

"Are you sure? I can't guarantee these will be anywhere near what you're used to." I pointed to the rack against the front of the store where generic-looking mountain bikes were lined up waiting to be rented.

"I think I'll survive, Fred."

"You say that now, Herb, but don't blame me when you're walking funny tomorrow."

I followed him into the store. Jay told the guy behind

the counter that we needed two bikes, and he handed Jay a form to fill out while he went to the back to get us some helmets.

"How much is it?" I asked Jay, reaching into my backpack for my wallet.

Jay shook his head. "I've got it, going for a ride was my idea."

He looked as if I wouldn't be able to change his mind even if I tried, so I zipped up my backpack and rested it back on my shoulder.

"So which way?" Jay asked me once we had our helmets on and we were walking our bikes across Main Street toward the bike path.

"How about taking West Tisbury Road and seeing where we feel like going from there?" I suggested, and Jay agreed.

The bike path was wide enough for both of us, but when other bikers came toward us from the opposite direction, Jay would slow down and fall behind me, letting them pass. Then he'd be right beside me again, until the next group of bikers appeared in the distance. We pedaled out past Morning Glory Farm, sharing the bike path with families and couples and a few lone cyclists dressed as if they really knew what they were doing, with special shoes that snapped into bindings and aerodynamically engineered helmets.

Every time Jay pedaled up next to me, he asked how I was doing. And each time I told him fine. Which was true. Until we'd gone almost three miles and were still a mile from the airport, where I figured we'd hang a right and head over to Edgartown–Vineyard Haven Road to make our way back. At that point I was ready for a rest.

"How about stopping when we get to Airport Road," I suggested.

Jay erupted, "Finally! My God, I'm dying. Why the hell didn't we remember to bring any water? I was beginning to think you were a camel or something. Aren't you hot?"

"Yeah, I'm hot." I was sure he could tell from my red cheeks. "I think I might have a bottled water in my backpack."

"Then break it out, Fred. I'm dying over here."

We pulled off the path and rested our bikes on the ground. I removed my backpack and sat on a long, flat rock at the edge of the woods.

"Can I ask you a question?" I unscrewed the cap on the bottled water, took a sip, then handed the bottle to Jay.

"I guess that depends what the question is."

"Why didn't you go to Colorado with your friends?"

Jay took a swig of my water, then spit it out onto the dirt. "That's gross, it's warm."

"I said I had water. I didn't say it was cold."

He put the bottle to his lips again and chugged. This time he swallowed.

"If you don't want to answer, you don't have to." I figured if he was willing to down a bottle of warm water with my backwash, he was willing to go to great lengths to avoid answering my question.

"I was uninvited." Jay screwed the cap back onto the half-empty bottle. "Well, maybe uninvited isn't exactly true. It's a long story."

"Unless you're ready to get back on that bike, I have plenty of time."

Jay smiled and sat down on the rock beside me. "I was

supposed to play lacrosse at school. It's the whole reason I went there in the first place. But after a pretty crappy first semester my grades sucked, and when it came time to play, they wouldn't let me. I didn't tell my dad, of course, since lacrosse was the whole reason I went there in the first place. He wanted me to go to Harvard."

Lacrosse, it explained the body. "You got into Harvard?"

"Is it that hard to believe?"

"Honestly, yeah."

He shrugged. "Anyway, I'd been hanging out with some guys from the team, and they were all planning to spend the summer out West, mountain biking, hiking, that sort of stuff. When I went home for Christmas, I told everyone that's what I was doing. But then when I couldn't play and they were all doing team stuff, we sort of stopped hanging out . . ." Jay's voice trailed off.

"Why didn't you just tell your dad? Didn't you think he'd find out?"

"Well, he still doesn't know. I have no idea why he thinks I'm here."

"Hasn't he asked?"

Jay shook his head. "I'm sure you think my family is screwed up. This sort of crap doesn't happen on the island, does it? It's like this place is removed from all the bullshit that happens in the real world."

"Actually, you'd be surprised." I shook the bottle of water and watched the bubbles rise to the top. "I think my parents are going to split up, and you know the worst thing, well, besides the obvious? I don't even think they care. I mean, how do you just give up and stop even trying?"

"Maybe they tried."

"They've pretty much lived apart for three years. I think you have to be under the same roof to *try*, don't you?"

"You're asking me for advice?" Jay laughed. "Haven't you learned anything today?"

"I learned that taking a ten-mile bike ride gets old after about the first three miles."

"A valuable lesson, Fred." Jay stood up and held out his hand for me to join him. "I just wish we didn't have to learn it with seven miles still to go."

We made it back to the bike shop, but by the time we got there Jay and I had sworn off any future activities that required pedaling, hand brakes, or small leather seats.

"Thanks for the afternoon, and the rental." I ran my fingers through my hair, trying to fix any remaining helmet-head effect. "I'm going to go catch the bus."

"You're going to walk to the bus? I can't believe you can even walk that far." Jay shook his head. "Why don't I give you a ride home. You've had enough exercise for one day."

The way my thighs ached, I wasn't about to argue.

"Thanks again, Jay," I said when we reached my house. I unbuckled my seat belt, but didn't open the door. "I guess I'll see you tomorrow."

"If I can move. I have a feeling I'm going to be awfully sore."

"I thought you were a lacrosse player. Aren't you supposed to be in shape?"

"You missed the point of the whole story, Fred. *Former* lacrosse player."

"But you can still play this year, right?"

"Only if my grades are better. And if I make it onto the team after a year off, and who knows if that will happen."

"Do you want to play?"

"Well, yeah, but that's not exactly up to me."

"Well, if you want to play, you can't just give up, not if it's what you want."

A breeze blew through the front seat of the Jeep, messing my hair, and even though I pushed most of it out of my eyes, a strand remained stuck to my lip.

Jay brushed his fingers against my face, moving my hair back, and I found myself moving toward his touch until our lips were pressed together, his tongue gently parting mine, his hand moving to the skin on my neck and pulling me against him. And instead of moving away I slid across the seat until there was no space between us, because it felt amazing and wonderful and even though every muscle in my body ached I wanted to be near him.

Finally, Jay pulled away, a look of surprise and delight on his face. "I wasn't sure you were going to let me do that."

"Is it that hard to believe?" I asked, and he laughed, remembering that he'd asked me the same thing earlier that afternoon.

"Honestly, yeah," he answered, and this time we both laughed.

I sat there for a minute, trying to process what had just happened, to understand how I was sitting in the front seat of Jay's Jeep with a ridiculous smile on my face. Yeah, I could have asked him why he kissed me, I could have tried to analyze why I kissed him back, and we both could have sat there for hours trying to figure out what it all meant. But I didn't really want to.

I reached for the handle and pushed the door open. "I guess I'll see you tomorrow, Herb."

"Not if I see you first, Fred."

Chapter 14

The Oceanview camp program pretty much ran on autopilot at this point, even if the kids tried their best to make it unpredictable, such as this morning when a hungry eight-year-old named Max couldn't wait until snack time and decided to try one of the apples in the basket on the coffee table in the lobby. Only he didn't realize they were wax until it was too late, and Rachel and I had to floss the kid's teeth for fifteen minutes to remove the red flakes that clung to every tooth better than most glue.

"It can't get much worse than this, can it?" Rachel asked me as she washed her hands with antibacterial soap for the third time. "My boyfriend will not believe that I spent my morning with my fingers in someone else's mouth."

I handed Rachel a paper towel. "You have a boyfriend?"

She looked up at me as if trying to figure out if I *couldn't* believe she had a boyfriend or I *didn't* believe she had a boyfriend.

"I just meant, you've never talked about him before."

Rachel turned off the faucet and took the paper towel. "Mark Bottner and I started going out right before school ended."

I knew Mark Bottner. He was on the hockey team and we had a history class together our freshman year.

"He's a nice guy," I told Rachel, although I didn't tell her I was at the game against Scituate when a senior about twice Mark's size hip-checked him into the boards and knocked Mark unconscious. When he came to, Mark kept asking for his mom, and needless to say for the next few weeks nobody at school let him forget it.

"Do you have a boyfriend?" Rachel asked me, tossing the paper towel in the garbage can. She turned toward the door and I followed her out of the bathroom, but instead of walking toward the activity room she stopped in the hallway, waiting for my answer.

If she'd asked me the same question last week, I would immediately have said no. If she'd asked me four days ago, I would have said the same thing. But everything changed on Monday when Jay dropped me off at my house. That kiss changed everything.

Ever since our kiss, Jay met me at the VTA bus stop every day and walked with me to the Barclays' house—his house. It was barley ten minutes, but from the moment I stepped off the bus until we came within view of the house, our bodies were touching in one way or another. The first day when I looked out the bus window and saw Jay standing by the tree in front of the building on Church Street, I felt a surge of anticipation so great and so unexpected I was standing at the door before the bus even pulled to a stop. I'd stepped off the bus and Jay was right there, reaching for me, pulling me aside and pressing me up against the twisted trunk, the rough surface of the bark against my back and the firm, warm feel of Jay against the rest of me. When his lips reached mine, the urgency and necessity was so overwhelming it almost verged on desperation, our tongues pushing and probing, our eyes squeezed tight as we felt our way around one another until a boy's sarcastic voice yelled out, "Get a room," and we broke apart and laughed, embarrassed.

Our hands locked the entire way to the Barclays' house, and we stopped at least twice to try the kiss again, those times more tenderly than at the bus stop but no less enjoyable. The thing is, when we were in the house or around Cassie, Jay and I made sure we didn't touch, even if sometimes I'd catch him looking in my direction in a way that made me wish we could sneak away to an empty room and just be alone, the two of us. Once we even did, although it was just while Cassie went downstairs to get herself a snack.

"Yeah, I do," I told her.

"So who is he?" Rachel wanted to know, taking a seat on the bench against the hallway wall. She was obviously stalling for time before we had to get back to the kids. I couldn't imagine she was that interested in my love life. "Do I know him?"

"His name is Jay, and you don't know him. He's in college."

"So? I might know him. I knew a few of the older guys." Rachel was leaning back against the wall, making herself comfortable as if we had nowhere to go and nothing to do but sit here and shoot the breeze.

"He didn't go to school with us." I paused, bracing myself for Rachel's reaction, and I was sure there'd be one. "He's just here for the summer."

"A summer guy!" Rachel practically shouted, and I looked

down the hallway to see if any of the guests in the lobby had heard her. But either Rachel wasn't as loud as I thought she was or the guests didn't realize the significance of Rachel's words. "You're dating a summer guy? What are you thinking?"

"I'm not thinking anything, we're just spending time together." I knew I didn't have to justify my relationship to Rachel, but I felt that I had to say something. I didn't want her thinking what I knew most people thought, that summer romances were as fleeting as the season itself. "His family has a house here, so it's not like he's *just* here for the summer. He'll be back again."

Even as I said the words, I wanted to believe they were true. I wanted to believe that whatever Jay and I had just started, it wasn't simply a result of convenient circumstances, our proximity to one another and the fickle sheen of the season.

"You're right." Rachel nodded her head more vigorously than she had to. "I mean, he has a house here. He'll probably come back every summer."

I recognized the tone of Rachel's voice. It was the same tone I'd used our first day of camp, when Rachel described the extent of her experience with kids. And I knew she was thinking the same thing I'd thought when I told Rachel that going to the bathroom in the vicinity of story hour counted: I was screwed.

"We better get going. Marla's probably wondering where we are." I started down the hallway toward the activity room, not even waiting for Rachel to catch up with me—partly because we were already way later than we should have been, but mostly because I didn't want Rachel to see that I knew she was right.

"Can I ask you a question, Winnie?" Anne stood over the kitchen sink washing Cassie's lunch plate.

"Sure."

"I know it's none of my business, and I don't want to butt in where I'm not supposed to, but I feel I have to ask." She took the dish towel off the counter and dried her hands before turning around to face me. "Is something going on between you and Jay?"

I tried to remember where Anne was that time Cassie went downstairs to get a snack, or even another instance when she might have noticed the glances Jay and I exchanged with one another, and that's why I didn't answer Anne's question right away.

And when I didn't say anything, Anne took that for a yes. She came over to the kitchen table and sat down across from me. "Look, there's a lot about Jay that you don't know."

"He's different than you think, Anne. He's different than I thought." I knew I sounded defensive, but I felt that Jay deserved to be defended. And all of a sudden I wasn't all that comfortable talking about Jay with Anne, as if I were being disloyal just by talking about this with her.

"I don't know what he's told you, but he had a really rough year last year."

"He told me."

"He told you about his mom and how he was put on academic probation and how he was kicked out of the dorms?"

Okay, I didn't know about the dorm thing. "He told me everything," I lied.

"Just be careful, okay, Winnie?"

"Okay," I promised. "I will."

I forgot my backpack in the break room at the Oceanview, so Jay offered to take me there when I was done watching Cassie, and I gladly accepted his offer. That's why, at four o'clock, Jay and I were backing out of the Barclays' driveway when I noticed Anne in the front window, watching us, but before I could wave, she'd walked away. Even though I knew it was crazy, a part of me felt that I was betraying her by being with Jay. If I was going to be forced to make a choice, I'd chosen Jay.

While I went to the break room to get my backpack, Jay wandered around the resort grounds. I found him a few minutes later in the courtyard standing beside the larger-than-life-size chess set.

"The guests are always asking us to take their pictures beside the pieces," I told him. The bishop came up to my waist, and even though the guests loved to try to move the pieces from one square to another, I'd actually never attempted it.

"You ever play?"

"I doubt I could lift the pieces, even if I did know how to play chess."

"Then I guess I can't challenge you to a game."

"You could, but I'd have to say no."

Jay left his place beside the king and came over to me. "How about taking a walk down to the beach instead?"

I accepted the offer, because even if I didn't know how to play chess, I did know how to go for a walk.

Jay and I took the path we counselors usually used with the kids, crossing the footbridge over the wash that dried up when it hadn't rained for a while. Then we made our way up to Atlantic Drive, which runs along South Beach, with the dunes on the beach side and brush on the other. Although a few summer homes were set back along Atlantic Drive, huge sprawling houses with decks and balconies hanging off every room, mostly the street saw beach traffic and an occasional jogger. This late in the afternoon we were more likely to see joggers than cars on their way to the beach, so the road was deserted as far as we could see.

"Come on, we can walk along the street," I suggested, taking Jay's hand. "We can still get the view without the sand in our shoes."

We walked along the edge of Atlantic Drive, moving over onto the sandy grass lining the pavement whenever a car passed. When a bright red biplane took off from the grass runway at the Katama airfield up ahead of us, Jay and I stopped to look up, reading the word RIDES in white block letters on the underside of the wings.

As we approached the split-rail fence surrounding the airfield, Jay slowed and let go of my hand.

"Did you know them?" Jay asked, stopping to look down the incline to our right, where a makeshift memorial was crowded by tall grass.

I shook my head. "They were older. I think my sister, Shelby, knew them."

Jay stood there, staring at the small wooden crosses no

taller than my arm, the public markers of someone's private grief.

"Who do you think takes care of them?" he asked.

"I don't know. Probably their family and friends come by every once in a while to clear the brush."

"On the way from Greenwich to school there are a few of these along I-95. Last September, on my way to school, I passed a bunch of cars lined up in the breakdown lane, and I figured there had to be an accident or maybe a car ran out of gas or something. But as I drove by, I noticed the cars were empty and there was a small crowd of people standing around a wreath of flowers they'd nailed to a cross."

I pictured those people standing along the side of the highway, how they had to climb over the guardrail to get to the spot where someone lost his life, feeling the rush of air hit them every time a car passed.

"I remember thinking of my mother's oncologist's office," Jay continued. "Wondering if that was the equivalent of the bruised and mangled tree beside the cross with flowers. I kept thinking maybe a cross should be erected in the waiting room of his office every time one of his patients died, because honestly, Winnie, I didn't know what else to do."

I reached over and took Jay's hand, and he wove his fingers between mine and pulled me closer, so our hips were touching and I could feel the humidity clinging to his bare arm.

"Now every time I pass that spot on the highway I always look, every single time," Jay told me. "Only I don't just see the cross with its handwritten letters or the faded artificial wreath. I see those people who went back because they needed to remember. Do you think it makes them feel better?"

"Maybe not better, maybe just like they could do something at a time when they were feeling pretty helpless."

"They probably had no idea they were going to die." Jay nodded toward the memorial. "My mom knew. And she knew I wasn't there."

"Why weren't you there?" I practically whispered.

"Because my dad told me to stay at school." Jay spit out the words, and when I looked over and saw the pained expression on his face, the cold, hard look I saw that day he'd turned his back on me and walked up the stairs, I felt my stomach constrict, almost nauseated as I envisioned Jay sitting in his dorm room while his mother lay in bed alone, her body ready to give up its fight. And for the first time I understood why Jay was so angry with his father, and it made me want to shake Mr. Barclay, to scream at him, to let him know what he'd done to Jay when he took that moment away from him, the moment he could have said good-bye to his mother one last time.

Jay stepped back, away from the memorial and back onto the street. He held on to my hand, not letting go, and I followed him.

"I know it doesn't help, but I'm sorry." I leaned my head against his shoulder as we walked.

"Thanks." Jay squeezed my hand. "I don't mean to be so morose. I just haven't talked about it much."

This time I led and Jay followed as I walked him across Atlantic Drive and up the dunes to the beach, where I sat and pulled him down beside me.

"You can talk to me. So talk."

Jay bit the side of his cheek and stared out at the water as if trying to decide where to start, or even if he could start at all. "She'd already beaten it twice, the first time when I was twelve, and the second time when I was fifteen. But this was different."

Jay remembered every detail in a way that I couldn't imagine, how she was so small, her arms so thin Jay could wrap his fingers around her wrist and still have extra room. He touched his thumb and forefinger together, forming a circle to show me what he meant.

"And I knew. By the end of the summer, when it was time for me to go off to school, she couldn't even get out of bed. Her hair had been gone for a while by then, and all she had was this grayish white fuzz that reminded me of my grandfather's stubble when he'd forget to shave, but so much softer."

I listened as Jay described his mother, how she lost so much weight even the children's nightgowns they bought her hung loose around her shrinking frame. He remembered the smallest details of her last weeks, her cracked lips that never healed no matter how much lip balm he applied, how she'd slip so easily into sleep only to awake a few minutes later, moaning. He remembered everything, although I was sure he'd rather forget.

I thought how so many people died in similar ways, and yet the details separated them and made each exceptional.

I couldn't begin to imagine what Jay had been through with his mother, but still, in a way it was similar to how I felt about my parents. It was the details of when they were together that I remembered, the way my dad used to rub my mom's shoulders when she'd be grading her students' work at the kitchen table, or how my mother would cut my father's horoscope out of the newspaper and slip it into his camera bag, and how he'd always come home from a photo shoot and say something like "Don't worry, Lydia, they say this year is going to be a breeze after the planetary pummeling I've just been through."

It was those details, those moments, that went away when he got the studio in the city. Or maybe they didn't go away. Maybe they were just replaced by new details, moments that they created on their own, separately, without the other person. The same way Jessie and Nash had moments together that I didn't know about, and how Shelby was creating her own details far away from us. And I knew that when I looked back on this summer, it would be the small moments with Jay that I'd remember, the way he'd placed his finger against my lips at the Fuller Street beach and how afterward my lips had tasted slightly salty when I'd run my tongue against them, or the look on his face when he'd pulled away from me after our first kiss. But it was that moment right then and here on the beach with Jay that I'd remember most vividly, because it was the moment I realized just how much we needed each other.

Chapter 15

"Aren't you going to ask me in?" Jay asked as we sat in my driveway, the Jeep still idling.

I leaned against the door. "You want to come inside?"

"Well, you spend almost every day in my house, but I have no idea what your place is like." Jay nodded toward the front door, where my mom had hung a decoupage wreath she'd made out of a discarded Jell-O mold and some silk flowers.

"You've dropped me off before," I reminded him, thinking if he knew that the wreath was just the beginning of my mother's talents, he might actually want to stay in the car.

"Okay, I take it back. I know your driveway like the back of my hand. But unless your house has gravel floors and reflectors to keep me from running into trees, I have no idea what the inside of your home looks like."

I'd spent the whole summer intertwined with Jay's family, but this would be the first time Jay was exposed to mine, unless you count that day at the Pot Belly, and I didn't. I hadn't even told my parents about Jay and me, how things had developed between us. It was something I wanted to keep to myself, someone I didn't want to have to share.

Besides, after everything I'd told him about my parents it was a giant leap of faith to let him see what it was like in person. It was one thing to speculate with Jay about what was going on with my parents, but quite another to have him experience the situation firsthand and have him confirm everything I suspected.

But it was a chance I was going to have to take, because it didn't look as if he was going anywhere anytime soon. "Would you like to come in, Herb?"

Jay cut the engine. "Love to, Fred."

I gave Jay the grand tour, which took all of five minutes and consisted of taking him counterclockwise around the first floor. Our last stop was the dining room.

"What's all this?" he asked, peering in through the swinging door.

"My mom's craft room, which, in other people's homes, is better known as the dining room."

"That's kind of cool." He walked into the room and over to my mom's latest creation, a fishbowl she'd decoupaged with pictures of fish and then turned into a lamp with some kit she'd bought at the hardware store. I had no idea where she planned to put it because every table in the house already had more than one of her crafty creations on it.

"At least the fish in that bowl won't die, right? Hey, what's this?" Jay picked up the box I'd been working on.

"My contribution to the Dennis family's gallery of useless crap."

He turned the box over in his hands, scrutinizing my work

as if it were a fine piece of art. I waited for him to comment on the movie tickets or the corner of our Island Wheels receipt, but he just placed the box back on the table.

"I like that better," he told me. "Even if seeing the receipt for the mountain bikes just made my thighs hurt all over again."

"And those cone wrappers from Mad Martha's just made me have to loosen the button on my shorts," I replied, and Jay laughed. "Come on, I'll show you the upstairs."

But we didn't make it that far. Instead we bumped into my mom in the kitchen, her arms piled high with *discards*.

"Mom, you remember Jay," I told her, taking a tin umbrella stand from her arms before she dropped it on the kitchen floor. "You met him at the Pot Belly."

"Hi, Jay." My mom walked over to the counter and laid down the rest of her goodies, which included a glass picture frame, a huge terra-cotta flowerpot, and a statue of a cat. I didn't even want to know what she was going to do with that, maybe sit it next to the fishbowl lamp.

"Where's Dad?" I asked her.

"The yacht club, shooting a nautically inspired poodle."

I pictured a poodle in a white captain's hat sitting at the helm of a boat with his paws on the wheel.

"I'm going to take Jay upstairs," I told her.

She nodded slowly, shifting her eyes over to Jay. "That's fine, but can you help me get a few more things out of the car, Winnie? Jay, why don't you wait for Winnie in the living room. She'll be right there." My mom motioned me toward the garage and I followed her.

The back door to the car was still open, but when I bent down to see what other discards my mother had acquired, I noticed the seat was empty. "There's nothing else," I observed, and when I turned around, my mother was closing the kitchen door behind her, obviously not wanting Jay to hear what she was about to say.

"Isn't that Cassie's brother?"

"Yeah."

My mom paused, contemplating how to phrase what she wanted to say next. "Do you think that's smart?"

"I don't think it's not smart." I wasn't sure that was the most resoundingly positive thing I could have said, so I added, "It's not a big deal."

"Does Anne know?" My mom didn't look convinced.

"Yes, she knows."

My mom's expression relaxed. "And she's okay with it?"

"Absolutely." I sounded so convincing I almost believed it myself. "She's fine with it."

My mom gave me a flat smile as she reached for the door-knob and turned it clockwise, pushing the door open and stepping back into the kitchen. "Okay, as long as Anne doesn't mind."

If the downstairs tour took less than five minutes, the upstairs tour was over in half the time. Needless to say, we ended up in my room.

"Where's the hamster?" Jay asked, pointing to the empty Habitrail on the floor in the corner.

"There was never a hamster," I explained. "There was a mouse and he wanted nothing to do with that thing."

Jay sat down on the floor beside the collection of plastic

tubes and minitreadmills. "I don't see why." He peered inside the empty apparatus. "Looks like fun."

I sat down next to him. "Mostly he just sat there scratching at the plastic walls trying to get out. I finally set him free in our backyard."

I slid over and leaned against my bed, and Jay moved over next to me.

"Why'd you get kicked out of the dorms?" I asked him.

"Did Anne tell you that?" he wanted to know.

I hated that Jay automatically assumed Anne would tell me only bad things about him, even though she'd never actually elaborated on any of the details behind Jay's school troubles. "Does it matter?"

"I started a fire." I must have looked horrified, because he quickly grabbed my arm and backtracked. "Wait a minute, it's not like it sounds. I'd gone out to dinner with some guys from my dorm and brought home the leftovers, nothing great, just some potato skins, but you take it where you can get it, right? They were really good. So about two o'clock in the morning I can't sleep and I'm starving again, and I remember the potato skins. Only there's no microwave on my floor, so I decided to use the hot plate, which, as you can imagine, doesn't work. You can't reheat potato skins in a pot. So I took one bite of the skins and threw them out, but I left the hot plate on and the paper towels next to the hot plate must have fallen on top of the burner, and you get where this is going. Next thing you know, I'm the freshman arsonist."

I thought of Anne's warning, how she'd told me to be careful. Maybe this was what she was talking about. "But you're not, right?"

"No, Fred, I swear. Not an arsonist. Just a hungry insomniac."

Jay and I hung out for a few hours, listening to music and talking until it was time for him to leave. As I was saying good-bye to him in the driveway, my dad's car pulled in and he stepped out, coming over to us.

"Sorry I'm so late. Temperamental standard poodles are the worst." My dad held out his hand and Jay shook it. "I'm Peter, Winnie's dad."

"Dad, this is Jay." Jay frowned at me as if my introduction was insufficient, if not inaccurate. "My boyfriend," I added, and my explanation seemed to satisfy him.

"I've never been a fan of poodles," Jay told my dad, and he smiled. "But I've heard about your work."

"Well, I hope Winnie also told you about my upcoming show in town. You're more than welcome to come."

Jay looked to me and I nodded. "Yeah, you should come."

"I'll be there," he said, and my dad seemed pleased.

"Then I'll see you at the gallery in a few weeks. I should go inside." My dad sniffed his hands and made a sour face. "I think I smell like poodle."

After my dad left us, I walked Jay to the Jeep, where he wrapped his arms around my waist and held me. "They both seem nice."

"They are," I admitted. "But I think you talked to my parents more in the past two hours than they've talked to each other all day."

"Sometimes it's like that," he told me, but I didn't think that was an explanation so much as an excuse.

"Sometimes is fine." I turned to look at the house, trying to find my parents' figures inside the windows. It was the all the time that worried me.

Jay placed his hand under my chin and turned my face toward him, kissing me before stepping back and wrinkling his nose. "You know, I didn't want to say this in front of your dad, but I think he was right."

"He was?"

"Yeah, unless you're the one who smells like a poodle."

Chapter 16

"It's a big day today!" Marla announced when we gathered in the break room before heading to the lobby to get the campers. "The sand-castle-building contest on South Beach begins at nine o'clock, so we won't be having any morning activities. Let's gather up the campers, fill the wagons with supplies, and get moving."

Rachel and I hung back, letting the other counselors file out first.

"This is so dumb," Rachel told me. "We build sand castles every freaking day. And we can't even win!"

She was right. As always, the counselors were expected to help the kids build their castles, which would automatically disqualify our team from winning a ribbon. Instead the Oceanview had its own ribbons made up, lest our campers be deprived the thrill of victory. Each child would receive a first-place ribbon to take home to show his or her friends. So what if the campers didn't actually win anything or compete against other teams? Their friends didn't need to know that.

They may not have been competing to win a ribbon for real, but the way the kids were strategizing with one another in the lobby, you would have thought an international title was on the line. A few even brought their own water-spray bottles, because everyone knows the key to keeping a castle standing is well-hydrated sand.

Marla gave the parents her speech, which, luckily, she'd honed from that first day to just touch on the basics—*Your kids won't drown and we'll return them to you in one piece*—and we packed up the wagons with pails and spatulas and plastic funnels and any other contraption we could find to mold, scrape, or stack sand. Then we took the kids down the familiar sandy trail to the beach.

We were a fine-tuned machine that morning, focused on our own tasks, whether we were helping to build the foundation or collecting the decoration—seaweed, shells, and anything else that could adorn our growing fortress.

The kids and the counselors had a nice start going when I finally looked down the beach to see what the other contestants—the ones who really had a chance of winning—were making. While I was expecting the normal entrants, the sand turtles and mermaids that required dyeing the sand green with food coloring, I wasn't prepared for team number six, who'd staked out a plot of sand about ten yards from us. The guy was wearing a baggy surfer bathing suit and gray T-shirt with faded red letters that I immediately recognized, and the little girl had a terry-cloth cover-up over her pink-and-green-striped bikini. Jay was bent down telling Cassie something and pointing to a large green bucket that looked better suited to mopping a floor than the beach, but when he looked up, he noticed me staring at them and waved.

"Hey, can you watch my kids?" I asked Rachel, who was in charge of making the guard shack at the entrance to our castle.

"Do you have any idea how much sand I have in my underwear?" Rachel stabbed her shovel in the ground, just barely missing my toe. "Every night I go home and pour at least a pound of sand out of my clothes. My mother's started making me get undressed outside in the sunporch."

"Please?" I begged. "Just for a few minutes?"

Rachel didn't look terribly excited about watching three extra kids, but she agreed.

"What are you guys doing here?" I asked Jay when I went over to them.

Jay pointed to a sign stuck in the sand beside them, a rectangular piece of cardboard attached to a stick. The sign had a number 6 on it in thick black Magic Marker. "We're here to build a sand castle, of course. We're team six."

Cassie was kneeling next to her pile of pails, their sizes ranging from small to supersize, but when she heard Jay talking to someone, she turned around.

"Winnie!" she screamed. "Look, we're building a sand castle for the contest."

"I see that. It looks like you're doing a great job."

"Can you hand me one of the wooden spoons?" she asked Jay, who went over to the large canvas beach bag beside his beach chair.

"If you'll excuse us, we don't want any distractions. We're here to win." Jay winked at me, then pulled from the beach bag not one, not two, but four wooden spoons. I wondered if Anne knew they'd raided her kitchen.

I took the hint and went back to my own team, but for the next hour I kept an eye on Cassie and Jay. I guess they did really want to win, because Cassie was the only one working on the castle, while Jay observed her progress. I noticed him walk around the growing fortress, pointing out areas for rein-forcement and handing her one of the many tools they had stashed in the beach bag—a spatula, a shovel, even a spaghetti strainer Cassie used to form a dome in the center of the cas-tle. Watching them together, laughing, I found it hard to be-lieve that was the same guy who'd told Cassie she shouldn't leave her toys in the hallway. I don't know that I'd say they acted like brother and sister, because every brother and sister I knew couldn't spend three hours on the beach together without fighting, but they definitely acted as if they had a spe-cial bond. I noticed how Jay started to anticipate Cassie's re-quests, handing her a tool before she had to turn around and ask for it, how he hovered over her almost as if he were pro-tecting Cassie, making sure she was okay.

At one point I noticed the photographer from the *Vine-yard Gazette* walk up to Jay and say something. She must have asked to take Cassie's picture, because once Jay nodded, the photographer stood down by the water and aimed her lens up toward their castle, a proud Cassie posing for the camera. The photographer waved to Jay, calling him over to get in the pic-ture, but he shook his head no, preferring to stand off to the side and let Cassie have all the glory.

"Friends of yours?" Rachel asked me, standing over my shoulder and watching as Jay finally pulled the gray Wesleyan T-shirt over his head and laid it across the back of the chair. I thought I heard Rachel inhale, and even though I knew it was ridiculous, I smiled, because I knew she was checking him out. So was I.

"Yeah," I answered. "That's my boyfriend."

"*That's* the boyfriend?" Rachel pushed me away with both hands as if she were pissed I'd been holding out on her. "*That's* the summer guy?"

I nodded, enjoying Rachel's reaction.

"You didn't tell me he was gorgeous."

"He's gorgeous?" I repeated, as if I didn't notice Jay's bare chest, the way you could see the muscles in his stomach contract and ripple when he bent over to look at Cassie's handiwork.

Rachel rolled her eyes. "Please. The little girl is cute, too. But her brother isn't hard on the eyes."

"Yes, she is," I answered, although what I was thinking was, *No, he isn't.*

We had to pack the kids up at eleven thirty, and the judges wouldn't announce the winners until noon, so I had to leave the beach before I knew how Jay and Cassie did. I could see that Cassie had about twenty upside-down pails of sand forming a circle around the spaghetti-strainer circles in the center. Sticks and shells and seaweed and even a couple pieces of driftwood were stuck in the front of the castle, which I assumed were supposed to be pillars of some sort.

"Bye!" I yelled down the beach, and Jay and Cassie both looked my way. "Good luck!" I held my crossed fingers in the air for them to see and reluctantly followed my campers toward the path that led back to the Oceanview.

"Well?" I asked later, finding Cassie and Jay at the kitchen table eating peanut-butter-and-jelly sandwiches. "How'd you do?"

Cassie reached for the yellow ribbon beside her plate. "We won!" she exclaimed, holding up a ribbon with 3RD PLACE embossed in gold in the center.

"We did!" Jay seemed almost as excited as Cassie. "Well, we came in third, but that's as good as first, right, Cassie?"

She nodded. "Right."

"Nice job." I reached down and gave her a hug, getting some peanut butter and jelly in my hair in the process.

"Here." Jay handed me a napkin, and I wiped the sticky clump away. At least most of it.

"Can I go put it in my room?" Cassie held up the ribbon.

"Sure, it's all yours." Jay reached for her plate, to eat the crust she'd peeled away.

Cassie hopped down from her chair and skipped the entire way down the hall.

"Why'd you do that today?" I asked Jay, pulling out a chair and sitting next to him.

"What?" He acted as if he had no idea what I was talking about. "You mean the contest?"

"Yes, of course that's what I mean."

"Anne can't do much with her these days, and I figured Cassie was going a little stir-crazy when I heard her having a tea party with the croquet mallets."

I laughed but Jay kept a straight face.

"Seriously, she named them all. The blue one was named Posey. I had to tell her it was a boy. Just about broke her heart." I could see Jay was struggling not to laugh now, too.

I grabbed the crust before he could stuff it in his mouth. "Come on, really. You didn't have to do that."

"I know I didn't have to do it. But I broke the girl's tea set. It was the least I could do." Jay looked over toward the hallway as if still listening for the sound of Cassie skipping. "I owed her one."

I reached under the table and rubbed his knee, feeling the rough grains of sand still clinging to his skin. "You are the best brother, Jay."

Jay shook his head and smiled at me. "Not the best, but according to the judges, good enough for third place."

I obviously wasn't going to get Jay to be serious with me, but that was okay. Even if he wouldn't admit it, I knew why he did it. He took Cassie to the sand-castle contest because he was her big brother, and that was something a big brother would do if he really cared about his little sister.

"It was really nice of you," I acknowledged one last time. "You're a good guy, Herb."

Jay reached for another strip of crust, and I swear it was so I wouldn't see him smile.

"Don't go around spreading that nasty rumor, Fred," he warned me, narrowing his eyes as if I should fear his wrath. But no way would those eyelashes let Jay look the least bit menacing. "Posey still thinks I'm a badass."

Chapter 17

The morning of the Chilmark Road Race, Jay picked me up and we drove to Jessie's house. I knew we'd hit traffic on the way to the race, but luckily the weather was gorgeous, and as we drove to Chilmark with the top down and the sun shining, I couldn't imagine a more perfect day for the race. Even though it was early, the temperature had already hit eighty, and I didn't envy Jessie, who had more than three miles of hilly terrain ahead of her.

When we finally reached Chilmark, Jay and I parked the car at Jessie's house and walked to Bettlebung Corner. And we weren't the only ones. The whole town was packed, with buses transporting racers from the ferry to Chilmark, and spectators and family members milling around waiting for someone they knew to come into view before cheering them on across the finish line, encouraging them those last few strides. We'd missed the starting gun when the pack of racers took off up Middle Road, but I'd already warned Jessie we might be late, and she was fine with that. She didn't expect everyone to be a morning person, as long as Nash was.

I hadn't seen Jessie in almost three weeks and felt we hadn't shared much time this summer, and unless you counted that night we all hung out at the beach, we hadn't shared our boyfriends, either. We had just a few more weeks to go before Jay and Nash left, and even though we knew Labor Day was inevitable, we both kept them to ourselves, as if we could keep the reality of the outside world at bay by limiting our exposure to it.

As far as the eye could see, discarded paper cups littered Middle Road where runners had dropped them, staying hydrated before making a final push to the finish line. The runners coming toward us wore a sheen of sweat, their skin glistening under the sun, but as soon as they heard the crowd, their feet ran a little faster, their arms pumped harder, and when they raised their arms over their heads and their names came over the loudspeaker, I don't think any of them regretted a single day of training. Although Jessie had told me we could wait for her in the postrace area at the Community Center, I wanted to be there as she crossed the finish line at Beetlebung Corner, next to Town Hall.

With all of the brutal hills along Middle Road, I knew Jess had be dying out there no matter how much she'd trained. When I spotted her black ponytail bobbing toward us, I put my hand on Jay's shoulder and pointed her out to him, then instructed him to cheer as if his life depended on it. Jay and I yelled for Jessie at the top of our lungs, chanting her name and clapping so hard my hands stung. But for all her training, when Jessie finally came running down the center of the road toward the finish line, she looked as if she were going to vomit right there on the pavement all over her sneakers.

The announcer called Jessie's name, and when we heard it ring out over the speaker, officially ending her race, Jay and I left our spot along the side of the road and went to find Jess among the crowd of racers walking around trying to catch their breath. We found her bent over gasping for air.

"Oh my God," Jessie stammered, reaching for the water bottle I held out for her.

"You did great," I assured her.

She narrowed her eyes at me. "I sucked. What the hell? It's less than four miles." Jessie attempted to guzzle the water between gasps but ended up choking. "I ran twice that on Thursday and I barely broke a sweat."

"It's hot," I tried again, but she was having none of it.

"Where's Nash?"

I pointed over toward the tent.

"When did he finish?" She looked up at the official race clock, watching the bright yellow numbers tick up one second at a time.

"A few minutes ago," I told her.

"How few?" she demanded.

"Five minutes twenty-two seconds."

Now Jessie seriously turned green.

I started to reach for her back but then stopped, realizing that maybe rubbing Jessie's sweaty back wasn't the best way to calm her. "Come on, it's not that bad."

But it must have been, because the next thing I knew, Jessie grabbed her stomach and doubled over, spewing half-digested energy bar and Gatorade into the grass.

"It's just five minutes, Jessie," I repeated, and another wave of nausea swept across Jessie's face. Only this time I was smart enough to turn away, so I got the audio, but not the visual.

"I must be coming down with something." She gagged. "This is so not like me."

I turned around and laid a hand on her back, rubbing in wet, sweaty circles. "Do you need something to eat?"

She wiped her mouth on her sleeve and tugged at my shorts.

"What?" I crouched down to see what she needed.

"Does he have to stand there and watch me throw my guts up?" She rolled her eyes in Jay's direction.

I stood up and faced Jay. "Hey, why don't you go see if you can find Nash. We'll be right there."

"It's just a race," I told Jessie as Jay walked over to the tent.

"I've felt crappy lately. I probably shouldn't even have run in the first place. I think I'm coming down with something. Yesterday I almost threw up a bag of Doritos."

Eww. Just thinking about it almost made me want to throw up.

If she were anyone else, I would have asked why she even ran the race in the first place if she wasn't feeling well, but I knew the answer. She wanted to win. "Why don't you sit down?"

Jessie spit one last time and then stood up, holding my arm to keep her balance. "Let's just go get the guys, okay?"

The tent area was packed, and standing on a makeshift stage, an announcer was holding a microphone, preparing to announce the winners in each age category.

Jessie didn't even stop to listen. She knew they weren't going to be calling her name. Instead we made our way through the crowd until we found Nash and Jay over by the water table.

Nash had already stopped sweating, if he even sweated in the first place, and I wasn't convinced he did.

"Do you want to go get a bite to eat with us?" he asked, and Jessie gave him a look as if he had to be kidding.

Jay reached for my hand and pulled me next to him. "Actually, I was going to take Winnie to Aquinnah."

"You were?" I asked, surprised.

"Yeah."

"Just as well, I don't think I could hold anything down anyway." Jessie rested her head against Nash, and I realized Jay hadn't even told him Jessie had been throwing up. Nash looked completely oblivious. For a minute I couldn't believe Jay didn't tell him so Nash could at least show some sympathy. But then I looked at Jessie again and realized that Jay probably knew what he was doing, because Jessie wasn't someone who liked people feeling sorry for her. Jay realized that.

And that's when I realized just how amazing my boyfriend really was.

Although it's just on the other side of the island, with its scrubby green brush and rocky, jagged coast that always reminded me of a broken beer bottle, Aquinnah feels almost like a different world. As we left Chilmark and wove our way toward the southwestern tip of the island, the houses fell away, replaced by water on either side as we crossed between Menemsha and Squibnocket ponds, then up toward the sheared, orange clay cliffs that hardly needed the No Trespassing signs, but carried the warning anyway.

"I can't believe it's still like this," Jay observed as we drove up toward the top of the cliffs, the lighthouse perched perilously at the edge as if just waiting for one final push to tumble into the water where the Atlantic Ocean met Vineyard Sound. "I thought it might have changed, but it's exactly like I remember."

"When's the last time you were here?"

"My mom used to bring me to see the lighthouse when I was younger. Did you know it's the only brick lighthouse on the island?" He sounded a little like a tour guide.

"Yeah." I smiled. "I think I've heard that somewhere before."

When we got to the top of Aquinnah, Jay parked the car and we walked through the grass to the lighthouse.

"It seemed a lot bigger when I used to come here," Jay told me.

"Probably because you were so much smaller."

Jay shrugged. "Maybe."

I started walking down the worn path toward the lighthouse, but Jay lagged behind me, and when I turned around to see where he was, he stood gazing at the lighthouse as if the intermittent light making its way around the top might offer him answers.

"Are you coming?" I called.

"Yeah," he answered, taking his eyes from the light swinging around toward him one more time. "I'm coming."

On the way back to the Barclays', Jay and I decided to play a game of croquet when we got home, our way of making up for being the type of people who would watch a road race on a Saturday morning instead of being the type who would actually run in such a race. Not that you could compare swinging a mallet to running five kilometers, but we'd convinced ourselves it was the next best thing. Jay was assigned to wicket duty while I was going to make up a fresh, cold pitcher of lemonade. Athletes need to stay hydrated.

When Jay and I walked into the house, we could hear Mr. Barclay banging away at the keys on his laptop in the library. Jay walked right by the door, not even turning his head to look at his father, and I finally understood why, even if I wished there was a way to change the situation.

I let Jay get ahead of me, and when he turned the corner toward the kitchen, I poked my head inside the library.

"Mr. Barclay?"

He looked up from the screen, but kept his fingers on the keys. "Hi, Winnie. What's up?"

I stepped into the room, my flip-flops descending a good inch into the thick carpet until I could feel the wool pile tickling the tops of my toes. "Jay and I just got home from the road race, and I was wondering if maybe you and Anne and Cassie wanted to join us for a game of croquet."

Mr. Barclay sat back in the brown leather chair and rested his hands on his lap. "That would be great. When were you thinking?"

"How about five minutes?"

Mr. Barclay placed his hands back on the keyboard. "That sounds great, just let me finish this and I'll be right there."

I decided it was probably best not to tell Jay what I'd just done, but to have him set up the court and let Anne, Cassie,

and Mr. Barclay come out to join us. When I found Jay outside in the backyard, he was already setting up the wickets
with Cassie.

"Where's your mom?" I asked Cassie, helping her push a
stubborn wicket deeper into the lawn.

"She's upstairs resting."

I bent down and cupped my hands around her ear. "Why
don't you go see if she'd like to join us?"

Cassie nodded and ran inside the house, the screen door
slamming behind her.

Jay had created a playing area that was bigger than it
should have been, which is why he was halfway between the
harbor and the patio and still pushing wickets into the stubborn ground.

"Hey, are you sure that's regulation size?" I yelled out, and
Jay waved away my question.

"Don't pull any of this girly stuff with me, Fred," Jay teased
as he came up the stone path toward me. "You're probably a
ringer ready to take me for everything I have."

Before I could respond, the kitchen door opened and Mr.
Barclay stepped out onto the patio.

Jay looked from Mr. Barclay to me and back to Mr. Barclay again, trying to figure out why his father was selecting a
mallet from the set resting against the table.

"I just passed Cassie. She went to see if Anne was up for
playing." Mr. Barclay took a practice swing and came over to
me and Jay. "I hope neither of you wanted the blue one. It's
my lucky color."

I wondered if Jay was thinking the same thing I was. He'd
picked Posey.

"I'm a yellow girl myself," I answered as Jay said nothing.

"Hey, Jay, have you decided which classes you're going to take this fall?" Mr. Barclay asked.

I noticed Jay's body stiffen, as if preparing himself for a blow. "There's still time."

"I know there's no rush, but you should at least be thinking about what you'd like to take." Mr. Barclay found the blue ball to go with his mallet and started hitting it around. "You have a lot to prove this semester, you know."

Jay's face was tight and still, but his lips still managed to frown. "I am fully aware of that."

Mr. Barclay lined up the mallet and smacked the blue ball all the way down to the farthest wicket. "There's a lot riding on this semester, Jay."

This time Jay was silent, but he clenched his hands and held them at his side, pressing against his thighs.

Mr. Barclay watched the ball slowly come to a stop, then turned to Jay. "If this semester doesn't work out, I don't know what will happen."

I saw it coming before Jay even opened his mouth. I saw it in his eyes, how the gold flecks seemed to light up, how his body moved toward Mr. Barclay almost as if uncoiling from the building tension. I knew what Jay was going to do because I'd seen him look like this once before, that day in Cassie's room.

"What do you want from me?" Jay snapped, his voice flaring. "I'm going back. I know what's at stake."

"I'm just saying—"

"I know!" Jay shouted, and I stepped back, moving away from the center of the storm.

Jay didn't even appear to notice I'd moved aside. "I know it's all thanks to you, okay, Dad? If you hadn't talked to the dean, they wouldn't even have let me back this semester." Jay's voice was loud but his words trembled, as if he was struggling to keep composed but was losing the battle. "You're the reason they're letting me back in the dorms. Is that what you want me to say?"

Mr. Barclay didn't even attempt to answer, he didn't have a chance. Jay pushed past him and tore the kitchen door open, slamming it behind him.

It was a Jay I'd only seen once before, but I knew this was the person Anne was talking about when she told me to be careful.

"I'm sorry about that, Winnie." Mr. Barclay rubbed the bridge of his nose between his fingertips, closing his eyes for a minute before looking up at me.

"I better go see how he is." I hesitated, almost hoping Mr. Barclay would stop me, tell me that he'd go inside and talk to Jay. Instead, he nodded and stepped aside so I could go find my boyfriend.

"What just happened out there?" I asked when I found Jay upstairs in his room, pacing back and forth in front of his bedroom window, his eyes alternating between staring out at the harbor and staring at the rug beneath his feet.

"He can be such an asshole." The edge in his voice was even sharper than before.

"What are you talking about?"

"That remark about school. I'm so tired of it, so tired of him always having to be right. Like if it isn't done his way, it's wrong. Well, I did it his way and what did it get me?"

I wanted to tell Jay that this time *he* was wrong, that this time he couldn't blame his dad because his dad didn't do anything wrong. But I also wanted him to know that I was on his side. I knew he needed me to be.

"I think you're overreacting." I walked over to Jay, wanting to touch him, calm him down, but he stepped back.

"Look, Winnie, it's been like this between us long before you came along. So leave it alone, okay? This is one problem you can't fix."

I recoiled, pulling back even before my hand reached his shoulder. "What's that supposed to mean?"

"I know you think it's your job to fix everything for everyone and make it all better, but real life isn't perfect like it is on the island."

"Are you kidding me?" I practically sputtered. "How can you say that?"

"You want this flawless view of everybody, a picture-perfect life where everyone gets along and nobody ever does anything to hurt anyone else."

"How can you even say that?" I shook my head, disbelieving. "Tell me, Jay, what is so perfect about having parents who don't even live together? Or a friend who hasn't called me in weeks? Or a sister who hasn't been home in almost a year?"

Jay waved me away. "You don't understand, Winnie."

"Then I guess you're going to have to explain it to me, Jay, because after what I just saw back there, it looked like you were being the asshole, not your father."

Jay stopped pacing and watched me, his mouth open but no words coming out.

I knew it wasn't his father Jay was mad at. Jay was angry with himself because he knew he'd had a choice to make when his mother was dying and he'd made the wrong one.

"On second thought, forget it." I started to leave, but spun around when I reached the door. "You know, Jay, staying angry with your father is a pretty lame way to keep your memory of your mother alive. And if that's all you have, then maybe you should be looking in the mirror instead of at your dad."

I walked out and ran down the stairs and this time I didn't look back.

Chapter 18

Monday morning on the bus on my way to work, I received a text message from Jessie telling me to meet her between clinics at the Community Center. Mr. Barclay was in all week from the city on his big summer vacation, so Anne didn't need me to watch Cassie. Which was just as well. After Saturday I didn't want to see Jay, and since he didn't call me yesterday, I figured he didn't really want to see me either. I finally understood why Anne had warned me about Jay. She knew that eventually he'd end up breaking my heart.

Summer was winding down and I figured Jessie was probably beginning to feel like me, that it was time to get back to real life, where it was just the two of us again. I texted Jess back, telling her I'd take the bus straight to Chilmark after camp. At least that was my plan until I walked out the side door at noon and found someone waiting for me.

"Can I talk to you?" Jay asked. He looked terrible, as if he'd been up all night. Or maybe as if he'd just woken up. Even now I couldn't tell the difference.

I didn't stop. Instead I kept walking across the resort's grounds toward the bus stop. "What do you want, Jay?"

"Can we just go somewhere and talk?" He moved in front of me, blocking my path.

"I have to go see Jessie." Every time I stepped to walk around him, Jay moved over, not letting me pass.

"I just need a few minutes, okay?"

I turned around and started walking in the opposite direction, toward the courtyard, where the oversize chess set was flanked by oversize chairs that made an average-size adult look as if she were sitting in a high chair. Jay followed me.

Three little kids I didn't recognize were trying to lift the rook and move him to an empty space on the chessboard. They managed to tip it slightly when they all crowded on one side, but finally gave up and ran in the direction of the pool, leaving Jay and me alone.

"Want to sit down?" He gestured to one of the chairs and attempted to get me to smile.

I didn't. "Why are you here?"

Jay stood beside the chair, which made him appear small and out of place. "I want to say I'm sorry. To apologize. I'm sorry about what I said. I know it hasn't been an easy summer for you. I don't know what I was thinking, I was totally out of line."

Jay stepped toward me but I backed away, just out of his reach. "Yeah, you were."

Jay licked his lips and rubbed his hand along the stubble on his jawbone. "I guess there are some issues between me and my dad that I need to figure out."

I moved toward Jay, challenging him, knowing he had nowhere to go, cornered between me and the chair, his back against the thick wooden leg. All of a sudden I wasn't afraid of hurting his feelings. I wanted to treat him as carelessly as he'd treated me.

"Can I ask you a question, Jay?" I didn't even wait for him to answer. "Why didn't you go to see your mom? I mean, I know your dad told you to stay at school, but you didn't have to listen to him. So why?" My final word echoed in the courtyard.

Jay was silent.

"All you had to do was get in your Jeep and drive," I pressed. "So why didn't you?"

Jay looked at the ground, at the chess pieces, the chairs. He looked everywhere but at me. That's when I realized that Jay didn't just look small, he looked fragile, as if he were about to break from the sheer force of my words, as if he needed protection.

"You were right, Winnie." Jay inhaled sharply, as if he needed to catch his breath before continuing. "I wasn't there with my mom and it's not my dad's fault. It's mine."

Jay looked at me then, and I could see the pain in his eyes each time he blinked, each time his eyelashes swept downward, giving him a moment of relief before he had to face me again.

My resolve dissipated, and as much as I wanted to hate Jay, to see him as the aloof, indifferent guy he was those first few days, I couldn't. I knew that wasn't really who he was. "That's not what I said."

Jay slid down to the ground, resting his back against the wooden leg of the chair, his left arm folded across the tops of his knees. "You didn't have to, Winnie. Maybe I knew that all along. I mean, I could have just gotten in the Jeep and headed to the hospital. I was an hour and a half away and I didn't even get in the car."

I knelt on the lawn next to Jay, but I didn't reach out to touch him even though he laid his right hand on the grass next to me. "Why not?"

"If you had seen her—she wasn't even my mom anymore. She looked so tired and thin. When she laid her head on the pillow, she barely made a dent. The skin on her cheeks hung back against her ears. It was horrible." Jay's face twisted as he remembered standing by his mother's bedside, as if he were there all over again. "I couldn't stand to see it, and I should've been there and I know I should've been there and I wasn't, and it's nobody's fault but mine."

I felt myself softening, but, still, I kept my hands on my knees.

"You can't keep beating yourself up over this, Jay. Or your father."

Jay grazed my bare knee with his as he stretched his legs out in front of him. "You know, my dad went to the funeral, well, he went to the church. I remember turning around and seeing him standing all the way in the back, next to the entrance. And I remember thinking that it was his fault I wasn't there, but it wasn't. It was mine."

This time when Jay moved his hand toward me, I took it, and he held my hand tight and firm, as if he would never let go. I moved over to him and he laid his head on my shoulder. "It's nobody's fault, Jay."

"I'm sorry, Winnie, I really am," Jay apologized again, and this time I was ready to believe him. "I never meant to hurt you."

"I know you didn't," I assured him as we sat there, being watched by a couple of three-foot-tall knights, the word *checkmate* going through my head. "I know."

As much as I wanted to spend the afternoon with Jay, I'd promised Jessie I'd meet her after work. So Jay drove me to Chilmark and dropped me off at the Community Center, where I found Jessie sitting cross-legged on the grass under a tree beside the tennis courts. She wasn't eating, but I could see an unwrapped peanut-butter-and-jelly sandwich sitting on the ground in front of her, splayed out on top of a crumpled brown paper bag.

"What's up?" I asked her, settling on the ground across from the uneaten sandwich. She hadn't even begun pulling it apart yet, which meant it was still up for grabs. I reached for it so I could have a bite.

"I'm pregnant." The words seemed too thick for Jessie to get out, as if they were stuck somewhere deep in her throat where her vocal cords couldn't even allow her to form the words.

"You're pregnant?" I discovered I had a hard time saying the words myself. There was no way. Of all the people in the world this could happen to, I would never have guessed it would happen to Jessie. She knew how to take care of herself. She wasn't some naive girl whom Nash had seduced into having sex. "How is that possible?"

Jessie squeezed her eyes shut as if trying to visualize exactly how it was possible, the precise moment this happened. "I don't know, we used condoms, I thought we were being careful, I have no idea." She opened her eyes and stared at me. "What am I going to do?"

I knew she didn't really expect me to answer, to lay out her options and take her through them one by one pointing out the pros and cons of each. We both knew there was only one choice.

"Does Nash know?" I asked, putting the uneaten sandwich back on top of the crumpled brown paper bag. Like Jess, I'd lost my appetite.

She nodded. "I told him last night."

"When did you find out?"

"Yesterday. I took one of those home tests. Actually two, but it didn't matter, they both said the same thing."

I thought about all those pregnancy-test commercials where the woman ecstatically discovers the plus sign on the easy-to-read window, and I couldn't imagine Jessie giving a crap about whether the stick had a comfortable thumb grip or splash-guard-protected results or any of the other new and improved features the commercials touted. I just pictured Jessie standing alone in her bathroom, crossing her fingers as she waited for her future to appear in a urine-soaked window.

"I must have spent twenty minutes in the aisle at Stop and Shop choosing which test to use. You can get digital home tests now, did you know that? I went the regular route, though, because the idea of peeing on something digital made me afraid I'd electrocute myself." She tried to smile but it didn't work.

"You went alone?"

Jess nodded, making me feel even worse for not being

there, as if I should have known. And if I'd called her last night as I'd wanted to, I would have known. Only I didn't call Jessie. I didn't want to tell her about Jay, to repeat what he'd said to me only to have her tell me I should have known better. Only now I realized Jessie was in her bedroom thinking the same thing, afraid to call me for the same reason.

"Why didn't you tell me? I would have gone with you to buy the test. I would have waited with you for the results."

"I don't know. I guess we haven't seen each other much this summer and I didn't want to seem like some stupid girl who got herself pregnant."

"You're not stupid," I told her.

"Yeah, but I am pregnant, and right now they feel like the same thing." Jessie glanced at the sandwich, then looked away. "Can you please cover that up? Just looking at food makes my stomach churn."

I picked up the sandwich and stuffed it inside the bag. "So what did Nash say?"

"Oh, you can just imagine—*how did this happen? What was I going to do?*"

"What are *you* going to do?" I repeated, not believing what I'd heard. "The last time I heard, it takes two to get pregnant."

"That may be true, Winnie, but I'm the one who has to . . ." She didn't finish her sentence, but she didn't have to.

"Will you come with us?" she asked. "The appointment is next week, in Boston."

I laid my hand on her knee and squeezed, noticing how much tanner her leg looked next to my hand. "Of course I'll go with you."

"Don't tell Jay, okay? Please?" She placed her hand

over mine and held it there. "Can we just keep this between us?"

It was already August and the summer was winding down.
Soon it would be just the two of us again, our summer boyfriends no longer around, just me and Jessie. I knew this was her
way of preparing us for the beginning of the end. "Okay."

I asked Marla if I could have Wednesday morning off and
told Anne I needed to help Jessie with something Wednesday
afternoon. Neither of them asked me for more details or an
explanation for my unexpected request, although I almost
wanted them to. Not so I could tell them about Jessie, but so
that when I returned to work on Thursday, they wouldn't ask
me how my day off was and expect me to say it was fine.

"Anne said you can't watch Cassie tomorrow. What's up?"
Jay asked me when he found out I wouldn't be babysitting. I'd
promised Jessie I wouldn't tell him, so I lied, completely aware
of the irony that to prove that my best friend could trust me,
I had to prove my boyfriend couldn't.

"Jessie asked me to hang out with her, maybe play a little
tennis," I explained, focusing on a sailboat slowly working
its way toward the yacht club, so I wouldn't have to look Jay
in the eye. "We haven't seen each other much this summer."

"I thought you didn't play tennis," he reminded me, and I
remembered our conversation down by the harbor, a talk that
seemed so long ago, before everything had changed.

"Maybe it's time I started again."

Jay cocked his head and scrutinized me as if trying to figure out whether I was telling him the whole story. "What are
you guys really planning to do?"

I hated lying to him. "We haven't decided yet, maybe go to Chappy and hang out on the beach, maybe play tennis. I swear, it's no big deal."

Jay had no choice but to believe me, and because I owed it to Jessie, I believed I had no choice but to kiss my boyfriend and pretend it really was no big deal.

Chapter 19

"**W**here is he?" Jessie asked for what had to be the tenth time. She glanced at my watch again, as if the minute that had passed since the last time she'd looked would dramatically change the result.

"We better get on the boat," I told her. "We don't want to miss it."

I had no idea what we'd do if Nash really didn't show up. He was supposed to drive us to the city. Even if Jessie and I got on the ferry, how we'd get to Boston once we reached Woods Hole was a whole other problem.

"What if something happened, like he got in an accident?" Jessie's voice was almost hopeful, as if an accident at least gave Nash a reason for not showing up, a reason for her to still believe in him even though it was beginning to look as if he was bailing on her. "Maybe I should try calling him again, just one more time."

"Look, you've already tried three times. His battery probably ran out."

Jessie bit her lip and looked toward the intersection, expecting to see Nash's car turn the corner.

It didn't.

"Come on." I laid my hand on her elbow and led her toward the ramp to the ferry. "He can always catch the next one." But even as I said it, I wasn't holding out hope for Nash to catch anything other than a bunch of shit once I found him.

"Yeah, it's just an hour, right?" Jessie moved her eyes away from the intersection and toward me. "It shouldn't be a problem to get his car on the ferry midweek, so he could make it on time."

"Of course." I gave her a smile I hoped was more convincing than I felt. "It's just an hour."

Jessie's eyes were blinking too fast. "What are we going to do?" she asked, her voice cracking midsentence.

Shelby was in Boston, but there was no way she could drive down to Woods Hole and pick us up in time for Jessie's appointment. We could probably catch a bus at Woods Hole and take that into the city, but the trip would take almost two hours, and we'd still have to find our way from South Station to the clinic. Our options were slim, and I could only think of one way to get us to Boston in time.

"I'll be right back," I told her, then squeezed her shoulder. "It's going to be okay, I promise."

Jessie nodded and turned back hopefully toward the intersection.

I walked over to the Steamship Authority building and stood there watching Jessie chew on her fingernails as I dialed Jay's cell phone.

Was it conceivable that Nash would drive up in the next fifteen minutes? Sure it was. But he'd told Jessie he'd meet us at the ferry over twenty minutes ago. The traffic on the island wasn't that bad, even if it was August. So was it conceivable? Yes. Was I willing to take the chance that we'd miss the ferry? No way.

"We're all set," I told Jessie, startling her as I laid my hand on her shoulder. "Jay's coming and he's going to take us. I just bought the ticket for the car, and he should be here in time to make the boat. If he hurries." I hoped he didn't hit any traffic.

"I can't believe this." Jessie hung her head in her hands and rubbed her eyes so hard I wasn't sure if she was trying to keep the tears from coming or helping them along. "I can't freaking believe this is happening."

"Look, if you need some help, I can get money out of the ATM when we get to Boston."

"I told him we could split it, fifty-fifty."

"That seems fair." Or at least it did when Jess actually thought Nash would show up. "But if you need me to help out, I can."

Twelve minutes later Jay pulled into the ferry lot where Jessie and I were waiting with his ticket in hand.

"Wait here," I told Jessie, even though she didn't make a move to get up from the bench. "I'll give Jay the ticket at the check-in booth and we can meet him in line."

The cars at the head of the line were already turning on their engines as the ferry staff began walking down the lanes asking for tickets. I started walking faster.

"Thanks," I told Jay, leaning in through the open driver's-side window and handing him the ticket.

"Is she okay?" he asked, nodding toward the bench where Jessie was still seated. She didn't look over at us.

"As okay as she can be. They're already loading the cars, so we'll meet you in line."

Jay nodded, took the ticket from me and pulled up to the ticket booth.

"So he knows?" Jessie asked as we walked to the end of the line of idling cars.

"I had to tell him."

"I know." She looked down at her feet. "Ironic, no? I'm the one whose boyfriend gets her pregnant, and your boyfriend is the one who shows up."

"Don't talk like that, Jessie. Once we get back, we can figure out what happened with Nash. Right now, let's just get on the ferry and make it to the appointment on time."

The ride to Boston was quiet. I offered to let Jessie sit in the front seat, but she declined, instead sitting in the back, resting her head against the padded roll bar and looking out at nothing in particular. After a few tries Jay and I stopped attempting to include her in our conversation. Jessie didn't feel like talking, and I couldn't blame her.

An hour and a half later Jay pulled off I-93 and wove his way through the city toward Commonwealth Avenue. The clock on the dashboard clicked away the minutes until Jessie was no longer pregnant.

"I need to stop at a cash machine, so can you pull over when we see one?" I asked, scanning the storefronts ahead for an ATM sign.

Jay nodded and glanced up at the rearview mirror, watching Jessie as she stared out the plastic window. "I can give her the money," he told me, his voice low so Jessie couldn't hear.

"They were going to split it fifty-fifty. She already has half."

"So I'll take care of the other half."

"No," I told him. "Thanks, but no."

"Why don't you guys go ahead and I'll park the car," Jay offered, pulling up to the front of the building, which looked like any other building on the block.

I twisted around in my seat and faced Jessie. "Sound good?"

She shrugged, slid across the backseat to the curbside, and waited for me to open the door. "Let's go."

The waiting room wasn't big, about the size of our living room at home. However, there was no mistaking this room with anybody's home, even if the artificial floral arrangements and framed posters attempted to make it look less like a doctor's office and more like the foyer of a midpriced hotel. The waiting room didn't have any windows, and I wondered if there was a reason for that. Instead the posters on the wall were prints that replicated windows, complete with curtains falling in front of the artificial views of mountains and gardens and waterfalls, things far away from the reality of where we were.

Wooden chairs lined the perimeter of the room, their upholstered seats just thick enough to verge on comfortable, but industrial enough that you wouldn't want to spend too much time on them. I headed toward three empty chairs at the far corner.

We weren't the only people, which made me feel better, although how I felt wasn't exactly paramount at the moment. Everyone in the waiting room kept her eyes downcast as if completely engrossed in a *Good Housekeeping* article on getting bubblegum stains out of a tablecloth or in a pamphlet on gonorrhea.

Jessie went up to the receptionist's window and a minute later came back and sat down next to me. "Paperwork." She held up the clipboard in her hand.

When the door to the clinic opened, the entire waiting room looked up, and eight pairs of eyes landed on Jay, the sole male in the room. He came over to us, but instead of sitting down next to me, he sat on Jessie's other side, so she was between us.

When the nurse finally came out and called Jessie's name, she didn't move.

"Remember back in the beginning of the summer when I said we should go to Boston in August?"

I nodded.

"This isn't what I meant." Jessie tried to smile at her joke, but only the left side of her lips raised at all, so the effort was lopsided. "I guess I'll see you in a little bit," she finally said, standing up and walking toward the waiting nurse.

"Good luck," I called after her, knowing that if she'd been lucky, Jessie wouldn't be here right now.

Jay moved over into the seat Jessie had left vacant. "She'll be okay," he told me.

"I know." I wasn't sure though.

"Why didn't you tell me this is where you two were going?"

"She asked me not to."

Jay didn't remind me that he was my boyfriend or that I should have trusted him regardless of what Jessie wanted. Instead he reached for my hand, weaving his fingers between mine and setting our joined hands on the armrest between us. "Okay."

"Do you know anyone who's ever had one?" I asked.

"I don't."

"Me, neither. At least I don't think I do. Until now."

Jay squeezed my hand. "I do know someone who got pregnant her senior year of college and had the baby."

"Who?"

Jay scratched at his jean leg, picking at a frayed spot with his finger. "My mom."

"You never told me that."

"It hardly matters nineteen years later, right?"

"I guess not. Did she tell you?"

"I could do the math, it didn't take a genius. They got married as soon as she graduated, and seven months later I arrived."

"Maybe you were early," I pointed out, thinking it was a pretty logical explanation.

"Have you ever known me to be early for anything?" he asked, and I couldn't help but crack the smallest of smiles.

"Thanks for sitting next to Jessie," I told him.

"No problem. I didn't want her to think that all guys are assholes."

Five to seven minutes was all it was supposed to take, but the person Jessie spoke to on the phone told her to expect to be at the clinic for about two hours. After the first ten minutes I knew Jessie wasn't pregnant any longer, but it didn't make sitting there any easier knowing she was in a back room by herself while her boyfriend was probably sailing around the island, not a care in the world.

The clinic was on Shelby's street, probably less than a mile away from her small studio apartment within walking distance of Fenway Park. My dad's photography studio couldn't have been more than two miles away. I wondered what they'd think if they knew I was in the city, a short cab ride away, although it would be cheaper and probably just as fast to hop on the Green Line. I wondered if Jay had told Anne he was taking us to the city, or if Jessie's parents had any idea she'd called in sick for her tennis clinics. For two hours I had nothing but time to wonder.

Discomfort, that was what the woman on the phone had told Jessie to expect during the procedure. She recommended Jessie take ibuprofen after it was over, which is why Jessie had a brand-new bottle of Advil in her purse. I had an extra bottle in my backpack, just in case.

When Jessie finally emerged from the door beside the receptionist's window, she looked tired and pale. If I didn't know what she'd just been through, I would probably have assumed she just wasn't feeling well, had maybe gone to the clinic to have one of the doctor's test her for strep throat and prescribe some antibiotics.

Jay and I stood up and the three of us walked to the door, which Jay held open for us as we left.

Jessie stopped in the doorway and turned to Jay. "Hey, thanks."

Jay nodded. "You're welcome."

On the ride home I wanted to ask so many questions,

what it was like, if it hurt, how she felt. But when I turned around to say something, Jessie was asleep, her head resting against the back of the seat, her hair suspended in midair from the static.

An hour later as we were crossing the Bourne Bridge, Jessie's cell phone rang. I turned and watched as she glanced at the number on the display.

She looked up at me. "It's him."

I was about to ask what she was going to do when Jessie flipped open the phone and said hello.

Jay reached over and turned up the radio. Then he adjusted the speakers so that all of the sound was concentrated up front where we were, giving Jessie the privacy she needed for her conversation with Nash.

"He said he wants to talk," she told us after she'd snapped the phone shut. "Now he wants to talk. Where the hell was he this morning?" Her words were angry, but her voice didn't have the strength needed to make her sound anything but weary.

Jay and I knew she didn't really expect an answer to her question.

"He said he'll be waiting at the ferry when we get in," Jessie continued, but she didn't tell us that she'd told him not to bother or that she didn't want him to be there.

I looked over at Jay and he pressed his lips together in a flat smile, and I knew that he was thinking the same thing I was, that he didn't want Jessie to get her hopes up. Nash hadn't shown up this morning, and chances were he wouldn't be there when the ferry docked, either. With everything she'd gone through today, the last thing Jessie needed was to look out the backseat window and find that Nash had once again let her down.

But when the Jeep drove down the ferry ramp in Vineyard Haven, Nash was there, leaning against his car. Jay pulled up next to the curb and Jessie climbed out of the backseat, giving my hand a squeeze before walking over to Nash, who held her as she broke down in tears.

On the drive to my house Jay didn't say anything and neither did I. I wanted to hate Nash for what he'd done to Jessie, how he'd made her go through today alone, how he didn't have the balls to show up this morning and go through it with her. Maybe Jay was thinking the same thing, or maybe he was wondering what he would have done if that was me.

When we pulled into my driveway, Jay put the Jeep in park and turned to me, his face serious and eyes focused. "I'd never do that to you, I hope you know that."

"I do." I believed him.

Jay leaned over and took my face in his hands, holding them there so I couldn't look away. "I've done some shitty things, but I would never, ever do that to you."

Chapter **20**

"**I** feel so guilty," Jessie sobbed, her hands covering her face. She'd called me after Nash dropped her off at home, and I immediately went over to see her.

When her mom answered the front door I waited for a sign that she knew we'd gone to Boston, an indication that she had some idea of what had happened that day. But she just let me in and told me Jessie was upstairs in her room. And that's where I found her, lying on her bed staring at the ceiling and the glow-in-the-dark stars she'd stuck up there two years ago when she'd thought they'd help her fall asleep easier. Only now the lights in her room were on and the stars just looked like pale yellow cutouts instead of celestial bodies.

When she heard me come into the room, Jessie moved over, making space for me on the bed. I lay down next to her and fixed my eyes on what I thought was the North Star.

I put my arm around Jessie's shoulders and pulled her against me. "Come on, Jessie, you didn't do anything wrong. It was a mistake."

She wiped her eyes and looked over at me, her cheeks red

and tearstained, her eyes shiny and waterlogged. Then she let out what sounded like a choked laugh.

"I don't feel guilty about the abortion," she sniffled, saying the word out loud for the first time since she'd told me the results of her home tests. "I feel guilty because it feels so great not to be pregnant. For the first time in over a week I actually feel like myself again."

I wasn't expecting that.

Consoling I could handle. Cheering up I could manage. Putting things right was practically my specialty. But what was I supposed to do with someone who says she feels great to be like her old self again, but has snot running down her lip from crying so hard?

"Well, that's good right?" I asked, sure her response had to be normal for someone in her situation, even though I didn't feel that this was a situation where anything could be considered normal.

"You know what I kept thinking? The whole time I was standing there waiting for my pee to make a plus or minus sign show up in that window, I kept thinking, 'I'm too organized to get pregnant.' Do you believe that?"

Knowing Jessie, I could.

"And then, when that plus sign showed up, I wasn't scared, I wasn't freaked out—that came about a minute later. I was mad. I was pissed I'd fucked up."

I could completely picture Jess in the bathroom swearing at the stick, telling it to go to hell right before her knees gave out and she sat on the toilet and cried.

"What does Nash think?" I asked.

Jess curled up onto her side, her knees and elbows pulled

in tight as she talked. "You know what he said to me when I got back? He said, 'I told you I'd be here,' and I just lost it because you know what? He'd also told me he'd be there to take us to the appointment, but where was he? And then there he was at the ferry this afternoon waiting for me, after I spent the whole ride convinced he wouldn't show up."

I didn't tell her that I wasn't expecting him to show up either. Apparently Nash had surprised both of us.

"So now what's going to happen with you guys?" I asked.

"I guess we'll try to go back to the way things were, but I don't know if we can. Maybe there are some things that you just can't forget."

"Maybe you don't have to forget about it. Maybe you just need to figure out how to move past it."

Jessie sighed and turned away from me, fixing her eyes on the spattering of stars above our heads. "Well, we've got three weeks to go, so I guess if we can't, it doesn't really matter."

But I knew it mattered. And I knew Jessie knew it, too.

The next afternoon when I arrived at the Barclays' house, I spotted Mr. Barclay down by the harbor wall in the same Adirondack chair Jay had been in when I'd taken a chance and gone to talk with him. I decided to give Mr. Barclay the same chance.

Maybe my talk with Jessie yesterday had made me think that if she and Nash could try to work through their ordeal, then maybe if I understood why Mr. Barclay had done what he did to Jay, then I could figure out a way to help them work through their situation, too.

"Hi, Winnie." Mr. Barclay took a sip of the iced tea he had

resting on the arm of the chair. "Boy, the summer has gone fast, hasn't it?"

I looked at him and he smiled. Only I didn't smile back. Instead I tried to imagine how the man who played croquet with Cassie on the lawn and helped to build a Coke-bottle rocket could justify letting Jay's mother die without her son beside her, how he could defend his decision to keep Jay at school when he'd needed to say good-bye one last time.

Just thinking about it made my chest tighten, my breath start coming quicker. It wasn't fair. And if Jay wasn't going to ask him, then I was.

"Why'd you tell Jay to stay at school when his mother was dying?"

Mr. Barclay placed his glass on the arm of the chair and inhaled slowly, filling his lungs so that his chest rose up, and I wondered if he was preparing to yell at me. Instead his voice was low and steady, and if I hadn't heard the wounded tone in the words he spoke, I would have thought he wasn't even fazed by my question. "Is that what he told you?"

I nodded, afraid that if I spoke, I might say something I'd regret.

Mr. Barclay brought his hand up to his temple and rubbed it slowly, as if he was finally beginning to make sense of something that, until I'd asked the question, he couldn't quite understand. He sat there, his chin resting against his chest, his eyes fixed on his outstretched legs.

"In July, when we pretty much knew she was losing her fight, Jay's mom called me." He paused and finally turned to look at me. "Let me tell you, if there's one thing you can never prepare yourself for, it's the sound of a voice you once knew better than anyone else's calling to tell you she's going to die."

Mr. Barclay wrapped his hand around the glass and held it there, as if steadying himself, the condensation sliding down the sides and over his skin. "But that wasn't the reason for the call. Jay's mother wasn't looking for sympathy. She wanted to make sure that I wouldn't let Jay put school on hold. She was worried he'd put all his energy into trying to save her and end up missing out on a time in his life he was supposed to be enjoying. Jay's mom was dying, but she didn't want her ending to keep Jay from starting school. So she told me to make sure he stayed at school, and that's what I did."

"But he wanted to be with her."

Mr. Barclay motioned for me to sit down on the chair beside him, but I shook my head.

He went on, "His mom wanted Jay to be at school, where he'd be starting something new, his life after high school, maybe even his life after his mom. Look, Winnie, maybe I wasn't right, but what did I know at the time? I tried to do what she wanted. At that point who was I to tell her what was right or wrong, regardless of what I thought?"

"But he blames himself for not being there. He thinks he let her die alone."

"He shouldn't think that," Mr. Barclay insisted. "She didn't think that."

"But he does. Didn't you ever tell him that's why you said he should stay at school instead of going home that weekend?"

Mr. Barclay looked down into his lap. "I didn't."

"You have to," I implored, gripping the back of the empty chair, feeling the sharp edges of the slats dig into my hand. "He has to know that his mom talked to you. Jay blames you."

"Maybe I should have told him, but I didn't want Jay to

think his mother didn't want him with her. Because she did, Winnie, I know she did."

"Then why'd she tell you he should stay at school?"

"Honestly, Winnie, I didn't ask her." Mr. Barclay bit his lip and paused, chewing on the chapped pink skin as he looked out at the water, not focusing on anything in particular. "I have to imagine it was because she knew there was nothing he could do at that point. Or because he'd just started college and she wanted him to settle in and start making friends. Maybe because she knew he'd need people to rely on when the inevitable happened and she realized those people would be at school."

I thought about his answers, his guesses as to why Jay's mother had called her ex-husband to have one final conversation.

"You need to go talk to him," I told Mr. Barclay. "He needs to know."

Jay's dad reached to the end of the armrests, one hand gripping the glass while the other grasped the under edge of the chair, gaining leverage. "Where is he?"

"Probably in his room."

Mr. Barclay pulled his body forward, then he stood up and looked at me for a second before walking up the path toward the house.

He took a few steps, then turned to me, his body at an angle between the harbor and the house. "She wasn't ready to leave him, Winnie, but she knew it was time to let him go."

Chapter **21**

The gallery was just off Main Street, a few doors down from the fudge shop, and as Jay and I walked past the familiar chef figure in the window, I couldn't help but think that this was the last week Cassie and I would take our afternoon walks around town, the week we'd sample the last remaining flavor of fudge.

Jay and I had decided to walk to the gallery from the Barclays', even though Mr. Barclay had offered to drive us. He was dropping Anne off at the gallery, then parking downtown and meeting us at the event. Jay suggested that we invite them, and I knew my parents wanted to meet the family I'd spent so much time with all summer, so I told him it was a great idea.

When I'd left the Barclays' yesterday, I wasn't sure what would happen with Jay and his dad, but I knew it was time for me to leave and let them figure it out. As I walked down the gravel driveway, I listened for the sound of raised voices coming through the open windows, but all I could hear was a family coming down the sidewalk on their way into town, the little kids running ahead of their parents as they screamed something about ice cream.

I was home for two hours before Jay called, and when we finally talked, he didn't get into the details of their conversation. He just asked if I thought it would be okay if his dad and Anne came to the opening night at the gallery.

"I think that would be great," I told him. "I'll have my dad put their names on the list."

"Don't do it yet," Jay cautioned. "They don't know if they'll be able to find a babysitter on such short notice."

I wasn't about to let something as simple as child care keep Jay and his family from coming to my father's opening night. "Don't worry. I know someone who'd love to do it. Just tell them it starts at seven."

"Ready?" Jay asked, stopping in front of the window stretching across the entire width of the gallery. Condensation clung to edges of the glass, small drops of water seeming to bubble up before losing their grip and sliding to the bottom of the sill. Centered in the window, three of my father's photographs hung in frames suspended from the ceiling, the thin wires disappearing against the backdrop of the crowd gathered inside.

"Wow, there's a lot of people in there." I hung back as a couple passed us and pulled the gallery door open, a burst of cool air rushing past us before the door closed behind them.

"He's a pretty well-known photographer," Jay said. "Even if people don't know his name, they know his dogs."

"It's weird, you know. My whole life I grew up walking by this window, looking at paintings and sculptures and photographs by people I didn't know, people I thought had to be famous or special, and how they probably had everything they ever wanted. And now my dad is one of them."

"Come on." Jay reached for the door handle and held the door open for me. "They're waiting for you."

The gallery was packed with people I recognized and strangers I didn't. In one corner my dad was surrounded by admirers, while in another my mom talked with some friends. Jay and I mingled, and when Anne and Mr. Barclay arrived, they joined us, although Anne spent much of the time sitting down in a chair the gallery owner offered her. The event was catered, so every few minutes we were offered bacon-wrapped scallops and stuffed mushrooms and crab cakes. Before long I was stuffed, and when someone tapped me on the shoulder, I was ready to decline another offer of tuna sashimi.

"No more, thanks," I said, turning around to face the server, only it wasn't one of the girls in white tuxedo shirts and black skirts. It was my sister.

"No more? But I just got here." Shelby nudged my shoulder, and all of a sudden I felt like crying, as if I had so much to tell her and yet had no way to go back and explain everything.

"What are you doing here?" I demanded. "Why didn't you tell me you were coming?"

"You didn't think I'd miss the big event, did you? I thought I'd surprise everyone. Besides, when I heard it was being catered, I thought it would be a great way to gather a little competitive intelligence."

Jay was standing beside me, waiting for an introduction. "This is my sister, Shelby. Shelby, this is Jay."

Shelby paused, looking from me to Jay and then back again, giving me a curious look like *Am I supposed to know this guy?*

"Jay is my boyfriend," I added, and Shelby's confusion

seemed to dissipate some, although she still looked as if she expected a more elaborate explanation at some point.

"It's nice to meet you, Jay." Shelby grabbed a crab cake from one of the servers, then provided us with her professional opinion: "Not bad. Not bad at all."

Jay tapped me on the shoulder and pointed to the front door. "Look."

Jessie had just come into the gallery, her hair springing out around her cheeks from the humidity. She glanced around the room looking for a familiar face, which she found when she spotted me.

"You made it," I told Jessie when I reached her. "I thought you were babysitting."

"I am." Jessie wiped the back of her hand against her forehead. "God, it's brutal out there."

"You look nice, Jess." Jay knelt down until he was eye level with Cassie. "And you look pretty nice, too."

"She kept begging me to bring her. I figured a few minutes wouldn't kill the party. Want to go find your mom and dad?" Jessie asked Cassie, and they wandered away into the crowd.

"She seems like she's doing okay," Jay observed

"Jess will be fine."

"What about her and Nash?"

I shrugged. "They talked, she let him say what he had to say. I guess we'll have to see what happens from here. He's leaving for school soon."

Neither of us said more, but I knew we were both thinking the same thing. That soon Jay would be heading back to Wesleyan, too.

My mom pulled me over to talk to some friends of hers,

and Jay went to find Anne and his dad and Cassie. I spent some time saying hello to people I knew, but then I slipped through the crowd on my way to the front door. Once outside I crossed to the other side of the street where a stone wall ran to the corner of Winter Street and sat down.

They were all inside, my parents, Jay, Jessie and her parents, Anne and Cassie and Mr. Barclay, my parents' friends. Even Shelby. But one by one they'd be gone. Jay and Shelby would go back to school, the Barclays would head home to Connecticut, my dad would pack up his closet and drive to Boston.

My father had already told me I was welcome in the city whenever I wanted to take a break from the cold, gray winter of the island, but who knew what the school year would bring.

"Hey!" Jay was standing on the sidewalk outside the gallery, watching me.

"Hey," I called back.

Jay looked to his left to make sure no cars were coming, then crossed the street. "What are you doing out here? Shouldn't you be inside celebrating?"

He sat down beside me on the wall and placed his hand on my knee.

"I was getting a little claustrophobic," I admitted. "What's your excuse?"

"I just wanted to get a little fresh air. Your dad drew quite a crowd."

I nodded, catching a glimpse of Shelby through the gallery window. "It was great of Shelby to come back, wasn't it?"

"Well, it's a big deal. She seems nice, although she kept critiquing the hors d'oeuvres. Apparently the stuffed mushrooms should be firmer to the touch."

I laughed and Jay did, too. "That's Shelby."

"So why are you really out here?" Jay asked. "I could see you from the gallery. You were definitely thinking about something."

"I was thinking about how great it is to have everyone together. And how soon you'll all be leaving." My voice shook and Jay moved his hand up to my cheek.

"I can't speak for anyone else, but I can tell you that I don't want to leave any more than you want me to. Probably less."

"Things will be better for you at school this year," I told Jay.

"You say that, but you don't know how bad it was last year. Everything would be so much easier if I could just stay here with you."

I didn't disagree with him.

"There's your dad." Jay nodded toward the gallery.

I looked up and saw my father coming toward us.

"What's with that?" I pointed to the camera my father held in his hand. "Can't you stop even for your own party?"

"Old habits." He smiled.

"I'm going to head back inside." Jay squeezed my hand, then let it go. "I'll see you in there."

I nodded, and he left me alone with my dad, who sat down next to me. Across the street we could see the party going on inside the gallery, my mom laughing at something her friend Marcy said.

"It's strange, isn't it?" my dad asked. "I can't say I ever imagined this would happen."

"A party in your honor?"

"Well, yeah, but everything. Remember when you were little and you used to beg me to let you come to work with me? I used to let you hold the film canisters, and you'd grip them so tight in your hand, afraid to drop them in the sand. Of course that was before everything went digital."

"I'd forgotten about that," I admitted, suddenly remembering those early mornings on the beach. I loved it when he'd load the film and hand me the black plastic cylinders with the gray caps. "I always took the empty containers home and lined them up on my dresser, filling them with marbles and jewelry and stuff I'd collected."

"I know. Your mom and I couldn't figure out what the smell in your room was until we discovered the baby spider crab you'd decided to house in one of the containers."

I laughed, recalling the morning my parents finally decided to scour every nook and cranny to solve the mystery of the smell emanating from my room. "I wanted a pet."

"It was dead," my dad pointed out.

"I didn't know what to feed him," I explained, and my dad grinned at me. "So are you moving to the city full-time?"

He looked down at the camera in his hand, his finger tracing the circle of the lens. "I think for now, yeah."

"So what's Mom going to do," I asked, when what I really meant was *What are we going to do?*

"I think if the past three years have shown us anything, they've demonstrated that your mom is more than capable of taking care of herself."

"So is this it?"

"I don't know, Winnie. I guess we'll have to wait and see what happens."

"Are you going to stay in the studio?"

"I think I'm ready for another room. I'll start looking after Labor Day."

"So it's all decided?"

He nodded and laid his arm over my shoulder, pulling me against him. "It is."

Through the plate-glass window I saw my mom deep in conversation with Marcy. Jessie and Jay were intently listening to a uniformed server describe the hors d'oeuvres on her silver tray, and I wondered how Jessie was going to manage picking apart a slice of bruschetta.

"We should probably go back inside," I told my dad, resting my head against his chest, where I could hear the thumping of his heart against my ear. "They're probably wondering where the guest of honor is."

I stood up, but Dad just sat there, not moving. I wondered what he saw when he looked through that window, if he saw his dreams coming true or his dreams coming apart. "Come on." I nudged him. "Let me buy you a celebratory glass of champagne."

"It's an open bar." He cracked a smile.

"Really?" I feigned surprise. "Then I guess I'll have to get you next time."

"Yeah. Next time."

Chapter 22

The next morning I woke up to the click of the coffeemaker, which was eventually followed by the smell of dark-roasted beans and the rush of water through the floorboards as the hallway bathroom door opened and footsteps made their way down the stairs.

I tumbled out of bed and went downstairs to the kitchen, where I found Shelby already dressed, in the same jeans and white T-shirt she had always worn. Her hair was a few inches longer than when she'd left. It grazed her shoulders for what I think was the first time since she was seven years old and my mom left one of her craft scissors on the kitchen counter, the kind with the sharp, V-shaped teeth instead of a straight blade. Needless to say my mom wasn't thrilled with the results of Shelby's do-it-yourself haircut or the three inches the salon had to cut off just to make it even all the way around.

"I was thinking of going to the Willow to see Wendy," Shelby told me, sliding a pan of muffins out of the oven. "Do you want to come? I hardly got to see you at all last night."

I peered over her shoulder to see what she'd decided to bake for breakfast. The pale yellow top with orange flecks gave it away. Shelby's famous sunshine muffins. Wendy, the owner of the Willow Inn, where Shelby had worked before heading off to Boston, loved Shelby's sunshine muffins. Pretty much everybody did. "Can I take a muffin with me?"

"Go get dressed, and they'll be cool when you come down."

With Shelby around it almost felt the way it used to, everyone settling into their routines, the house filled with familiar sounds and smells as if it were waking up from hibernation.

"So talk to me." Shelby stared through the windshield, not even looking over at me as she drove into town. "You can start with Mom and Dad or you can start with the guy who had his eyes on you all night."

I decided to start with my parents. It seemed easier than trying to explain Jay. "What have they told you? I'm always the last to know anything."

She gave me a sideways glance, as if she didn't believe me. "Only because you don't want to know."

"They don't fight," I began, because at least that was one thing that hadn't changed. "It's more like they coexist. Remember that race-car set Drew Carlson got for his birthday that one year?"

She nodded. Drew Carlson was our neighbor until his family moved to Michigan.

"You know how the two cars went around the same track,

hugged the same curves, but even if they were right next to each other, they didn't touch? Well, that's what they're like. If you didn't know any better, you'd think they were sharing the track, but they're really just running their own races."

"Drew Carlson always had bad breath, do you remember that?" Shelby put on her blinker and we turned right toward downtown.

That was it? Our parents were splitting up and she wanted to talk about Drew Carlson's poor oral hygiene?

"The thing is, he didn't even know it," Shelby continued. "He was so used to it that he couldn't even tell anymore. The same thing happened with Mom and Dad."

"They didn't floss?"

"They got so used to being apart they forgot what it was like to be together, and being apart just started to feel normal."

"So do you think this is it? They're splitting up?"

Shelby took a right at the Willow Inn and waited as a car pulled out of a space. Shelby always had good parking karma.

"Look, I don't know what's going on any more than you do, but if you're going to try to define what it is they're doing, or solve the equation that is our parents, you're going to be disappointed. They're not a postulate, Winnie, and not everything can be figured out by solving for x."

I didn't tell her she was mixing her math. "So it's not as simple as just flossing?"

Shelby cut the engine and turned to me. "I'm afraid not, Winnie. But flossing never hurts."

• • •

"Blueberry pancakes." Shelby wrinkled her nose, inhaling once more just to make sure. "A little cliché for a Saturday morning, don't you think?"

Personally, I liked blueberry pancakes, even if they were a little obvious in a bed-and-breakfast on a Saturday morning on Martha's Vineyard.

"Who's been cooking with you away?" I asked as we walked past the Willow's front desk and headed toward the dining room.

"Some guy," Shelby answered, not even bothering to retain his name. I knew she'd never think anyone could do breakfast as well as she could.

She left me in the dining room while she went to find Wendy, and a half hour later she found me on the porch sitting in a rocking chair watching tourists stroll down Main Street.

I figured Shelby would tell me it was time to go, but instead she sat in the chair beside mine and rested her foot along the porch railing.

"So who's Jay?" she asked, tapping the other foot against the floorboards. "Mom told me you were babysitting his sister this summer."

"His half sister," I corrected, as if it mattered.

"And what's going on with you two?"

"He's getting ready to go back to school, so I guess whatever has been going on won't be going on much longer."

"Should it? Do you want it to?"

I wanted to tell Shelby about that day in the city with Jessie, how he'd sat beside her and then waited with me. Or explain how I felt when we were together, as if he were the one person who understood, the only person who made me feel less alone, as if no matter what he'd always be there for me. Instead I just said, "Yeah, I do."

Jay was waiting for me at the kitchen table when Shelby and I got back.

"What are you doing here?" I asked him.

"Want one?" He took a bite of the muffin he'd been holding in his hand. "This is my second one. They're amazing."

"Third," my mom corrected, coming into the room. "He's had three."

"I lost count."

"I have to work this afternoon, so I'm heading back to the city." Shelby set her overnight bag on the kitchen floor and came over to me.

"Hey, Shelby, do you take mail orders?" Jay asked, brushing the crumbs from his fingertips, then pushing tiny morsels into a yellowy orange mound on the table. Jessie always made a huge mess with Shelby's sunshine muffins, as you can imagine, but she never left a stray crumb behind. Never.

"Sorry, Jay, maybe one day."

"Call me if you need to talk, okay?" she told me, her voice low, as if only I was meant to hear.

"Okay." I hugged her good-bye.

The horn sounded out in the driveway. "Mom and Dad are taking me to the ferry. And there are more muffins in the Tupperware on top of the fridge," she said, as if she knew that's exactly what Jay was going to ask.

I walked Shelby to the kitchen door, then watched as she slid into the backseat, pulling her bag in behind her and slamming the door shut. Through the driver's-side window I could see my dad preparing to back out of the driveway, one hand on the steering wheel, the other slung across the back of the passenger seat, his wrist resting behind my mother's shoulders but not close enough to touch. Two summers ago I wouldn't have thought anything of it; the three of them could have been on their way to Morning Glory Farm for fresh corn or heading into town to pick up a pizza. Even last summer I probably wouldn't have noticed the distance between my parents, how my mother leaned against the inside of the passenger door, resting her head against the spot where the seat belt disappeared inside the doorframe, how my dad kept two hands on the wheel, his eyes fixed straight ahead.

"I'm taking you somewhere," Jay informed me, although he didn't mention where. "Let's go."

"Are you sure I can drag you away from those?" I pointed to the Tupperware container sitting atop the refrigerator.

"Aw, Fred, you don't have to drag me away." Jay stood up and came over to me, laying his hands around my waist, lifting the hem of my shirt so he could feel my skin. "I can always pack a few to go, right?"

"Where are we going?" We'd started out heading toward Oak Bluffs, and I thought, maybe, we were going to State Beach. But then we passed the beach, and even when we got to the center of Oak Bluffs, Jay didn't stop. Instead we drove past the Flying Horse carousel on our left, the boats tied up to moorings on our right.

"It's a surprise," Jay teased, taking a right onto East Chop

Road. As we drove along the water, I saw it appear up ahead at the top of the hill, its tapered, white body topped off by what looked like a black crown.

"The lighthouse?" I guessed, and Jay didn't answer, which meant I was right.

After pulling over to the side of the road, Jay parked the car and we stepped out onto the grass.

"Come on." He grabbed my hand and pulled me up the incline behind him, leading us around the lighthouse to the edge of the bluff. Down below us the water of Nantucket Sound stretched out between the island and the mainland, and from up high the mainland looked close enough to touch.

"When my parents got divorced, the one thing my mom said she'd miss was the lighthouses on the island."

"Nantucket has lighthouses," I pointed out.

"Yeah, but when I was younger, before we even had the house in town or the jet to avoid the whole boat thing, we used to come here on the ferry. And as soon as the East Chop Lighthouse came into view, my mom would stand me up on her knees and tell me we'd arrived."

I tried to picture Jay as a little kid, his hair blowing in the wind as the ferry rounded the bluff and the lighthouse rose up from the waves.

"So that's why you took me here? So I could try to believe that you were once a little kid eating soft pretzels on the deck of the ferry?"

Jay shook his head. "No, although I did always get a pretzel, even though most of the time they were stale."

"Then why?"

Jay moved around to face me, Nantucket Sound creating a watery blue backdrop behind him. "I wanted to bring you here because whenever I came to the island with my parents, I always knew we were really here when I saw the lighthouse. That after the four-hour car trip from Connecticut and the ferry ride over, we'd finally made it. And on the ferry ride back to Woods Hole, it was the last thing I remember seeing, how I'd always wish we had one more week. Or two. Or three." He paused, building to what was beginning to feel like a big announcement. "And that's why I've decided to stay."

"Stay?" I repeated.

"On the island." Jay nodded, and then added, "With you."

On the island with me. As in not going home. "You can't be serious. What about school?"

Jay stepped back, almost as if he knew I needed some space to grasp what he was telling me. "What about it? Last year sucked. The only reason I was even allowed back this semester is because they're hoping my dad will fund a new science building or something. Besides, school will always be there."

Jay didn't finish his sentence, but I knew what came next—*but you might not.*

I'd never even considered that Jay could actually stay on the island, just choose not to go back to school. Even if I'd thought a million times about how great it would be to have him around, to come home from school and be able to not just talk with him but actually be with him, touch him, to fill up the empty days while my mom was grading her kids' work and my dad and Shelby were in the city pursuing their dreams.

And Jay was right. Just because he wasn't going back now didn't mean he'd never go back. It was just a semester. Or two.

"Can you do that?" I asked, both hopeful and doubtful at the same time. "Can you really stay?"

"Sure, why not? The house is empty all winter. Besides,

we've seen four of the five lighthouses on the island. I thought I'd stay and we could see the fifth."

"But what will you do?" I still couldn't believe he was serious or that staying on the island was as easy as deciding not to leave.

"I'll find a job doing something."

I thought about it. Jay on the island all winter. No matter who left, no matter how long people were gone or even if they didn't come back to the island for good, Jay would be here.

"Hey, look." Jay pointed toward Oak Bluffs, where the ferry had just made the turn and was heading out into Nantucket Sound toward Woods Hole.

We stood there watching the ferry slowly make its way through the water, spitting whitecaps out to either side, creating a frothy white foam that dissipated in its wake. It was the twelve-o'clock ferry, and Shelby was on it, on her way to the city where she'd finish her summer job, begin school, and one day probably head up her own kitchen. She wasn't coming back. And soon my father would be on that side of the sound as well, driving toward Boston and away from us.

But no matter what happened with my parents or where Shelby ended up, Jay would be here. He'd be with me.

"You're really serious?" I asked.

"Completely."

"Did you tell your dad?"

"Not yet. I wanted to tell you first. Why?"

"I was just wondering what he said. He's not going to be happy."

"This isn't about him. It's about us."

"You're really staying?" I repeated, just to make sure I wasn't imagining it.

Jay moved closer to me and laid his hands around my waist, squeezing gently before clasping his fingers together around my back. "Yes, Fred. I'm staying."

"So now that I'm going to be around, what do you want to do for your birthday?" he asked on our way back to the car.

"I have no idea, I've had all of two minutes to think about it." As I ran through the months in my head, I kept coming up with new things Jay and I would be doing together, new experiences we could share that would never have been possible if he went back to school. My birthday was just the start. Even the simple idea of having him around to carve pumpkins in the fall was mind-boggling, not to mention spending the holidays together.

"Well, think about it."

"What'd you do for your eighteenth birthday?"

He didn't even need a minute to think. "I shaved my mom's head."

We'd reached the Jeep at that point, but instead of walking over to the passenger side, I stood with Jay and looked at someone who'd spent his eighteenth birthday in a way most people couldn't even imagine. "Really?"

"Yeah. It was all falling out at that point, so she handed me a pair of scissors and a clipper and told me to go to town."

"Well, I can tell you one thing. That is not how we'll be celebrating my birthday."

Jay reached over and tousled my hair. "That's too bad. I bet you'd look good bald."

Chapter 23

It was Cassie's last tennis lesson and Jessie had stepped it up, challenging Cassie to keep pace with her. For a six-year-old, Cassie had got pretty good, and not just because Anne had promised her a cute new tennis skirt if Jessie gave her a good report. I think even Jess was impressed when Cassie returned Jessie's backhand, even though Jessie was obviously taking it easy on her.

"Jay's not going back to school," I told Jess when she walked off the court for a drink of water.

"Are you kidding me?" she asked, pushing her damp curls out of her face as she lifted the water bottle to her mouth.

"Nope. He decided to stay on the island."

"Because of you?"

"Not *just* because of me," I told her, sounding way more defensive than I'd intended. "He isn't ready to go back to school yet. Last year was tough. I think he just wants to take some time and figure out what he wants to do."

Jessie pushed down the cap on the water bottle and dropped it onto the grass. "What about you?"

"What about me?"

Jessie watched Cassie practice a serve. "Do you want him to stay?"

"Of course I do." I couldn't even believe Jessie would ask such a thing. "Come on, how would you feel if Nash told you he wasn't going back to school, that he was going to stay on the island instead?"

"Let's not use Nash as an example here, Winnie. I think we both know that's not going to happen." Jessie tapped the water bottle with the toe of her sneaker.

"You're right. I'm sorry. I just meant that if Jay leaves, I'll miss him. Really, Jess, I don't know what I'd do. If he goes back to school, who knows . . ." I didn't want to finish the thought. We both knew.

"And what happens next year when it's your turn to leave? What happens to him?"

"I hadn't thought that far ahead. I guess we'll deal with that when the time comes."

Jessie still wasn't convinced. "And what's his dad say?"

I knew what Jessie was implying, that Mr. Barclay would get Jay to change his mind. She obviously didn't know Jay as well as I did. "I don't think Jay's told him yet. But I also don't think it matters. Jay said he's staying."

Jessie shrugged, then shouted, "Cassie, fix your grip!"

We watched as Cassie turned the racquet around in her hand, eventually settling on a grip that seemed, if not right, at least not as wrong.

"So what's going on with you and Nash?" I asked.

Jessie reached down for the water bottle again and took a long sip before answering. "I don't know. I believe him when he says he's sorry about that day, I really do, but what's the point? Every time we're together, I try to forget, Winnie, and sometimes I do, but then it's there again. It's just not that easy."

"Maybe it's not supposed to be."

"Jessie, come on!" Cassie yelled from the court.

"Sure, get all Zen on me." Jessie took one more sip of water, then punched down the cap on the water bottle. "And if it's not supposed to be easy, how come it seems to be so easy for you?"

I spread the last coat of varnish across the top of the box and set it down on the table. I still hadn't decided what to do with the Corona bottle cap, but other than for that I'd covered the entire outer surface with pieces of my summer. And even if the box lacked the colorful hodgepodge look of my mother's pieces, I thought it was way more practical than a hot pink, yellow, and brown ceramic cat.

I took the paintbrush into the kitchen and set it in a jar of water while I went to show my mom the box.

"I finished the jewelry box," I announced when I found her in the backyard wiping the patio table, which had a thin layer of pollen fogging up the glass.

"What do you think?" she asked. "It was fun, wasn't it?"

"Yeah, it wasn't so bad." I held the box flat in my hands, careful not to touch the still wet edges.

"You could keep going, you know. That's the thing with decoupage, you never have to stop." She thought about this for a second. "Unless you run out of materials, I suppose."

"I guess I could always find more stuff to add, but I just decided it was time." I held the box out so she could take a closer look.

"Well, I like it." She inspected each of the pieces torn from my summer and reached out to touch the front.

"It's still wet," I told her, pulling the box away.

"I was just going to point to the piece of wrapping from the fudge shop. It's got a nice texture to it."

"Yeah, it's one of my favorites, too." Then I added, "Jay's not going back to school. He decided to stay on the island."

My mom took her eyes off the box and fixed them on me. "Why?"

"He just doesn't want to go back. Last year was tough."

"So he decided to drop out of college?" She slid a chair out from the patio table and sat down, motioning for me to do the same.

"He's not dropping out of college, Mom. Can you just not be a teacher here and try to understand?" I continued standing. "Jay would just rather stay with me."

My mom pressed her lips together and nodded, not saying anything.

"I know what you're thinking," I told her, because I did know. "You're going to tell me that Jay needs to stay in school, and I know that, and he'll go back. Just not yet."

"That's not what I was going to say, although you obviously know that's part of it." She stared at the box in my hand, tilting her head to read the pieces I'd pasted on sideways. "I think right now having Jay stay on the island probably sounds like an easy solution, but sometimes doing what's right isn't always easy."

The words sounded vaguely familiar, and then I realized I'd said something just like that to Jessie at the tennis courts earlier. But this was a totally different situation. Wasn't it?

"Everyone's changing their living arrangements, so I don't

even know how you can act like what Jay's doing is so wrong. Isn't Dad moving to the city?"

Her eyes moved off me and to the glass table, where she found a spot she'd missed with the paper towel. "For the time being," she conceded, although that seemed like a nonanswer to me.

"So why don't you go, too?"

"I have a job here, Winnie, we have a house and friends, not to mention *you*." She looked up at me. "Did you forget that? It's your senior year and I want you to enjoy it. I don't want to make you move to a new school when you have enough to think about with college and all coming up."

"Then why can't Dad wait another year? Or why can't he just keep doing what he's been doing?"

"Because it's not fair to any of us, Winnie. It hasn't been easy, as I'm sure you know." She reached for my hand and pulled me down into the chair beside her. "We didn't mean for this to happen."

"I thought absence was supposed to make the heart grow fonder."

My mom laughed, but it sounded sad. "I guess it can. It can also make the heart forget."

I thought about Jay staying on the island, how I couldn't stand to think about him leaving, to know that with every passing day he thought about me less, missed me less.

"So why now?" I wanted to know, still believing that maybe there was a fix to all this, if only I could think of it. "You survived for three years, so why now?"

"It's what he's always wanted, Winnie." My mom laid the balled-up paper towel in her lap and pulled at it with her fingers, tearing it like a piece of tissue paper she was preparing for one of her projects. "It's what I used to want for him, until it meant making choices I didn't want to make."

"So you're just going to let him leave?"

"I guess I could force him to stay, tell him if he goes, it's the end, but what would that prove? Look, I know this isn't easy for you, especially with Shelby gone. I know it's easy for me to say that this is between your father and me, but I know that's not true. I know whatever happens to us happens to you as well. But he's got to see if he can do it. And I've got to let him try." She swallowed hard, as if she needed to take a break before continuing. "Otherwise, what's the point?"

I knew she was talking about my dad and his photography, but I couldn't help but think about Jay and school. And even if I wanted to think she was wrong, a part of me knew she was absolutely right.

Chapter 24

Even before he saw me sitting beside the small rectangular window, I spotted Jay leaning up against the twisted tree trunk, his hands stuffed in his pockets as he waited for my bus, just as he did every day. I'd grown so accustomed to seeing him there, and I loved that I always caught a glimpse of him first, just a few seconds when he didn't know I was watching. As soon as he spotted the bus rounding the corner onto Church Street, Jay stood up and searched the row of windows for me, and by the time the double doors opened and I stepped down onto the sidewalk, he was there, his hands out of his pockets as he waited for me to walk into his arms.

Unlike so many afternoons before, the urgency in his touch had subsided even if the desire hadn't. Since he'd decided to stay, Jay was more relaxed, less rushed, as if he realized we had plenty of time. But as he wrapped his arms around my waist, I knew better, and so I held on even tighter, holding the warm bare skin of his neck against my own, burying my lips in the soft fleshy spot where his collarbone disappeared into his shoulder. I closed my eyes, committing the smell of his hair to memory, the feel of his rough cheek, the taste of his salty skin. And when we pulled apart, I smiled, as if, like him, I believed we had all the time in the world.

"So I thought, why wait? Why not just go today?" Jay was talking about the lighthouse, how there was no reason for us to wait until everyone left the island. "There's plenty of stuff for us to do once everyone's gone."

"Why today?" I asked, as he led me up the front walk of his house to the door. "We can always go tomorrow."

Jay lifted up the mat and took the silver key out from under it, ignoring the water bugs that had also made the moist area beneath the mat their home. Jay hadn't bothered to get his own set of keys and instead always used the one Anne had made for me.

Anne had taken Cassie to a play date in Vineyard Haven, and then she was meeting some friends for lunch, so Jay and I had the house to ourselves. We'd been alone in the house before, but this time it was different, even if I couldn't tell Jay why.

"I know. We can go whenever we want, but it's gorgeous out and I thought maybe we could grab some lunch in Oak Bluffs." Jay replaced the key under the mat and I followed him inside.

I didn't give him a chance to bring up the lighthouse again. Instead I grabbed his hand and led him around the foyer table toward the stairway.

"Come with me," I ordered, and Jay reluctantly trailed behind.

I took one step up, but Jay stopped, preferring to remain on the foyer's hardwood floor.

"What are you doing?" Jay stayed at the bottom as I continued to the next step. "Anne won't be back until three at the earliest."

"I know." I turned around and took one step down so that I was still one step away from Jay but we were at eye level. I took both his hands in mine and held them, our palms pressed together. I said the words slowly and looked into his brown eyes, willing him to understand what I was saying without making me say the words. "We have two hours."

Jay looked as if he was about to protest again, but then he stopped. "Are you sure?" His expression was serious, as if he knew what a big deal this was.

I'd be lying if I said that what had happened with Jessie and Nash hadn't scared me a little, but I wasn't Jessie and Jay wasn't Nash.

"I'm sure," I said, believing it with every fiber of my being. "I'm absolutely certain."

We lay there in his bed, the blanket falling off us, a breeze coming in through the open window.

"So when do we get to hit the last lighthouse?" Jay asked, stroking my hair. "If you're watching Cassie the rest of the week, we could go this weekend."

As I lay there with my head on Jay's bare chest, my eyes wandered around the room, taking in the seemingly ordinary pieces of Jay's life—the wallet on the dresser, the magazine on the night table, his sneakers in the corner of the room. It was a different room from the one I peered into at the beginning of the summer. It was lived in. Jay may have thought the island had become his home, but it had nothing to do with where he was and everything to do with how he felt.

"Go back to school, Jay." I kept my head on his bare chest, my ear pressed against his skin listening to determine if there was any truth to the idea that you could hear a heart breaking.

He was silent, and when I turned my head to look at him, Jay was staring up at the ceiling, his eyes barely blinking.

I propped myself up on my elbow and turned onto my side.

"I mean, I don't even know why you want to stay. You've obviously never spent the winter on the island. It's pretty damn cold." I tried to smile, and Jay tried to reciprocate. Neither of us succeeded. "There's nothing here for you, Herb."

"You're here, Fred," he reminded me, as if I'd forgotten. "Besides, it's not that easy."

"It might not be easy, but it is simple. You need to go back to school."

"What about you?" he asked, looking at me for the first time.

"What about me? I'll be fine. It's my senior year. I'll have a million things to keep me busy."

Jay reached over and stroked my head, pushing the hair away from my face and then holding it there so it wouldn't fall forward and cover my eyes.

"But that means we only have a week left," he reminded me, although I'd already done the math and I knew exactly how much time we had together.

"It's a whole week," I told him, as if that were more than adequate, when it wasn't nearly enough. "Seven whole days. You'll be sick of me by then." I tried to laugh, but the sound got stuck in my throat and instead it sounded like a hoarse cough.

Jay locked eyes with mine, and even though I wanted to look away, I couldn't, my gaze held there by the sheer force of his will to hold it. I waited for Jay to say he could never get sick of me, that he needed more than one more week with me. But we both knew he couldn't, even if he believed that, and I really trusted he did. So instead of saying anything Jay leaned over and gently pressed his lips against my forehead, taking a deep breath as if trying to inhale this moment, capture it deep in his memory so he could remember what it was like.

"You can always come visit me, check out Wesleyan," he offered, pulling away and facing me.

"Sure," I agreed, but I think we both knew that promising anything beyond Labor Day was more hope than anything else. "I can always visit."

He rested his hand under my chin and lifted it up so that I was looking directly into his eyes, into the fringe of lashes I'd noticed for the first time in the kitchen, and at the real person I'd noticed for the first time that day we sat beside the harbor.

"I love you, Winnie." Maybe if he'd called me Fred, the knot in my throat would have dissolved, but hearing him say my name lodged it so tight I could hardly swallow, no less speak.

Instead I nodded, unable even to say his name.

Anne was due home shortly, so we got dressed and went downstairs, where I challenged Jay to a game of croquet on the back lawn, a diversion until we heard Anne's car pulling into the driveway.

"It's getting to the point where just walking into the house makes me want to take a nap," Anne told us when she found Jay and me taking the wickets out of the lawn.

Just looking at Anne, I could see why. She was huge. It wasn't just her stomach anymore, it was everywhere, as if she'd swelled up. Her ankles were barely noticeable, her face was almost completely round, even her arms were puffy. "And that's exactly what I'm going to do right now." She covered a yawn with the palm of her hand and left us to go upstairs and sleep.

But twenty minutes later Anne was back, standing in the doorway leading to the patio, where Jay and I were having lemonades. I just thought she couldn't fall asleep until I saw her hands gripping the underside of her belly, almost as if holding it up, cradling the baby inside.

"Something's wrong," she practically whispered, her face white.

That's when I noticed the red stain seeping from under Anne's palms, the edges spreading outward beyond her grasp in almost a perfect circle, the blood highlighting the rough grain of her linen dress.

"Oh my God," I gasped. "What do we do?"

"I already called the doctor in Connecticut. She said to get to the hospital." Anne inhaled sharply, pursed her lips, and let out a long, controlled breath. "So, Winnie, if you could take me to the hospital, that would be great. Jay, Cassie will be home from her play date in an hour, if you could just wait for her."

"No," Jay answered, and Anne and I both turned to him. "I meant, I'll take you to the hospital. Winnie can stay here with Cassie until we know what's going on. Is that okay?" he asked me.

"That's fine. Let me get some towels and I'll meet you both at the car."

In less than five minutes we had Anne in the passenger seat of the Mercedes, where I'd placed some folded-up bath towels for her to sit on.

"I'll call you when we know something," Jay told me before putting the car into gear and backing out of the driveway.

I stood there watching the car until it hung a right and disappeared up the street, wondering what I was going to tell Cassie when she came home.

Chapter 25

The bleeding stopped but the doctor decided to keep Anne in the hospital overnight for observation. On their way there Jay called his dad at work to tell him what had happened, and Mr. Barclay flew up from New York. He went straight to the hospital from the airport, but when he finally got to the house, around ten o'clock, I was still there with Jay.

"Cassie's in bed," I told Mr. Barclay, sitting up and shifting my weight off Jay. Jay and I were on the couch watching TV, the light from the flat screen casting a blue glow around the dark room.

Mr. Barclay reached over to the end table and turned on the lamp.

"How's Anne?" Jay asked.

"The doctor doesn't think it's anything serious, but he wants her on bed rest from now on." The harsh glare from the lamp accentuated the circles under Mr. Barclay's eyes, making them appear even darker. He'd obviously had a long day, and if the look on his face was any indication, he was preparing himself for a long night. "I'm going to take Cassie and

Anne back to Connecticut tomorrow. She shouldn't be flying, so we'll probably catch an early-afternoon ferry."

His announcement wasn't surprising, but, still, I winced. Jay noticed and reached over and pulled me nearer him.

Even though I knew it was going to happen eventually, that every day that passed was one day closer to the day we said good-bye, I wasn't prepared for the Barclays to leave tomorrow. I thought I still had six more days.

Mr. Barclay moved over in front of the couch, standing between us and the TV. "You don't have to go, Jay. It's up to you."

I turned to look at Jay, who was watching his father. Mr. Barclay and I waited for Jay's answer, the sound of the TV providing background noise in the silence.

"I'll let you know tomorrow," Jay said.

Mr. Barclay nodded and yawned, covering his mouth with his hand as if it required more strength than he had. "I'm going to bed. I'll see you in the morning, Jay. Good night, Winnie."

We sat there listening as Mr. Barclay's footsteps faded down the hallway.

"What are you going to do?" I asked, practically holding my breath.

"What do you think I should do?"

I shook my head. "I can't make that decision for you, Jay." I wanted to tell him to stay, to spend the next six days with me as we'd planned. But I couldn't. Not any more than I could have asked him to stay on the island with me.

"Can't we just enjoy tonight?" Jay asked, reaching out and laying his hand across the back of my neck, pulling me into him and resting my head on his shoulder.

"Yeah, we can," I practically whispered over the lump in my throat. "Let's do that."

"We're going home early," Cassie told me. She was waiting on the steps when I walked up the front path to the door. I'd wanted to leave camp early, but with Labor Day coming up the resort was packed and we had twenty kids waiting for us this morning. I ran out of the inn as soon as camp ended and was in such a rush to get to the Barclays' I didn't even bother changing out of my Oceanview shirt.

"I heard." I sat down next to her.

"We didn't do it." I must have looked confused because she added, "The fudge. I made a list. Here."

Cassie handed me a piece of paper where she'd written down every flavor of fudge we'd had over the summer. It was on the same dragonfly notepaper I'd found on the refrigerator what felt like ages ago.

She ran down the list: "We had chocolate, rocky road, chocolate toffee, chocolate cheesecake, chocolate marshmallow, Butterfinger blast, vanilla toffee, peanut-butter chocolate swirl, mint chocolate swirl, butterscotch bliss, and chocolate-chip-cookie dough. But we never got to have chocolate coconut."

"It's just one flavor. That's not so bad."

"I guess." She didn't sound convinced. "I have to finish packing. Daddy said we're leaving in an hour for the ferry."

An hour. After almost three months it came down to one final hour.

"Come on." I took Cassie's hand and together we stood up. "I'll help you pack."

. . .

Jay was upstairs in his room, the familiar duffel bag out on his bed.

"How's it going?" I asked.

He gave me a sad grin. "It's going."

He came over to the doorway and pulled me into the room. That morning Jay had called and told me he wasn't leaving on today's ferry. I'd felt a rush of relief, but it was fleeting, as I knew he was just buying time. He had to leave eventually, and eventually turned out to be tomorrow. He'd decided to stay one more day before heading down to Connecticut for a few days to help out at home. Then he'd go back to school.

"Hey, I like the shirt, especially that." Jay pointed to a purple stain in the vicinity of my belly button.

"It's Kool-Aid."

"Did you ask for tomorrow off?" he wanted to know.

"Marla said it was okay, but she wasn't happy about it. The place is swarming with kids now that it's the last week before everyone starts school." I glanced around the room. "It looks like you're just about ready to leave."

Jay shook his head. "Not yet, Fred. Not yet."

By two o'clock the car was packed and Cassie was buckled in the backseat, ready to go. Anne claimed to be feeling better, but on the way to the car she moved slowly, uneasily, as if unsure of each step.

"Please keep in touch," she said, easing herself down into the passenger seat.

"I will, I promise."

Anne took my hand and squeezed it. The strength of her grip surprised me. "Thanks for everything, Winnie. Really."

"You, too." I squeezed back, then poked my head inside the open backseat window. "And you be good, okay? Help your mom."

Cassie nodded. "I'll miss you, Winnie."

"Me, too, Cassie," I told her, wishing we'd had a chance to get that chocolate-coconut fudge.

Mr. Barclay and Jay came outside with the last of the bags and piled them into the back of the SUV before slamming the tailgate shut. I walked to the back of the car and stood there with them, surveying the contents of their summer stuffed into a single space.

"Have everything?" Mr. Barclay asked Anne and Cassie, and I could see each of them running down a mental tally of items they didn't want to forget.

"I think so." Anne didn't sound sure. "I hope so."

"I'll go do one final sweep of the house," Jay offered, and turned back toward the front door, leaving just Mr. Barclay and me alone on the driveway.

"I don't know what we would have done this summer without you, Winnie," Mr. Barclay said, then reached out and wrapped his arms around me. I let him, then reciprocated the hug.

When we pulled apart, I looked through the car's window and saw Anne lay her head back against the headrest and close her eyes.

"Do you think she's going to be okay?" I asked Mr. Barclay, my voice low and hopeful.

"I think so." He nodded his head slowly. "I think we're all going to be okay, Winnie."

Jay came back outside and declared the house all clear.

"Then I guess this is it." Mr. Barclay walked around to the driver's side of the car and Jay followed him, while I stayed where I was.

I couldn't see them over the roof of the car, so I watched Anne instead. Although I couldn't hear what Jay and his dad were saying to one another, I knew from her vantage point she could. When I saw a satisfied smile make its way across her lips, I knew Mr. Barclay was right.

Chapter 26

"It's weird, isn't it?" Jay took the spatula off the counter and folded over the omelet, shaking the frying pan so the edges lined up perfectly and a little cheese oozed out over the sides. "I can't believe I'm about to say this . . ."

"You miss them," I finished for Jay. "Admit it."

But he wouldn't. Instead he reached for the skillet on the back burner and moved it forward so he could flip over the bacon that had been sizzling on high and splattering grease all over the stove top.

We'd been alone in the house before, but this time it was different, emptier. Cassie's toys were put away for the winter, the dresser in her room bare except for the third-place ribbon, which she'd left out so it would be waiting for her when she returned. If I hadn't told Jay to go back to school, he would have spent all winter here, alone, waiting for me to come over after school and fill the vacant rooms.

"Do you want pepper on your omelet?" He held the frying pan in one hand and the pepper mill in the other.

"Sure."

It was our last day together, and we'd decided to start with breakfast, and although I'd expected nothing more than a bowl of cereal, Jay had surprised me with eggs, bacon, and, if the juicer and six oranges on the counter were any indication, fresh-squeezed orange juice.

"Before I forget, can you do me a favor?" I slipped a bag filled with chocolate-coconut fudge out of my backpack and laid it on the kitchen table. "Can you give this to Cassie? We had one more flavor of fudge to go. Now she can say she had them all."

Jay turned the front burner off and came over to me. "Why are you so wonderful?"

"You got some grease on your shirt." I pointed to a watery brown spot near his chest. "Do you know what my mom would say?"

Jay shook his head. "That I'm making you one hell of a breakfast?"

"You're thinking of my sister, and given the smell of burning bacon over there, I'm not sure she'd actually say that."

Jay moved the pan of bacon off the burner. "Then I can't imagine."

I stood up and walked over to where Jay still stood, holding the pepper mill in one hand, and wrapped my arms around his neck, pulling our noses so close my vision blurred and his eyes blended together. "You should have worn a smock, Herb."

Jay had the whole day planned out. First breakfast, then a quick trip over to Chappaquiddick, where we'd spend the morning at the beach. Lunch at the Pot Belly Deli, and we'd finish up the afternoon with a visit to the West Chop Lighthouse. It was a lot to do before he left to catch his five-o'clock ferry, and I told him that, but Jay insisted, almost as if he needed to make just a few more memories to take with him, in case the ones we had started to fade.

So at nine thirty we washed the breakfast dishes, put them away, jumped in the Jeep, and drove up the street to the Chappy ferry.

But only one ferry was running, and we ended up having to wait in line for forty-five minutes for the three-minute trip across the inlet.

"Why don't we just go to South Beach instead," I offered, watching the next three cars in line slowly boarding the ferry. "It's just a beach."

But it wasn't just a beach to Jay, and I knew that. It was someplace we hadn't been before, at least not together, and that's what he wanted, so we waited for the ferry over and waited for the ferry back, which meant we didn't even get to the Pot Belly for lunch until close to two o'clock.

I knew Jay had the whole day planned, but all I wanted to do was go back to the Barclays' and be with him.

"Let's just have lunch and then go home," I suggested as we stood at the counter at the Pot Belly reading the chalkboard sign with the sandwich listings. "We have two hours before you have to leave for the ferry, and I just want to be with you."

"What about the West Chop Lighthouse? We've only seen four, it's our last one."

"We can save it until next time."

Even though I knew he'd planned our visit to the lighthouse for the last day on purpose, Jay nodded.

Kendra stood behind the deli counter waiting for us to

choose. "What will it be?" she asked, a pen in her hand as she prepared to write down our orders.

"Two Santa Fe Gobblers, please," he told her, and then, as if warming up to the idea of just him and me being alone in the house for the rest of the afternoon, he added, "and make them to go."

Ten minutes later Jay and I walked down Main Street for the last time and took a right onto South Water Street.

"Do you know there are gravestones over there under the bushes?" I pointed to the rhododendron bushes along the side of his neighbor's house.

"No way." He let go of my hand and walked up the short brick driveway. "Where?"

"A little to the left," I directed him, and he pushed aside the branches until he found the flat, gray stones that reached just about to his knees.

"I had no idea these were here." Jay squatted to place his hand on a stone, tracing the carved letters with his finger.

"Come on. Somebody's going to come out here and yell at you."

Jay stood up and stepped back, letting go of the branches as he made his way back onto the grass. One by one the branches settled back into place, and by the time Jay reached me the stones were invisible once again.

"You could have gotten in trouble, you know. You can't just walk into someone's yard and start rifling through their bushes."

Jay reached for my hand and we started walking toward home. "They've got four dead bodies buried in their front yard," he answered. "I think they have more to worry about than their landscaping."

•   •   •

My first time in the Barclays' house I wondered what it would be like to wake up there every day, how it would feel to be surrounded by everything in the right place exactly as it should be. To have the perfect family who sat outside on their patio overlooking the harbor, a chilled pitcher of lemonade waiting to be shared. But then I learned that things are rarely as they seem, and even if they are, what you see is not always what you get.

Jay told me to go ahead to his room and he'd bring lunch up. Having spent most of my day on what amounted to a field trip, I wasn't about to argue. I took the stairs two at a time and flung myself on his bed, where I closed my eyes and listened to the water slapping against the harbor wall. I must have fallen asleep because the next thing I heard was Jay knocking on the doorframe.

"Wake up, Sleeping Beauty."

I sat up and saw Jay was carrying a tray with our sandwiches and two champagne flutes, each one filled halfway with a strawberry floating on top.

"What's that?"

"It's a birthday sandwich." Jay shielded the flame with his hand as he walked over to the bed.

When he reached me, he held out the tray and I recognized the long, white, tapered candle stuck in the center of my Santa Fe Gobbler. "Did you take that out of the candle-holder on the dining-room table?"

Jay ignored my question. "Just be quiet and make a wish before I set fire to our turkey sandwiches and we both starve."

I closed my eyes and blew out the candle, and I think we both knew what I wished for.

"I'm sorry I'm going to miss your birthday, Fred." He sat down on the bed and set the tray on the night table, reaching for the champagne flutes and handing me one.

"I know you are. But it's okay."

"It's not, but thanks for saying it is." Jay held up his glass and waited for me to do the same. "A toast."

I crossed my legs pretzel-style, sitting up straight so I wouldn't spill the champagne on the comforter. "To what?"

"To the fifth and final lighthouse?" Jay suggested.

I shook my head. "To the summer?"

Jay didn't seem too impressed with my alternative. "How about, to next time?" he proposed, his toast as much a wish as a promise.

I tapped Jay's glass with my own, and a high, crisp clinking rang out. "Until next time."

Jessie's sister, Kelsey, was sitting on the front steps of the Community Center fanning herself with a paper plate and looking as if she couldn't wait to get the hell away from there.

"Hey, is Jessie around?" I asked, walking up to her.

Kelsey pointed around to the side of the building. "Over by the courts practicing her serve."

I wondered if Kelsey knew about Jessie and Nash or if she just looked at her sister and saw the same person she knew at the beginning of the summer, the girl who practiced her serves and picked her food into pieces. It was definitely easier that way, just as it was easier to see my mom and dad as my parents instead of two people who had their own desires and interests and even their very own wishes they made each time Shelby placed a double-layer, butter-cream-iced birthday cake in front of them and we all waited for the candles to be blown out. It was way more difficult to acknowledge that it wasn't that simple.

"How was your summer?" I asked Kelsey. "I didn't see you much."

She set the paper plate down and ran a hand through her hair, lifting the brown waves off her neck. "Ever worked at a snack bar?"

I shook my head.

"Well, I can tell you this—next summer I'm doing something else, something totally different and way more interesting than handing out Snickers bars and making change for a dollar."

I had a hard time imagining next summer when this summer was just coming to an end.

"At least you only have a few days left."

"Thank God." She rolled her eyes at me. "What about you? How was your summer?"

Having so many ways to answer that, I wasn't quite sure what to say. Things at the Oceanview were already winding down. We had fewer and fewer campers each day, and on Friday we'd all say good-bye to Marla and she'd probably open her umbrella like Mary Poppins and fly away to look for new children to look after, and for her sake, and theirs, I hoped they understood the concept of an inside voice. I knew Rachel was counting down the days until camp ended, but at least I could sleep at night knowing she'd never again have to suffer the indignity of rubbing diaper-rash cream on her tender nose. Of course, the Oceanview was just one of my summer jobs. And even if Kelsey had the time to listen to me talk about my summer with the Barclays, she would never hang around long enough to listen to me explain what had happened to my family.

So how was my summer? It was good and bad and fun and terrifying. And if it was interesting that Kelsey wanted, I'd had more than my share. "It wasn't exactly what I expected," I finally answered.

I left Kelsey on the steps and went around the center to the courts. Jessie was there at the baseline, her back arched, her arm extended overhead, as the racquet came down hard on the ball, sending it across the net.

"Your serve looks good," I told her when I reached the court. I held on to the chain-link fence separating us, my fingers curled around the intertwined wire.

Jessie stopped serving and walked over to me. "He left this morning. The sailing team is having a preseason meeting and he needed to go back early."

I wondered if Jessie believed him or if it even mattered anymore.

"He invited me up to visit." Jessie tossed the ball up as if she were going to serve, but instead of raising her racquet head and connecting with the ball, she caught it again in her hand. "But I don't think I'm going to go. I think I'll e-mail Nash and tell him that with school starting, things will just be too busy. Coach called and said she talked to a few schools that are interested in me."

"That's great," I said, but it sounded like a consolation, as if we both knew that to have one thing she wanted, she needed to give up on another.

"Yeah, it is." Jessie attempted to say the words as if she really believed them.

"What about Jay?"

I glanced at my watch: 5:10. "Right about now he's probably passing the lighthouse at East Chop. He caught a five-o'clock out of Oak Bluffs."

Jessie gave me a resigned nod. "And here we are, right back where we started."

It was true in one sense. A few months ago I was standing in this exact spot, talking to Jessie about the summer, trying to figure out how I'd kill time after camp, wondering what would happen with my family, if she and Nash would actually last the summer or if I'd spend the next three months relegated to the backseat of his Saab.

"Every year when my mom gets a new class in the fall, she asks them to tell a story about their summer," I said. "You know, if I had to do that, I wouldn't even know where to begin."

"Are you kidding me?" Jessie snorted. "The beginnings are easy. It's the endings that suck."

I wasn't sure I agreed with Jessie. Maybe beginnings are easier, but I wouldn't say they're easy. My beginning with Jay was anything but easy. And I wasn't willing to concede the ending, not yet.

Chapter 27

The baby was born seven days early, on my birthday. They named her Abigail Louise Barclay. Abby for short.

Jay texted me from the hospital around six o'clock on Friday night to tell me that Anne had gone into labor. He'd driven down from school after his last class to be at the hospital with his dad and Cassie. Abby was born at 1:07 a.m. Saturday morning, and when Jay called to wish me a happy birthday six hours later, he put Abby on the phone, where she let out a cry so shrill I had to hold the receiver away from my ear.

"Did you hear that?" he asked, taking Abby away from the phone and laughing into the mouthpiece. "Did you hear it?"

"What?"

"She said happy birthday, Fred."

A week later I received a letter from Anne, written on a creamy white note card with her initials, AMB, in simple block letters on the front. When I opened the card, a photograph slipped out into my hand, and I held it, taking in the faces of one familiar little girl and one I'd never had a chance to meet. It was a picture of Cassie holding her new sister, who was haphazardly swaddled in a pink blanket that had fallen away, exposing Abby's pale, wrinkled skin. In the corner of the photo, I noticed a set of fingertips gently holding Abby's bare little leg, their grasp light enough so Abby could move comfortably but firm enough to make her feel safe. They were the same fingertips I'd held laced between mine, with the same soft, warm touch I'd felt against my face just before the first time he'd leaned in to kiss me. It was Jay.

I sat on my bed soaking in the image of the three of them, how small and fragile Abby appeared and how strong and firm Jay's hand was against her leg. It wasn't a family portrait on the dunes or a posed picture of the new family in their best clothes, but it captured the three of them perfectly. Jay wasn't standing front and center, but at least he was in the frame, and that was a start, even if the photo never ended up on the side table in the Barclays' foyer on South Water Street. And it didn't have to, because I had the right place for it, in the box on my night table, nestled inside the rest of my memories for safekeeping.

My birthday present from Jay arrived later on that day, a small, plain brown box addressed to *Fred*. I walked back to the house from the mailbox and sat on our front steps, where I slipped my finger under the clear tape and lifted the cardboard flaps open, exposing something carefully wrapped in tissue paper and bubble wrap.

I could feel the weight of the object even before I pulled apart the careful packaging that safeguarded my gift, and when the last sheet of tissue fell away, I held a small lighthouse, a replica of the one we never got to see in West Chop. It was no bigger than four inches tall and fit perfectly in the palm of my hand. I opened up the note that Jay had slipped inside the box, a plain piece of paper where he had written,

Until next time. I turned the lighthouse over and over in my hand, feeling the smooth cylinder of the base and the delicate decoration at the top, and not until I looked under the base did I notice the date someone had written in black Magic Marker: 1991. The year I was born. And that's when I knew Jay had gone to the storage and that he'd finally spent time with all the memories his mother had left behind and had his chance to say good-bye.

I sat on the step with the lighthouse in my hand and listened to the breeze rustling through the leaves on the trees outside the kitchen window, the branches scratching against the house, the birds shouting to one another as they fought for the insects hiding between blades of grass, even the biplane giving tourists aerial tours and the private jets landing at the airport. It wasn't really that quiet at all, even if it had felt that way for a while.

I slipped the lighthouse back into the box and went inside, where my mom was in the dining room putting things back to normal. She'd cleared away the tissue paper and jars of glue and paintbrushes, placing them in a large plastic storage container as she readied herself for another school year with her kids. The dining-room table was back to looking like a place that hosted Thanksgiving dinner, the surface gleaming as my mom made one final swipe with the cloth she held in one hand, a yellow can of Pledge in the other.

"Did you get a package?" she asked, nodding to the box I held in my hand.

"A birthday present from Jay."

She smiled and came over to me. "What did he send?"

I placed the box on the table and slipped out the lighthouse, holding it up so she could see.

"That's the lighthouse on West Chop."

I nodded. "It was the only one we didn't get to visit this summer."

"But you can go anytime you want. You could go every day if you felt like it."

She was right, I could. But I wouldn't. Because it wasn't the lighthouse that mattered so much as going there with Jay.

"I think I'm going to wait."

"What do you mean you're going to wait?" My mom stepped back as I passed her on my way out of the dining room. "Wait until when?"

Until next time, I thought, my fingers cradling the weight of the lighthouse. *Until next time.*

Read on for a sneak peek at *Local Girls,*
Jenny O'Connell's first book
in the Island Summer Series!

Available now in bookstores everywhere.

Chapter 1

I closed my eyes and inhaled just long enough to recognize the first sign of summer. Luckily, I opened them again in time to see the four-way stop ahead. But as I pressed my foot on the brake and came to a stop at the intersection, I inhaled again, leaning my head out the open window. I knew that scent even before I could see where it was coming from. The smell of summer. Skunk.

I glanced at the clock on the dashboard: 8:49. Mona's ferry would be arriving in eleven minutes. Almost ten months of waiting and I had just eleven minutes to go.

After looking both ways, I dropped my foot on the gas pedal and headed toward the ferry. Even without spotting the skunk, the slight burning in my nose told me I was getting closer, until there it was, pushed just off the road toward the bike path. Mona always complained when I lowered the car window at the first whiff of skunk. She'd crinkle up her nose and then pinch it shut, her index finger self-consciously rubbing the bridge of her nose and the invisible bump that wasn't noticed by anyone but her. Still, I always kept the window down and breathed deep, even knowing how much it bugged her, because eventually she'd always end up laughing, a nasally laugh that turned into a snort when she finally unpinched her nose.

But now, I avoided looking at the black-and-white mound next to the bike path and instead looked straight ahead at the sign announcing I'd entered Vineyard Haven.

It was near the end of June, and a Sunday, which meant there would be two types of cars at the ferry—the tourists leaving the island after a week's vacation, and the tourists arriving. The thing is, if it weren't for the fact that they were facing different directions, you probably wouldn't be able to tell which was which. But as someone who has lived on the island her entire life, I could tell. It wasn't the stuff they packed in their cars, because coming or going, the SUVs and sedans were layered to the roof with duffel bags, pillows, beach chairs, and boogie boards. If they were really ambitious, and unwilling to trade their expensive ten-speeds with cushy leather seats and spindly rearview mirrors for an on-island rental, there were always the bike racks hanging off the backs of trunks, wheel spokes slowly turning as they caught the breeze off the harbor. And it wasn't their license plates, because just about every other car was clearly labeled "tourist"—Connecticut, New York, New Jersey, and even a few Pennsylvanias tossed in for good measure. No, it was the difference between the shiny, sparkling cars with their polished hubcaps, and the cars coated with dirt and sand, their once gleaming exteriors dusted on-island like powdered donuts.

I made the left onto Water Street, following a BMW with WASH ME handwritten in block letters in the layer of dirt on the bumper. I patiently waited for the cars ahead of me to pull into the Steamship Authority parking lot and line up single file between the painted rows so they could board the ferry. Then I veered left and pulled Lexi's car into the row of spaces for people like me.

My sister knew I'd wanted to meet Mona at the ferry, and since she was planning to be at the deli early to let in the last of the contractors, she'd offered me her car. Even though July Fourth was almost two weeks away, which meant the worst of the summer traffic hadn't even started, I left the house early. Not as early as my parents and Lexi and Bart, who just *had* to be at the deli by seven, but early by a seventeen-year-old's standards, and *especially* early for someone whose last day it was to sleep late.

Mona's ferry wasn't in sight yet, so I walked to the edge of the water, where waiting families shared overpriced muffins from the Black Dog. They were all there, the Vineyard vacationers you saw in travel brochures and websites. There was the little boy who'd undoubtedly whined until his mom purchased the stuffed black lab puppy now clutched under his arm. His brother with the sharktooth necklace. The girl with the rope bracelet. A mom in Lily Pulitzer Capri pants.

They might as well have been wearing the same T-shirts—I WENT TO MARTHA'S VINEYARD AND ALL I GOT WAS EVERYTHING I ASKED FOR.

"Kendra!"

I turned toward the voice calling my name and recognized Ryan Patten down by the gazebo. He waved and started walking toward me. When you lived on the island, you didn't really expect to see people you knew at the ferry this time of year. Maybe in November when you were heading off-island to Target, or in March when everyone was going stir-crazy from the long, gray winter, but for three months during the summer the ferry was for strangers.

"What are you doing here?" Ryan asked, pulling a leash, and a very large dog, behind him.

"Mona's on the nine o'clock." I pointed to the golden retriever sniffing the grass and flicking his tail against Ryan's leg. "Who's that?"

"Dutch. He's along for the ride. My cousins and aunt and uncle are coming for a visit. You know how it is."

I nodded as if I did, but I didn't. Nobody in my family ever moved off the island. "So, what are you doing this summer?"

"Renting bikes at Island Wheels. What about you?" Dutch pulled at his leash and I followed along as Ryan let him continue sniffing the trail of whatever he thought he'd found.

"Working at the Willow Inn. We start tomorrow."

"We?"

"Me and Mona," I told Ryan, lowering my voice as if there was any chance she could hear me from the ferry.

I hadn't told her yet. The job was my surprise. We'd always talked about working at one of the inns for a summer. It met all three of our criteria. One, no lines. The idea of scooping ice cream while a line of exhausted parents and their demanding kids impatiently shouted out orders for Oreo cookie frappés wasn't exactly appealing, no matter how much free ice cream you could eat. Two, no retail (see number one, but replace pissy parents and their whiny kids with pissy women who don't understand why there are no more size 6 Bermuda shorts on the rack). And three, no nights. Serving breakfast at the Willow Inn was perfect. Technically, there could be times when people would be anxiously waiting for their morning coffees, but with only nineteen rooms, it wasn't like there'd be a line for the blueberry muffins. Besides, we'd always figured people were still optimistic that early in the morning, and therefore nicer to be around. By the end of the day they'd be sunburned, cranky from spending twenty minutes in traffic on Main Street, and downright rude after driving around for an hour, looking for a parking space, only to discover a ticket on their windshield when they returned. The Willow didn't serve dinner, just breakfast and picnic lunches for guests. Spend three minutes with a hostess trying to placate families who have been waiting over an hour for a dinner table, and you'd understand why.

Luckily, the guy who sold Lexi the cash register for the deli knew someone who knew the new owner of the Willow, and two weeks after Lexi placed an order for the Sam4s register with integrated credit card capabilities, I had secured jobs for Mona and me.

"Does Kevin know she's coming back?" Ryan asked.

I shrugged. "I don't know. She e-mailed me with her ferry time and that was it."

Mona hadn't seen Kevin since she left, that I did know. She only came back to the island once after she moved, last October for her grandfather's funeral, and I'm sure I would have known if Kevin had gone to Boston to visit her. Kevin went out with Melissa Madsen for a few months this winter, but I was still sort of hoping they'd get back together when Mona returned, and then everything would be just like it was before she left. At least for the summer.

"It's here." Ryan pointed past the houses hugging the

shores of the harbor and I could see the ferry come into view, white peaks of water cresting on either side of the bow as it made its way toward us.

"Hungry?" Ryan asked, and then pointed to the hand I had clutched against my stomach.

What could I say? That seeing the ferry coming toward us, the ferry with my best friend on it, had turned my stomach upside down? That all of a sudden the idea of seeing Mona again made me nervous because I didn't know what to expect?

"Yeah," I lied, and rubbed my stomach as if all I needed was a good bowl of cereal. "Starving."

We started walking toward the dock. "Where are you meeting your cousins?" I asked.

"Where they walk off. They got to Woods Hole late and missed their ferry, again. Couldn't get another reservation for the car until Monday, so they'll have to go over tomorrow and pick it up."

Ryan began telling me how his cousins missed their ferry every year, but even though I nodded in all the right places as if I was listening, all I really heard was the ferry engine revving loudly as it slid into place against the dock.

"You know what I mean?" Ryan finished. He looked to me for a response.

"Exactly," I answered, even though I had no idea what I was agreeing to.

We stood there with Dutch and watched as the front door to the boat's belly opened up to expose rows of idling cars. Once the guys working the controls for the ramp gave them the go-ahead, the cars slowly moved across the steel incline, forming a steady, orderly procession as they took turns driving off the boat and past the ferry building before accelerating in the direction of their rental house or relative's house or, in Mona's case, their new stepfather's summer estate.

I stood on my tiptoes trying to see if I could spot Malcolm's black Range Rover inside. Last summer, when Malcolm married Izzy in the backyard of his house overlooking South Beach, Mona and I wrote "Just Married" along the side of the car with a bar of Ivory soap. The soap was from Mona's grandfather's house. We couldn't find a bar in Malcolm's six-bedroom summer "cottage," where every bathroom had a bottle of L'Occitane almond shea soap on the sink and a matching bottle of body wash in the shower but not a bar of Ivory soap in the whole place. L'Occitane seemed to be the soap of choice in Malcolm's house, and it smelled amazing. It was actually the second thing I noticed the first time I went to Malcolm's house with Mona. The smell. It wasn't sweet like the air fresheners my mother seemed to have inserted into every electrical outlet in our house. And it wasn't comforting, like the lavender sachets the Willow Inn placed on the guests' pillows every night. The only way I could describe it was manly, like a combination of fresh-cut grass, seawater, and limes. Even though Malcolm had hired an interior designer from Vineyard Haven to decorate his summer home, it was definitely a house that had been occupied by a man. Malcolm didn't have any kids, even though Izzy told Mona he was married briefly to his college sweetheart. By the time Malcolm met Izzy, he'd been divorced for way longer than he was married, which is why the *first* thing I noticed about Malcolm's house was that it was way too big for a single guy with no kids.

"There are my cousins." Ryan nudged me and waved to a family walking toward us. "I guess this is it. Tell Henry I said hi and have fun with Mona."

"I will," I told him, realizing I'd almost forgotten about Mona's brother.

And that's when I saw it, the shiny black hood making its way out of the ferry doors and down the ramp. The back passenger window was open and I waited for Mona to poke her head out and scream my name. Instead I watched as Henry waved in my direction.

I waved back and walked toward the car, now pulling up against the curb to let the cars behind it pass by.

"Kendra!" Mona jumped out and ran toward me, her arms outstretched like in those slow-motion sequences in the movies. When she reached me, the force of her hug knocked me backward, quite a feat for someone who was at least four inches shorter, and fifteen pounds lighter, than me.

"You look so great," she told me, giving me one last squeeze before taking my hand and pulling me toward the car. "Mom, look at her, she looks exactly the same!"

Well, not exactly the same—my hair was longer and not as blonde as when Mona left the island last summer, but I didn't point that out. Instead I let her tow me toward the Land Rover.

"Kennie!" Izzy reached through the open passenger-side window and held her arms out.

I leaned in and let her hug me. "Hi, Malcolm," I said over Izzy's shoulder.

Malcolm smiled at me. "Hello, Kennie."

"I know you girls have a lot of catching up to do. So

don't let us stop you. Are you going with Kennie?" Izzy asked Mona.

"Yeah," I answered before Mona could even get a word out. "I can take you to the house, Lexi let me borrow her car."

"Great." Mona reached into the backseat and grabbed her purse with one hand and my elbow with the other. "Let's go."

MTV
MUSIC TELEVISION®

your attitude. your style.
MTV Books:
totally your type.

Phoenix is young and beautiful. And she's just been recruited to regulate alien mayhem in the Teen Alien Huntress series by Gena Showalter!

RED HANDED
There's blood on her hands . . . but it isn't human.

BLACK LISTED
Sometimes there are good reasons to do bad things.

IT'S NOT ABOUT THE ACCENT | Caridad Ferrer
Sometimes the greatest role you can play is yourself…
Sporting a new name and an exotic new Latina flair, she's ready for her college debut. But is the luscious Carolina really better than plain-Jane Caroline?

UNINVITED | Justine Musk
They give new meaning to the phrase Hell's Angels…
Kelly Ruland's small hometown is being terrorized by a group of bikers led by a charismatic leader. But is her brother's soul the only thing that can save the town?

AVAILABLE WHEREVER BOOKS ARE SOLD. | WWW.SIMONSAYS.COM/MTVBOOKS

PUBLISHED BY POCKET BOOKS
A Division of Simon & Schuster
A CBS COMPANY

16827

your attitude. **your style.**

MTV Books: totally your type.

NEW IN THE 310 SERIES!
Boy Trouble
Beth Killian

Is there really any other kind? Spring has sprung in the 310, and that means drama is in bloom—especially for Eva, who sees a bad boy looming on her romantic horizon.

The Book of Luke
Jenny O'Connell

There's no "how to" guide for love…so it's up to Emily to fill the void and write an instruction manual for dopey dads, bad beaus, and obnoxious brothers.

Graffiti Girl
Kelly Parra

Spray it—don't say it. A girl from the wrong side of town is drawn into the underground world of graffiti artists—but the lifestyle might be more than she bargained for.

Available wherever books are sold.
www.simonsays.com/mtvbooks.com

Published by Pocket Books
A Division of Simon & Schuster
A CBS COMPANY

16285